THE SOUL CAGES

By

Nicole Givens Kurtz

THE SOUL CAGES
Copyright ©2004 Nicole Givens Kurtz
Cover Design by Kim Tyburski
Copyright © 2004

Revised June 2005
All rights reserved
Printed in the United States of America
No part of this book may be used or reproduced in any manner whatsoever without written permission, except in the case of brief quotations embedded in critical articles and reviews, from the author or his/her agent.

ISBN 1-59146-010-7

For information about this and other books offered, address all requests to:
Crystal Dreams Publishing
P.O. Box 698 Dover, TN 37058
or
Visit us on the web at
http://www.crystaldreamspub.com/

E-Mail
crystaldreams@crimsonnova.com

This book printed in the United States of America

Crystal Dreams Publishing

If you found this book satisfying, please investigate the other books that we offer.

Come to http://crystaldreamspub.com and Explore our site and discover the fantastic authors that we are proud to present

TW Miller
Head Publisher
Crystal Dreams Publishing

Chapter One

It was not the fact that it smelled like smoke, or the fact that dried blood stained it. It was the color, an ugly green that reminded Sarah of the time she ate too much gosha and threw up everywhere. That was long ago before the cages robbed her of her taste and every other sensory experience.

But she had finally tricked them, and now she had regained her flesh and could taste the bitter sulfur that saturated the air.

"Come on, Amana. It is cold here. Put it on," Sarah urged as she gestured the green wool coat toward Amana.

"It is green…" Amana whined.

"You are being silly. Put the damn thing on before he gets back"

"But…"

"Now! We have to get out of here," Sarah insisted as she turned to search the sinister gloom for Valek or one of his henchmen.

Wrapping the ugly green coat around her, she followed Sarah as she crept along the dimly lit passage of the cave. They passed several sacks of skins that had once been human. Where the eyes once were there were now only burnt, empty sockets.

Sarah shivered. Her fingers were so cold she could barely move them. Blowing on them only warmed them for a second before they would chill again. She and Amana had not been able to feel, smell or anything else in years before their recent reincarnation into fresh flesh. Sarah secretly relished the numbness in her hands and the stench of the cages that even as they hurried further away seemed to race after them. These were the only signals she knew to be real. The times when she thought shadows were only shadows, they turned out to be Valek's henchmen or worse, Valek himself. She could never tell until it was too late.

"Where are we supposed to meet them?" Amana asked softly for third time that night.

"At the Circle of Allerton. How many times do I have to tell you?" She pinched Amana's cheek and winked, alleviating the sting of her words.

Leaving the soiled cages behind, they could still smell the filth and stench of the closed-in cages. Built beneath layers upon layers of the rocky surface of Solis, no light reached them. Their eyes had grown used to the dimly lit tunnels and passageways.

They scraped and cut their feet as they traveled the rough trail to the Allerton Circle. The pain, something else they were not used to, was welcomed now that they could feel the stinging pain, the sharp points of rock ripping skin.

The Allerton Circle was a passageway to other worlds. Sarah did not know who built them, but the older souls of the cages told stories that these circles were gateways. She wanted to be anywhere but Solis. Anywhere but the cages.

It had been many rotations since they had felt anything at all, so they welcomed the stinging pain of cut toes and bruised feet. Pain was a joy. They did not stop for food or drink as they hurried, as if there were any such things close by to obtain. There was no time. Any moment could be their last, any wrong turn could lead them back to the pits.

The murkiness strangled any green vegetation from growing, leaving only fungi and lichens to flourish. By the time they reached the last row of cages, the ground was heavily laced with minerals from the planet's poisonous surface industries.

"I think I see the blue light of the circle!" Sarah whispered excitedly; her heart sped up in anticipation.

Scurrying toward the azure glow, they reached the circle, just as one other arrived.

Sarah gasped as she yanked on Amana's sleeve. Fear crept into her stomach and a screamed died as she opened her mouth and no sound escaped.

"Hello there," Orono laughed as his bulging ice-blue eyes sparkled in the bleak and dismal night. The wind howled around him like a choir of madmen.

She became even more aware of the frigid air as she stepped in front of Amana protectively... instinctually.

"What is he doing here?" Amana stuttered from behind her.

Amana's breath rasped quickly and she held tight to Sarah's top. Orono had captured Amana before and the horror of the cages was too near for the young girl to forget.

The low humming of the mines filtered through the air in a sort of tribal beat. When she had worked in the mines, Sarah had listened to the beat of the same horrible drums. Drums made of human skin. Shaking off the memory, she crouched in an aggressive pose with both arms extended out in a ready-made karate chop No way were they going back without a fight. Too many had died already.

Orono smiled. Round and pudgy with a head much too small for such a bulky frame, his cheeks shook as they attempted to lift the heavy amounts of flesh to form his smile. It revealed three razor sharp fangs pointing downward toward a row of yellowing lower teeth. Despite the coolness of the air, his face was wet with sweat, giving his complexion the color of moist clay. The smell of decaying flesh followed him like a cloud of cologne

"You know why I am here." He kept his smile plastered to his face as his chubby paw opened to reveal a tiny blue glass ball.

Upon seeing the ball, Amana began to scream. Her voice pierced the night sky like an ice pick through the heart, drowning out the sickening call of the drums.

Hysterical and screaming wildly, she began to cry as she ran blindly for the Allerton Circle just twenty yards away.

"No!" Sarah cried out as she reached behind her for the place where Amana should have been.

But she was too fast and Sarah fell hard as she tried, in vain, to snatch Amana's coat sleeve.

Just as Amana leaped for the Circle, Orono threw the glass ball toward her and its blue stream of light suspended her body in mid-air before releasing it to collapse into a lifeless pile of parts, very much like a sack of potatoes, to the dead ground.

Where Amana's honey brown eyes used to be were now empty black sockets.

"For the heavens, no!" Sarah screamed as she raced to the spot where Amana's body lay. The hated green coat now covered a mound of vacated flesh...emptied of a soul.

The blue glass ball pulsated with an eerie pink color as it returned to Orono's sweaty palm through the crisp air.

"Back to the cages with you." He laughed as he pointed at the ball where Amana's soul was now trapped.

Gently placing the ball into a velvet red bag, he removed another blue glass ball from the sack.

Smirking under his giant cheeks and puffy pink lips, he said to Sarah, "Your turn. Back to the soul cages!"

Just as the blue glass ball warmed to a soft pink, in Orono's grubby paw, Sarah felt a rough shove in her back and she fell instantly to the unyielding ground.

A towering, broad man wielding a metallic shield with a raised silver 'M' stood over her. The glass ball's pinkish stream smashed against his shield and reflected back into the blackness of Solis' night sky.

"In to the Circle!" he ordered. The commanding voice did not seem to come from the massive man, but rather from the heavens. Indeed the man could have been a young god; his eyes covered by opaque glasses; his head devoid of hair and his skin the color of warm cocoa. As he defended her, his full lips were pulled back into a sneer, revealing clenched white teeth.

Scrambling to her feet, she slipped on the slick surface, scraping the delicate skin of her knees in her hurry to reach the circle.

Orono directed the glass's stream towards her, not to be outdone, as she hurried and slipped towards the Allerton Circle.

The man in the black leather pants threw his shield in front of her and the light's stream was again deflected. He was saving her again in less than a few moments. He raced over to her and retrieved his shield She got up and he joined her. Running along side her, the mystery man was the only thing between her and the soul cages.

Cursing, Orono adjusted his bulk and like a slow moving elephant lumbered towards the two. Heaving and huffing, he muttered curses as he hurried towards Sarah and her dark knight. His fangs ready to tear through the stranger's flesh.

"Whoever you are, you will surely despise the day you crossed me," he spat and swung a tight right fist towards the man.

Orono's fist landed squarely into the shield, knocking the man awkwardly and hard onto his back. He crawled on top of the man's shield, crushing the man beneath it with his extremely monstrous bulk, his fangs closing in on the man's exposed neck.

"For the heavens, into the Circle!" the dark man declared once more as he lifted the shield with ease as Orono went flying into a patch of grimy soil some ten feet away.

With her heart thundering in her ears, Sarah raced to the flickering glow of Allerton Circle and with one giant leap, was embraced by the tickling, dense feeling of the Allerton Circle's entranceway. She turned to look behind her and saw the massive mysterious man running towards the Circle.

Breathing heavily, he lowered his shield as he, too, entered the Allerton Circle.

Behind him, Orono cursed all the more as he, too, tried to enter the Circle. As soon as his foot slipped into the circle, smoke hissed and curled into the air. His face twisted in pain and mounting anger. He quickly retreated from the circle and growled in fury. The foul smell of burnt flesh floated into the Circle's ring.

"Bye-bye now." The man smirked as the image of Orono faded. The sheen of sweat glistened from his brawny shoulders and powerful chest. Hairless, his chest rose and fell in a hypnotic rhythm as he tried to regain his breath.

Sarah tore her eyes away from his torso and moved them up to the face of her rescuer.

"You had better hold on," he ordered as the whirling of the Circle began.

The mournful landscape blurred as the twirling increased, growing faster and making Sarah dizzy. Grasping for something, anything in which to hold on, she tried to stay awake and to keep her bearings. But the accelerated speed of the Circle grew to be too much.

It spun her into darkness.

***

The crisp, wintry air penetrated Sarah's lungs, icing the bronchial tubes that limited her breathing. Gagging and clawing for air, she awoke.

Motionless and seemingly unaffected by the chilly air, the knight, as Sarah decided to call him, squatted not far from where she had slept.

She noticed that the somber world of Solis had vanished and in its place was a world that was bitter cold. Colder than Solis.

Goosebumps blanketed her arms and legs. She glanced around her new environment and noticed that in place of Solis's moons was one full moon tinted the shade of purple. The sky, too, held tones of purple in varying degrees, and the vegetation presented a mixture of colors from lush, bold greens to gloomy grays scattered amongst the white, snow covered ground.

She heard loud chirps and looked above as large winged birds flew over them.

"Those are Wrangler birds." The dark man gestured to where the birds once where. In the distance, she could hear other birds squawk amongst the chirping of the wrangler birds.

No, this was not Solis, but where had the Allerton Circle taken her?

"You can stand now," The knight suggested in the same commanding tone in which he had ordered her into the Allerton Circle. He watched her from his crouched spot and he did not remove his glasses.

"I need to get my bearing." She drew the terry cloth blanket tighter around her shoulders. "What is your name?"

"I am Marion," Marion smiled. "And this," with his arms opened wide. "…is Veloris."

"Veloris?" Her breath caught as a bubbling started in her stomach. Surely it couldn't be...but what if it was Veloris?

Veloris was known throughout the secret circles of the galaxy as the Savior's Planet. It was the only planet from which Valek could not harvest souls due to Veloris's location and power. The route to Veloris was extremely dangerous; it involved travel through several rocky asteroid belts and past the Pixlis galaxy, which was also known as the Graveyard, the home of many pirates and thieves. If one got past those things, Veloris itself had a legendary navy and defense against any intruder.

"I am one of the Queen's Ministers." He turned and showed Sarah a tattoo on his left bicep. In a scripted "M" with a sword slashed through it, the tattoo labeled Marion as a Minister Knight of Souls.

She had heard of the Queen's Ministers of Souls. Everyone in the cages had heard the myths, legends and rumors that abound throughout about who they were, what side did they belong to and if they even existed. Valek could not be stopped some had declared, but still others believed and spread whispered tales about the battles the Ministers of Souls waged against Valek.

And won.

Marion moved closer to her and squatted down next to her; the leather stretched taut over his shapely, hardened thighs. She could smell a floral scent about him that reminded her of her childhood.

"Are you cold?" He asked as he reviewed her top and shorts. "Does the blanket not warm you?"

"Yes, a little," she stuttered and pulled the blanket closer. She felt awkward with his masked eyes on her. "No, not much."

"Come, we will start towards the castle." Standing, he offered his hand; he lifted her to her feet and she fell in step behind him. His stride took three steps of hers to keep up.

They walked for a few miles; she could not stand the silence. He marched on without stopping or even talking. It would seem his mind was elsewhere. She wondered several times if he had forgotten that she was even there.

"I thought you were a myth," she said as she rushed to catch up with him.

"I assure you; I am very real," he replied.

She waited for the dark Minister to continue. He did not.

"My sister, Amana, she was recaptured..."

"Yes, I am aware of that," he interrupted.

The ground crunched beneath their feet as they walked on towards the northern part of Veloris. If the tales were true, they were currently in the Northern Forest. Once they were through the forest and on the other side, they would reach the Queen's castle.

The Northern Forest had been almost completely cleansed of wildlife due to hunting. However, Queen Zoë had forbade any more hunting some three hundred rotations prior. Now, Marion explained, there were all sorts of wildlife, from the wrangler bird, Sarah heard earlier to the doggets with their packs of pups and den mothers. The forest was alive despite the icy temperatures and frozen lakes.

To the southeast, in which the Circle of Allerton had delivered them, was the Southern Forest, which had been decaying for years in part to the widening of the Circle. The Circle of Allerton's widening had begun only a hundred rotations prior but had ate the vegetation and the surrounding wildlife in order to sustain its growth. It drained all life within its grasp. He predicted that once the Circle reached the beginnings of the Northern Circle, Queen Zoë would have the Circle destroyed, which meant no others would be able to arrive via the Circle of Allerton.

Barefoot, Sarah walked slower than Marion, who wore boots of polished leather. The scrapes on her foot bled and left red footprints on the white, soft snow that peppered the ground. The cold numbed her toes and she could barely wiggle them. Marion's stride left her far behind, so far in fact that she could no longer hear his voice. Out of breath and tiring, she had to push herself to keep up despite the dizzy spells and her weakened condition.

"Then you plan to rescue her, too?" Sarah asked wearily, but loudly calling to him, drawing him back to the previous conversation before he changed it to Veloris's landscape.

"No." He stopped abruptly and turned back to look at her. He spun around to face her and took great strides to back to close the gap that had sprawled between them.

"What?" She stared into his blackened glasses. "But, but…"

Removing the tinted glasses, he revealed his pale gray eyes. The pupils were almost clear except for a shadow of gray. They were disconcerting; out of place among the smooth creaminess of his caramel-colored complexion.

"No. We are not planning to rescue your sister," he restated deliberately and firmly.

"Then take me back!" She pointed to the direction in which, they had come.

"I am not authorized…" he started.

"I don't care! Take me back to Solis; I will get her back!" She yelled as tears gathered in her eyes. They did not spill over. She was determined not to let them fall. Life had taught her not to reveal pain. She had learned that lesson well. He was not worth her most precious tears.

The forest fell quiet as if listening to the debate between the new arrival and the Minister. The sky had flushed to a deep purple, almost black, as night approached leisurely from the West.

He slapped down his glasses, turned around and marched forward. His pace quickened and Sarah's slowed. She stopped several times and searched her surroundings. She knew she was too weak to go back on her own, but

Amana needed her. And if he was a Minister, he could help her.

Suddenly, he turned around again and walked back to her. He chuckled

"You will learn to trust me." He smiled again for just a moment. Then his face turned serious when he said, "But it was I who rescued you. Do not forget it."

"And you can not do the same for Amana?" she pleaded. Her little sister, the only family she had left thanks to the slaving of the soul cages

He solemnly shook his head no.

"Then I will do this on my own," she swore defiantly as she dropped the blanket and took off running towards the south. She had very little strength, but she must try, even if it took her life.

As she raced south, she passed dense masses of evergreen trees that populated the southeast section of the forest. To the west, more trees of every color: blues, red and several shades of purple.

She had to get back to the Circle. The frosty air rushed into her lungs as she fled the presence of Marion. Looking up, the sky above had deepened even more as night crept closer.

A shadow suddenly appeared out of the corner of her eye and she almost collided with Marion who had flickered past her in a blur of black and walnut brown.

Her eyes grew wide in disbelief as he raised a black tiny glass sphere towards her face and said, "Sleep."

Chapter Two

" What happened to her?" Valek roared causing the hair on Orono's back to crawl and slither down his back. This made each and every strand on his fuzzy back ripple in fear.

"I-I already had the one," he hissed and sputtered. "Then this enormous dark man emerged from the Circle."

Valek slammed his skeletal fist into Orono's brunt nose, causing an outburst of pain from Orono and producing a splotch of blood.

"And you let him take her!" Valek slammed another of his pale, bony fists into Orono's floppy left ear, causing Orono to let out another howling shriek of pain and another shot of blood.

Valek spun around and went behind his gold desk. Dressed in a burgundy robe, ornate with hand-sewn rows of gold thread and hand-trimmed silver petals, Valek sat down gently in the desk's matching gold chair. He placed his burgundy leather boots on top of his desk as he watched Orono rub his injured nose and ear.

"You know I hate violence." Valek said softly. "I really hate violence."

Valek reached into the pocket of his robe and retrieved an orange rectangular box. It was a rare piece in that it was orange, not the slick, black lacquer of Solis.

No, this box was the last piece of Veloris Three that remained throughout the galaxy. The remaining evidence that there was ever a planet called Veloris Three.

Valek's slender fingers racked through the dried herbs gingerly as if cooling down from his anger sphere. Orono began to slink backwards towards the door — Valek's temper was legendary throughout the galaxy. Like the time Valek beheaded the servant wench on Earth 3012 with his sword because she clumsily stepped on his foot.

"I am not done." Valek calmly closed the box and turned to contemplate out the window.

Orono froze, and then dropped to his blubbery knees.

"Valek, I am sorry for-"

Whirling around, Valek's blonde ponytail slapped him lightly in the mouth, that at the moment was pulled back into a sneer that exposed two pointy teeth surround by even white teeth.

"Get up you sniveling maggot!" Valek ordered through clinched teeth. "And find her!"

Orono slobbered and scurried out of the office.

Valek sighed then turned his chair to face the window where outside the three moons of Solis were barely visible through the blackening clouds and smoke.

Valek hated Solis. The dreadful stench of the poisonous atmosphere only reminded him of how very much he hated Solis. From the dirty slick rocks and stony surface to the bleak, dreary days followed by the bleak dreary nights. Valek really hated Solis.

It was not the fact that Orono had lost an escaped soul. Orono frequently failed to recapture souls on the first try, on the rare occasions when one managed to escape. There had only been one other who had departed and had never been returned. Orono failed to recapture her as well and she, too, disappeared through the Circle of Granda exactly perpendicular to the Allerton Circle.

At the time, Valek had decided that Orono's talents and resources could be used in the capturing of more souls, but he probably should have tracked that one down.

Besides, he destroyed the Circle of Granda right after the soul escaped.

Perhaps he should have searched harder for the other Circles on Solis. Her escape was an omen and he had foolishly ignored it.

Now this new girl, too, had been rescued. He would not allow the matter to be unresolved, tempting others to try to escape. That would hurt business and business was the only thing that brought him pleasure.

And if that sorry sack of danker dung, Orono, was correct, the shield not only reflected the orb's power, but it also had a raised 'M' on it. Rumors from the cages of a group called the Minister Knights of Souls had such shields. The so-called saviors of souls. Rumor. Valek had initially denounced it as just that: rumor. He had now decided this rumor had its roots in fact.

"Manola, come here." Valek ordered to the seemingly vacant quarters.

Manola appeared from behind the shallow divider that separated Valek's office from his personal quarters.

"Yes," she slurred between rich red painted lips.

Valek smiled greedily as Manola made her way to his desk.

"Manola." He opened his arms wide as the heels of her thigh high boots clicked on the stony floor. She strutted over to him slowly at first, but the rhythm increased as she picked up her pace from a strut to a trot.

She reached his desk and hopped on it, pressing her naked buttocks against the cool, smooth surface of his golden desk. She crossed her legs and flipped back her red hair exposing full breasts partially contained by tight black velvet straps of her mini-dress.

Uncrossing her legs, she wrapped both around Valek's slender waist as she licked his face and purred.

"Why do you bother?" he whispered as he ran his hand through her hair. "I need information."

"Yes, my lord." She pouted when he continued to ignore her laps of affection.

An androgynous creature, Valek had only two pleasures: money and profit.

"Orono captured a soul, named Amana…"

"Yes." Manola licked her lips as she skillfully pulled him closer to her until her legs tightly locked around him.

"Her sister Sarah was rescued by a strange man at the Allerton Circle, and I want his name…"

Uncoiling from Valek, she leapt off the desk and made her way to the office door. The chilliness of the afternoon did not affect the scantily clad vixen, for she was dead. Valek kept her soul in a crystal bowl beside his bed.

"Quickly!" he demanded.

As soon as the office door closed behind her, Valek pulled open the desk drawer. The desk only had the one drawer; its purpose was more prop than use. He removed a blue orb, much larger than the orbs that Orono used to capture souls.

Indeed, this one was the 'mother' of the much smaller orbs. Valek was, above all else, a businessman. The violence and chaos surrounding the distribution of the potion Solance to the military groups of both Earth 3012 and Saturn Four was only remedied by the extremely generous amounts of funds donated to his establishment.

Not that the generals of both armies knew that he was selling the notorious potion to both sides, that was the beauty of commerce. All business deals were private.

The potion labeled "Solance" was creamy-white and tasted bitter and chalky, but it was not the potion's taste that sold bottles. It was the results.

Solance enabled whoever drank it to have the ability to read minds, an invaluable asset on the field of battle. Especially for Earth 3012 and Saturn Four, who had been warring against each other longer than he had been in existence.

But the Solance only lasted for 24 cycles before wearing off, leaving a bad aftertaste and an illness that caused one to return again and again to the potty house.

Sighing, Valek replaced the mother sphere into the desk and started towards his chambers. The day had been filled with demanding discussions with General Cullen from Earth 3012. He had used twice the Solance that he had in prior months and accused Valek of diluting the serum.

Chuckling to himself, he found the accusations humorous. He had done no such thing but the thought had occurred to him.

Diluting the serum would only ruin his dealings with General Cullen and he emphasized that. The General's bony face grew red and solemn as Valek informed him that his duty was to strengthen the serum and that he, Valek was doing just that.

He had said, "General Cullen, if you find Solance to be not what you are looking for, I can revisit our agreement and perhaps come up with a fair settlement."

The very mention of the revisiting of the contract meant a possibility that he would revoke the contract. That meant no Solance for General Cullen's army. If there was no Solance, General Cullen knew that he would lose the war.

General Cullen quickly said, "Oh, no, Valek, that will not be necessary. Forgive me, Valek."

He said, "Then can we discuss your next shipment?"

General Cullen nodded, "Yes."

Laughing at the memory, he opened the connecting door between his office and his private chambers. Pulling aside the wrought iron screen, he removed his leather boots immediately as he crossed the threshold.

Unlike most wealthy businessmen that he knew, he found guards, servants, and mistresses unnecessary and cumbersome. He had had servants before, but found that when he gave one specific orders, they would perpetually fail at delivering or carrying out those instructions, leaving him to have to go back and complete the orders. He found it more refreshing and satisfying when he carried out and completed his own desires, wishes, and goals.

But Valek believed it unwise to hold the notion that he could manage all matters himself. That was where Orono and Manola came into some importance. He oversaw each and every action they attempted, and the incident earlier in the day would have been better handled had he paid more attention.

Unfortunately, he had other duties to which he must attend to, like General Cullen's unexpected correspondence.

Sighing again, he passed through his outer quarters without taking a glance at the room or using the assistance of torches, candles or fireplace. Amazingly, he did not collide with the wooden bench made of acaia armata where Manola slept. Nor did he step into the only other furniture in the outer room, his square table of drink and herbs.

The outer quarters resided on the northern wing of Valek's castle, a modest, but heavily guarded castle that was built on the rocky plateau just above the soul cages and operating canyons of Solis's western continent.

The eastern, southern and most northern continents on Solis, although thriving villages and towns at one time in the planet's history, were now uninhabitable. The southern continent in particular at one time had an ocean to its western shore and mountains.

Industries found the tropical temperatures and scenic settings irresistible and before long, as it was with other planets and kingdoms, people populated the area in huge numbers.

Within several decades the people had abandoned the southern continent and migrated to the eastern continent, and eventually the most northern continents, destroying the environment and carelessly depleting Solis of its limited natural resources.

The story of Solis's destruction was as old and as common as the water that ran underground through her canyons and caverns, producing the impenetrable slick, oily rock that Valek called 'celleac'. He had found the one substance in the Pixlis galaxy that no one or nothing, not even a person's soul, could escape.

Leaving his boots in the outer room, he strolled barefoot to his inner bedchamber. Valek's feet fell silently on the stone floor due to the floor's coverings of human hair.

An extracted soul that is deposited immediately into the cages left a pile of lifeless skin, hair and body. Orono suggested that Valek use the hair for his personal floorings. A good idea Valek had responded, a rarity coming from Orono.

The remainder of the skin and body landed in a pit just outside the cages that was home to other garbage such as the remains of slaughtered fowls, beasts and henckens. The compiled waste of the potty-houses also ended up discarded in the pit.

Relief washed over Valek as he sat down on his polished wood bed. The bed contained no mattress nor pillow, neither quilt nor blanket. He never slept, his mind a prisoner of ideas and plans that swirled around in a chaos so fierce that his eyes remained open, unable to close and rest.

The three moons of Solis, full and bright and temporarily free of black clouds, illuminated a rectangular plot of Valek's quarters. Climbing onto the bed, Valek stared at the swirling patterns of the ceiling.

His mind returned again and again to the one who had escaped, the one called Sarah. No, the one that was rescued by another that came through the Allerton Circle.

It was not like him to second guess his decisions, but the nagging, relentless feeling that there were some things he had missed, an omen that he should have caught, would not be silent.

Whatever it was, it could only mean his destruction unless he identified it. He had learned over the years to pay attention to the details. Each time he had failed to watch the details, he had paid dearly.

He still remembered the old woman he threw rotting food at as a child. She warned him again and again to leave her alone. He ignored her warnings. He had ignored the wooden dolls she had hanging up in her windows with the knives and daggers stuck in them. He had ignored the details.

And one day he threw rotten food at her and she cursed him. He stood mesmerized as the old woman ran into her home, grabbed one of her wooden dolls and stabbed it.

Immediately Valek felt a sharp, burning pain in his stomach. He doubled over as bright red blood began to saturate his shirt. His friends raced for help and the local doctor had him fixed within the hour, but the pain remained.

He had ignored the details.

With eyes staring at the ceiling and sleep driven from him once again, Valek folded both hands across his bony chest and sighed.

***

Orono peeked into Valek's office and breathed a sigh of relief when he found it empty.

"He must have retired," he snorted before closing the office door and turning to MaxMion, a shorter, thinner version of Orono. Had MaxMion been taller than the average fig tree, he would be more intimidating.

His petite size deceived many and they found themselves rushing to the medicine man for herbal relief and balm, if they lived. He had enormous over pronounced teeth, two of which had been known to rip the tough flesh of wrangler birds without the aid of a knife, dagger or sword.

Legends abound that Valek discovered MaxMion on the home world of Earth 3012. He, with only two hands and a bumpy complexion, was a waif of a man who had the fighters of General Cullen frightened and fleeing when announced they had to face him in the tournaments of the King.

He had won so frequently in the tournaments that King Garison had decided to retire him to the slave mines on Earth 3012. Valek paid for his release and brought him to Solis to oversee the cages.

His compensation was neither money nor women, which he had difficulty finding due to his huge teeth. It was the flesh of some of the captured souls. Not all the bodies of the captured souls found their way to the garbage pit; some found their way to MaxMion's dining table.

Orono and MaxMion walked along the gloomy hallways towards the dungeons. The torches spaced out every five paces or so had been extinguished due to Valek's dislike for light. It hurt his eyes and often burned his pale skin when it was exposed to Solis's sun for too long.

For every step Orono's broad foot took, MaxMion, an entire head and shoulder shorter, had to take two. Barely out of breath, MaxMion maintained Orono's pace as Orono hurried to the dungeons.

"Are you sure it was her?" Orono asked for the third time that evening.

"Yes," MaxMion answered. "She altered herself then entered the cage with the one named Amana."

"Not another word." He placed a pudgy finger to his lips.

Valek's castle served one purpose and that was to provide shelter. Valek did not waste his wealth on fine, hand-sewn carpets, tapestries or furnishings. He did not entertain and he did not dance.

He did, however, believe that due to his growing wealth that others might attempt to take it. Therefore, the castle had been designed with many outlets to protect itself.

The location, high upon the rocky plateau of Solis's western continent, made the castle difficult to reach. The castle, called Vanor, rested behind a curtain wall that required the drawbridge be lowered to cross the moat which had been filled with a greenish liquid of questionable origin.

If an intruder had indeed passed all of these initial defenses, the castle itself was equipped on its roof with platforms that extended out from the castle that allowed for boiling oil, rocks, and other items to be dropped on attackers.

In addition to the platforms, the walls had parapets — slits on the roof that allowed arrows to be shot through to oncoming attackers.

As they rounded the final corner and descended the spiraling steps to the dungeon, Orono grabbed the sole torch in the staircase as they descended further and further below the castle.

The dungeon did not hold prisoners, but were the chambers of Orono, MaxMion and other henchmen who worked for Valek. Only Manola resided inside the official castle walls.

Entering the first square four paces-by-four paces cell, Orono placed his hefty bulk on the flat mattress on the stony floor.

"So, he did not trust me to locate the girl and the mystery man?" Orono asked.

MaxMion squeezed inside the cell that had seemed to grow smaller with Orono taking up more than three-quarters of it.

"That is the way I see it," he answered around his teeth.

"Fine, then I will show him." Orono patted his stomach. "I have had it up to here with his snide comments!"

MaxMion only nodded. He had heard these arguments from Orono before.

"Come, let us rest." Orono rolled onto his back, tossing the torch onto the cell's floor.

The torch sizzled then went out as MaxMion crawled onto Orono's lumpy stomach and slept.

Chapter Three

"Wake up," Marion's voice called. It sounded far away, like it was down in one of the pits of Solis where the echoes of the caverns amplified the moans and groans of the multitude of slaves. Amana was there now, adding her voice to the chorus of lost souls.

When Sarah opened her eyes, he stood above her with a worried expression that was hastily erased when he saw her eyes focus on him. He grunted as he stepped away. She sat up and rubbed the back of her neck where a purpling bruise had emerged.

"There is not a great deal of time for me to tell you all, so listen carefully."

Sarah stood shakily and held tightly to Marion's outstretched hand as the dizziness and nausea passed.

"Do not try to leave again," he ordered.

Sarah wondered how her rescuer could turn into a kidnapper with one swoop of her tongue and a simple suggestion.

"Do you understand?" he asked as he applied pressure to her slender hand.

"Yes." She grimaced as she tried to free her hand from his huge hand. It was rough and callused.

"Good." His solemn face lit up into a smile and he started again towards the direction of the castle to the north, but Sarah noticed that they were further north then before.

He went over to where the danker beasts, short and broad hairy creatures that were used as beasts of burden, waited near a small pond. The pond seemed to be partially frozen by Veloris's bleak climate. The danker beasts were prepared and well adapted to the harshness of Veloris. Their thick hairy hide covered all but their eyes and short pink nostrils. They snorted and passed gas on such a continual basis that it filled the air with the putrid odor of rotting food, yet they were dependable and quick despite their four trunk-like legs.

"Get on." Marion tossed a blanket over one of the smaller female danker beasts. "Thanks to you, we are now later than usual. We must use the danker beasts to reach the castle before nightfall."

He lifted her on to the smaller danker beast, careful to allow his hands to remain around her waist longer than necessary. She seemed so fragile that he wanted to be careful with her. She was a precious commodity, not to mention a pretty one.

The moon had sunk further in the sky, and the mountain ranges to the west seemed farther away where earlier they seemed closer. How far had they traveled while she was asleep?

"As you may not be aware, Solis is the home planet of Valek. He draws his strength from there," Marion said.

Sarah sighed. She knew this; she had been a prisoner on Solis.

"It was not by chance that you and Amana escaped the cages." Marion continued ignoring her displeasure at his history lesson.

"What?" she balked. "We distinctly planned for months and months on that escape. We hoarded as many sharp objects and rocks in which to saw through those damn chains..."

"Yes, yes," he interrupted impatiently.

"...The hours spent slowly crushing and destroying the objects." Sarah continued totally engrossed in the memory of the planning of the escape from the soul cages. There were four of them that dared to attempt an escape: Amana, Suzie, Margaret and Sarah. Margaret's soul number was called just one week into their plan. Then Amana's capture at the Allerton Circle. Suzie — well, Sarah did not know what happened to Suzie.

"The other you were to meet at the Allerton Circle," he interrupted again louder and more firmly.

"Was another in my camp, a female from Earth 3341 named Suzie."

"No, was I." Marion laughed. "Suzie was a decoy, a sacrifice if you will..."

"A sacrifice?" The words felt foreign on Sarah's tongue. There had been many that sacrificed themselves already for the cages. Did Suzie have to be one more?

"Many have given their lives for your arrival in this place." Marion took in a deep breath and secretly cursed Valek and his cages.

"You are very important, Sarah," he concluded. He then offered a silent prayer that she was all that they had risked, gambled and died for. She had better be that good.

***

The Northern Forest's landscape was pathetically beautiful due to its fantastic flowers, evergreens and colorful arrangements and vegetation that flourished amid the white snow. Every once in awhile the electric blue of Wrangler birds could be seen, or the pale whiteness of the owlers could be spooked from the trees. It gave the area the appearance of a detailed painting; the harsh numbing coldness did not give anyone the opportunity to stay around long enough to enjoy the view.

There were lakes and rivers the color of crystal blue, and then there were others that were as black as tar or as red as blood. It was beyond anything that Earth could produce.

Fish and other aquatic animals were plentiful in some of the lakes, deep below the icy surface and down into the depths of the lake. Most were poisonous; others had only been seen once or twice and never captured.

Marion had warned that some of the lakes were poisonous. Sarah was reminded of the legend of the Garden of Eden, where everything was beautiful but that one tree meant death if fruit from it was eaten.

This was not a pleasure trip and Sarah mentally slapped her hand for allowing herself to become distracted by Marion's knowledge of Veloris.

Many questions rolled around in her mind that were not answered by Marion's educational tale of Veloris's forest. Why was she chosen to be here? Who exactly was Marion? He said that he was one of the Minister Knights of

Souls, but she had never actually met a Minister Knight of Souls, so what if he was a fake? What if it was all a lie?

What if it was not?

There was only one way to find out some answers.

"Why me?" Sarah asked. "What am I really doing here?"

The stone castle peeked over the lush evergreen and powder blue hues of the thriving Northern Forest. Twilight crept slowly onto the home of the Ministers of Souls.

"All in good time," Marion responded. "Behold the palace of Queen Zoë."

He pointed to the tips of the castle's stone towers that seemed to be nestled into the violet purple sky. A few bright specs of distant stars lazily winked in the frigid night sky.

They moved closer to the castle and Sarah began to relax, as the arrival at the castle meant she could get away from the disgusting danker beasts. Not to mention, perhaps she would meet with Queen Zoë and persuade her to order Marion back to Solis to rescue her sister.

The snapping of twigs and the rustling of leaves were the only indication that they were not alone in the forest, as Marion had mentioned earlier. Just because they could not see the animals did not mean they were not there and when night completely blanketed the forest, those animals would acquaint themselves in the most violent way.

The trail snaked and circled upward towards the castle. It was worn despite the unyielding ground. The frozen prints of former danker beasts lined the trail that Marion and Sarah now marched over. She could only see the tip of the full moon above the alpine trees. This section of the Northern Forest was quieter and the snow seemed more recent. Fluffy and dust-like, the snow remained undisturbed.

The heavy breathing of the danker beasts and their expulsion of gas caused Sarah to choke. Their breath blew frozen clouds into the air; the sound added to the chorus of nocturnal creatures. The smell of decaying flesh spread with every breath of wind.

Marion snorted and finally allowed himself to observe Sarah. Since the rescue at the Circle, Marion had anticipated the moment when he would get the chance to observe her without the threat of her running away or throwing him one of her fiery looks.

Sarah had draped another heavy wool blanket over her shoulders. The edges, tattered and frayed, were pulled tightly across her slender shoulders. A thick braid hung to the small of her back and a few tiny spiral curls had escaped and floated along the front of her face.

Letting his eyes roam over her lovely oval face, Marion found it difficult to pinpoint what made Sarah so alluring. It was not just those green eyes, that when vexed grew large and round then dark like the deepest emerald. Nor was it just her skin, which was the color of honey and demanded that he reach out and run his finger along her cheek and taste her sweetness.

"What?" Sarah asked as she caught his heated gaze.

"Nothing," he gruffly replied with a small playful smile.

***

Sarah remained quiet; the dimly lit forest did nothing to comfort her. The blanket only slightly warmed her and she could no longer feel her feet or toes. It was not the vacant feel that was associated with the soul cages; it was the numb stinging and biting of nerves freezing.

"The evenings are the worst," Marion explained as he watched her shudder. He had no idea she would be so poorly dressed for Veloris's climate. He had only been to Solis once or twice and the slaves never wore clothes. Rags were more like it. Yet he should have been prepared to have more clothes for her. Orono's appearance at the Circle was a surprise.

Marion grunted to himself. He hated surprises.

"I will not be here long enough to find out," Sarah curtly replied.

Just the sound of his voice caused Sarah's teeth to clench. Valek she hated, but Marion she was growing to dislike as well. Not exactly the best way to embrace a rescuer, but he could easily turn into one of Valek's henchmen.

Sarah studied the brand on Marion's left bicep. The brand that had been burned into his flesh, the skin around the burn had scarred horribly. No one would voluntarily submit to such pain. The muscles under the tattoo caused it to appear to move around when they did, this was no magic; the tattoo was real.

"It is real; I am really a Minister Knight," Marion replied to Sarah's critical stare.

Sarah averted her eyes to the trail ahead, after a few seconds she observed Marion out of the corner of her eye.

It was now Sarah's turn to observe him. The danker beast was enormous, but the huge beast did not diminish his size.

Unaffected by the harsh climate, he only wore the black leather pants and the heavy boots. Around his waist was what Sarah could only call a sword. Indeed it was a sword, at least as long as her arm. On his back was the shield that had saved her from a return trip to the cages.

His glasses rested on top of his naked head, he had a commanding attitude, one commonly found on those in charge. Stern and unsmiling, Marion could be quite terrifying.

Sarah remembered his ferociousness during her rescue and shuddered. But at the same time, when he smiled, he lit up the forest. He was more handsome than any prince or king that Sarah had ever saw in the storybooks her mother read her as a child. That too was long before the cages.

After such a careful evaluation she discovered she was no closer to deciding if he was a knight in shining armor or a nightmare lying in wait

"There it is," Marion sighed in relief as if he did not expect to see it ever again. "Home."

"You are anxious to get there?" Marion called as Sarah coaxed her danker beast passed him towards the castle in a quickened trot.

Tapestries with gold and silver M's and white backgrounds hung from the outside walls. Shrubs the color of blue, red and orange lined the areas to the left and right of the door. Gray weathered stones stacked together in a pattern of interlocking rocks were cemented together and rose towards the sky, slivers of windows were sparingly scattered across the stony structure.

The thin air ripped violently through the trees, whistling and moaning as if disturbed by the presence of the two on danker beasts. Sarah shuddered as she waited outside the massive castle that stretched up towards the now full moon draped in darkening purple.

"This is it?" she asked in disbelief.

Marion guided the danker beast to the door. There was no need to knock for as soon as Marion approached the door disappeared.

Just across the threshold, he leapt off the danker beast. Inside the castle, people hurried about towards various duties despite the late hour. A group of young children noisily played a game of marbles; there were several enormous hearths that cast shadows across the walls. The castle was much more capacious inside than what one was lead to believe when standing outside.

Above the chaos, a shout of joy could be heard. Sarah descended the danker beast and watched as a young man shoved people out of the way as he raced towards them. He jumped over the fruit cart, and then sidestepped one of the bakers and a tray of hot rolls

The red leather pants threatened to rip as the man continued to run. He hurdled himself over a row of chairs and did not break a sweat.

Marion's face darkened like an approaching thunderstorm as he took off his sword. He watched with mounting displeasure at the young man's agility.

"Marion!" The young man yelled as the crowd of servants paid no attention to his yells, except to get out of his way.

The young man ran directly into him, nearly knocking off Marion's glasses. He then grabbed the slightly bigger Marion in a bear hug. He, too, was shirtless from the waist up. He was not even breathing hard.

Marion said, "Let go, Kalah, you are ruining my hardened image."

Sarah inched further into the foyer. She studied the young man that stood face to face with Marion.

He was only an inch or two shorter than Marion, but despite this his chest was just as wide and brawny. Kalah had a few tightly coiled blonde hairs sprinkled across his chest.

He had the same pale gray eyes, but his nose was skinnier and his lips thinner than Marion's. He was not unhandsome; he simply paled next to Marion.

"My apologies, brother," Kalah's voice held the hopefulness of youth. It was apparent to Sarah that Kalah had not been exposed to cynics or apathy.

Or the cages.

"Been busy in my absence?" Marion slapped Kalah affectionately on the back. "Little brother?"

He then reached to rub Kalah's bald head.

Kalah's youth reminded Sarah again of Amana. Amana, before the cages, was hopeful and full of life, goals and dreams. Her grief left a lump in her throat.

The delicious smell of roasted meat made Sarah's stomach growl loudly. It had been ages since she felt the pang of hunger, due to her life being vacant of a soul while imprisoned in the cages. Marion touched Sarah gently on the shoulder and said, "Come, let us eat, and then find you some warm clothes."

"My apology, my lady," Kalah said as he turned his gray eyes to Sarah.

"No problem," she said, as suddenly her feet had begun to thaw and ache from the icy trek through the forest. The day had been lengthy and she longed to rest. Despite Kalah's warm greetings to both her and Marion, she sensed tension in the air that seemed to come with his arrival.

Picking one of the torches from the wall, Kalah lead the way to the East Dining Hall. As they walked towards the East Wing, the noise of the main entranceway grew less. The hallway also grew narrower, only Kalah and Marion could fit the width of the hallway together. Sarah walked behind the two, silently watching the various paintings of persons draped in robes of rich colors and jewelry.

"Was the mission difficult?" Kalah asked in a more serious tone than that of the playful brother he had used earlier in the foyer. The excitement of Marion's return had died just as abruptly as it began.

"Orono was surprised!" Marion said proudly. "But Valek has destroyed several of the Circles on Solis. Escape from there will become nearly impossible before long. We will need to act soon."

"Impossible!" Kalah stopped short in disbelief. "Surely not…"

Shaking his head dolefully, Marion said, "It is true." Taking a deep breath, gradually letting it out, then said, "He grows stronger still"

"Queen Zoë must be told at once." Kalah pounded his fist into his huge palm. Thick fingers curled around into a clenched fist.

"How is she?" A concerned look wrinkled Marion's smooth complexion.

"She asks for you every rotation," Kalah grudgingly disclosed.

"What does Octiva say?" Marion turned to look at Kalah. Sarah noted again how much the two looked alike, almost mirror images of the other. Even now the concern for the Queen Zoë was reflected in both faces. But the younger one, Kalah seemed tense…almost angry where just moments…

Kalah did not answer and Marion searched his brother's face before turning to go back down the hallway, past Sarah and towards the main entranceway leaving her alone with his little brother.

Kalah turned to her and said; "I will show you to your room. Food will be brought in for you."

"My room?" she questioned as they started again down the hall towards the east.

"Why, yes," he remarked surprised at her question.

"But I thought..."

"You are not a prisoner; you are a guest," he answered Sarah's unasked question.

They reached the end of the narrow hallway, which led them to the East Wing Dining Hall. It was a sizable open room complete with three wooden dining tables, wooden benches and people cleaning the remaining scraps of meat and meal from the table and floors.

To the left of the hall was a staircase that led to the second floor Kalah pointed and the two started up the steps with him slightly ahead.

The dimly lit staircase curling along to the second floor felt chilly as her bare feet stepped timidly onto each step. Gritty patches were unavoidable and the grimy feeling when Sarah stepped on it would cause her stomach to turn. Candelabras secured tightly to the wall with iron-like brackets in the drafty stairway failed to cast enough light.

The second floor hallway was short. There were three doors: two on the right and one on the left. A sliver of a window covered with a greenish-white glass was at the end of the Hallway.

"This is your room." Kalah stopped at the only door on the left side of the hallway. Turning the knob, he shoved open the heavy wooden door as if it were a feather. Sarah could feel the fear stick in her throat making it hard for her to swallow. She inched into the room behind him, careful not to walk into him.

The room ran the length of the hallway. A window, identical to the one in the hallway, adorned the far wall.

Sarah let out a scream as her foot felt something furry and she jumped back from where she was standing. Kalah moved the torch toward her and in the illumination and she discovered a rug. It was furry and made of some animal, which she had never seen. Blushing, she chuckled nervously.

"It is a danker rug," Kalah said before moving to the fireplace just across from a huge sleigh bed. The room was soon washed in light once he tossed the diminished torch into the fireplace.

He said, "The bed is made of a heavy wooden frame and springs made with interlaced strips of leathers that have been overlaid with a feather mattress. You should find this room very comfortable."

Sarah sat down cautiously on the bed and touched the thick blanket. She eagerly pulled the blanket back and ran her hand across the crisp white sheets.

"Danker…as in danker beast?" she asked as she sniffed the air for the animal's distinct smell.

"Yes, but this one's fur has been washed several times and perfumed," Kalah explained with an amused smile.

The room held a warm glow as the fire chased the arctic chills away. It was sparsely furnished; the bed was the only major piece of furniture. The room was more long than wide with the fireplace and bed occupying the area closest to the door.

Further down the length of the room was an abandoned rocking chair with a woven basket beside it filled with balls of yarn and two knitting needles. Light from the nearby window illuminated the chair in a silver glow.

"This is it." He wearily waved his hand towards the window and behind him to the fireplace. The smell of rain and smoke stained the room, giving it the drafty smell of a dungeon.

Sarah crept over to the window and looked out. Whispers of cold air squeezed through the almost invisible spaces between the stone castle and the window's glass. Directly across from her room, she could make out a cluster of homely cottages, all one level and all constructed in a circular pattern. Some of the cottages had illumination; she could just make out flickering candles. To the left of the cluster of cottages, the beginnings of the Northern Forest stretched its blackening tree limbs towards the small cluster of homes as if reaching out for the light.

Kalah kneeled over the fireplace and placed a round, ceramic pot over the fire by taking a metal rod and suspending the pot via a metal loop over the fire. The pot was battered and dented...heavily used. She wondered how long it had been sitting there.

"What's that?"

"Evening meal, for you," he replied as he placed the utensils on the fireplace and around the poker. "Marion or I will come to notify you for meals in the future."

He moved closer to the door. "Do not leave the castle. Although you are a guest here, you are too valuable to lose."

"Why?" she asked as she squatted in front of the warm fire.

He sighed noisily before saying, "Later. Now, eat, sleep and rest."

He turned to go and she saw the brand on his left biceps.

"You are a Minister too?"

"Yes," Kalah answered before closing the door.

"But-" she stammered. The door slammed shut as Kalah left, before she could ask any more questions. She could not hear his boots as he walked down the stairs. Nice fellow, she smirked. She wondered if he got that attitude from Marion.

Two feather pillows and a couple of additional blankets lay on the bed. Beside the blanket a flannel gown and socks seemed to be casually placed. Sarah quickly took off her clothes and put on the much warmer gown and socks, noting the full softness and fuzziness. Her toes wiggled in the soft comfort of the socks and she felt the gown again and again, relishing her ability to feel and touch. The cages stripped her of those feelings and abilities for years. Each new sensation — the smell of the fire, the crackling of the wood as it burned, and the softness of her flannel gown overwhelmed her senses.

Kalah had started a pot of stew. She used her top to awkwardly remove the hot lid. Directly next to the fire were bowls, wooden spoons and a bunch of blue logs haphazardly piled together.

Using the spoon, she made herself a small dinner. She rolled the meat and vegetables around in her mouth before swallowing. Morsels of meat flavored with spices Sarah could not identify melted in her mouth and the enticing aroma soon filled the room. She decided the meal was good and greedily ate two more bowls before climbing into bed.

Her feet ached and had begun to dry. She removed her socks and climbed out of bed. She kneeled next to the cooling pot of stew and dipped her socks. The water was not hot but warm. She wrung the excess liquid from the socks and gently placed her injured feet back into them.

Yawning loudly, Sarah crawled beneath the blankets and finally slept.

Chapter Four

The sun rose with pale streaming rays of light that illuminated Sarah's room, forcing her to greet the new day. Blue smoke floated up, spiraling into the crisp morning air from the extinguished fire from last night.

"Wake up." Marion shook her gently allowing his fingers to straighten one of her corkscrew curls before releasing it to spring back into its taut spiral. Licking his lips nervously he squatted closer to her bedside.

"Up," she mumbled, as she remained buried beneath the blanket, only her curls could be seen.

"The room, is it to your liking?" Marion asked softly.

He touched her again, this time on the shoulder, sliding down the blanket with his fingers that seemed to have a mind of their own as they curled themselves around the free strands of her hair, across her parted lips and on to her smooth cheeks.

With a gasp, she opened her eyes and bolted upright in the bed. "What are you doing?"

Snatching the blanket towards her chest, she scooted away from Marion with a confused look of shock.

"Waking you," he stiffly responded as he turned his attention to the room's sole window, away from her.

"Did you sleep well?" he asked again.

"Yes." She moved the blanket cautiously down to just below her waist. "I had strange dreams of Amana and Solis."

"Yes, well, I am sure you did," Marion said. "You will meet the Queen today. She has a great deal to tell you, Sarah."

"Right," she mumbled just low enough to avoid being heard.

"I brought you clothes." Marion pointed to the rocking chair that now had clothes folded neatly, resting in its seat. "I will be outside while you change."

When she finally emerged some several minutes later, dressed in black leather pants, boots and a charcoal gray sweater, Marion felt his knees start to buckle, but he grabbed the wall anxiously to stop himself from collapsing to the floor.

Her hair, loose and free, only added an aurora of divinity to Sarah. Gone was the desolate woman he rescued from the cages only yesterday, here was a fantastic free woman.

A beautiful woman.

Perhaps beautiful wasn't right word. She was not a stunning princess beauty, but there was that something, just beneath the surface that intrigued him and plowed away at his restraint.

"Can I eat first?" she asked as she placed her hand over her flat stomach.

"You will be eating with the Queen this morning," Marion said.

"Oh," she said, which only brought a small smile to Marion's lips, but no additional commentary as he started down the staircase.

Following close behind, she asked, "Who is Queen Zoë exactly?"

She could hear Marion's surprised intake of air at the question.

"She is the originator of the Minister Knights of Souls," he said.

"Marion, why am I here?"

"The Queen will explain it," he said. "Trust me."

He had hoped the full night's rest would have softened her desire for answers, but it would seem it did not. Her innocence and her radiance this morning slowly nibbled away at his resolve to remain silent… and his tight control over his growing lust. He almost told her the true reason for her rescue just to erase the concern and fear that marked her face.

"Trust you?" She stopped as he turned around.

"Please, the Queen awaits," Marion started again down the hallway to the West Wing of the castle. The hallway partially lit by candles and hangings of alternating purple and black helped show the way. Huge banners scripted with the Minister Knight's crest lined the hallway opposite the windows and drapes.

"Patience," he whispered.

The early morning quietness made the castle seem sinister and surreal. Marion wanted Sarah to be told of her purpose immediately and in detail. He knew that Queen Zoë was very ill and it was she who knew the entire Antiqk scrolls and the predictions. Best Sarah get her answers from the closest source.

***

The open hearths, black and empty, gave the main foyer the feel of being deserted. The night before, the foyer was alive with children and people, but in the wee hours of the new day was vacant. Indeed the entire castle remained quiet and still. The only indication of life was the occasional passing of one of the servants burdened with the early morning chores of carrying the food to the kitchens from the storage cellars for morning meal.

The sweet aroma of sugary glaze and baked breads faint at first grew stronger as Marion and Sarah made their way to the West Wing Hall. The Great Hall as it was often referred to, was the only Hall in which the Minister Knights ate and celebrated. The Great Hall also had the larger of the two kitchens adjacent to it; the East Wing Hall had the smaller of the kitchens.

"The Great Hall," Marion announced softly as to not to wake the remainder of the castle. Strewn about on the floor were branches and various herbs speckled and colorful from the Northern Forest. She recognized some of the plants and flowers from her trip through the forest.

On the walls were elaborate carpets made from woven threads in charming colors of burgundy and pictures of Veloris landscapes. Dining tables set on trestles were covered with white linen cloths. In the middle of each table sat burned down candles and cooled wax statues. The morning sun streaming through the various windows and into the Hall provided plenty of illumination for the day's meals.

Just off to the right of the entranceway, an octagonal fireplace lazily warmed the enormous open room.

Marion took Sarah's hand as he led her into the Great Hall. Seated past the wooden benches and tables, up closer to the front of the Hall was a raised dais of stone similar to the stones used to construct the castle. It was away from the drafts and intrusions that came from people seated at the tables and coming and going through the entranceway during meals; it was far enough away from the belching, boisterous partying and celebrating of the Knights that went on each nightly meal.

Queen Zoë sat seemingly dwarfed by a massive chair with a sheer lilac canopy announcing her royalty.

Stunning and elegant, her intermingled black ringlets were streaked with silver and cascaded freely to her waist. Around her tiny waist was a golden interwoven cord. The somber purple robe appeared to be made of a heavy fabric that probably served one purpose, to protect the Queen against the wintry nights of Veloris.

"Good morning, child," Queen Zoë said calmly as she directed her full attention to Sarah.

She had thin, almost invisible lips and high cheekbones with pale gray eyes surrounded by wrinkles. Coughing, she held her robe tightly to her chest as Marion raced to her side. The Queen continued to cough and bark; it was a ravaging cough that caused her frail body to shake and shudder.

"Water! Get some water!" Marion shouted to one of the passing servants.

Before the servant could move, Kalah appeared from the side entranceway with a cup of water.

"Here."

Draining the cup of its contents, Queen Zoë patted Marion's head and gave the now empty cup back to Kalah who remained standing behind her chair.

Straightening her robe and running a hand through her hair, Queen Zoë cleared her throat and offered Sarah a smile.

"Come, closer." Hoarse and barely above a whisper, Queen Zoë beckoned Sarah to move closer and gestured for Marion and Kalah to leave. Silently they left the Great Hall through the main entranceway.

Kneeling before the chair, a fluttering of nervousness danced around in her stomach as the aroma of the morning meal from the kitchen scented the Great Hall.

"You have many, many questions," Queen Zoë said for it was hardly a question.

"Yes, Yes." Sarah said as she placed a hand over her squirming stomach.

"I can see them behind your eyes, waiting and moving about, rolling around again and again demanding to be asked." Queen Zoë smiled. "Go ahead...ask them."

"Can we go back to save my sister, Amana?" She held her breath as she waited for an answer.

"You will return to save her; yes." Queen Zoë answered.

"Yes! But Marion said—"

"Marion did not lie to you," Queen Zoë interrupted. "Morning meal will wait, no?"

Confused, Sarah answered quickly, "Yes..."

Queen Zoë waved off the servant who, unbeknownst to Sarah, had stood behind her and inquired about morning meals.

"Yes we can rescue her, but no we can not?" Sarah asked.

"It is best if we start at the beginning," Queen Zoë said as she took several deep breaths.

Nodding, Sarah waited for the Queen to gain enough strength to explain.

"Along time ago, long before the age of frost and cages, the worlds of Saturn Four and Earth 3012 were shared colonies of Earth."

"But Earth does not exist any more…" Sarah interrupted.

"Yes, but this is shortly after the colonizations," Queen Zoë smiled. "The shared colonies traded freely and were quite friendly towards each other. However, when King Nathaniel of Saturn Four wanted his daughter Amber to marry the son of King Tartan, Malcolm, a disagreement arose. You see, King Tartan's son was already promised to the daughter of King Ander of Veloris Three

"It came to pass that King Nathaniel demanded the unification of Saturn Four and Earth 3012 by the wedding of his daughter to King Tartan's son or else there would be a levy strapped to the trade of certain merchandise and goods.

"Well, King Tartan could not break his agreement with King Ander. King Ander's marriage to his son would unite Veloris Three and Earth 3012, which would give Veloris Three a larger army and outpost in the sector of that galaxy as well as access to more cultured items like ancient scrolls, books and fine carpets.

"Angered all the more at King Tartan's repeated rejections, King Nathaniel applied the levy. And for many years the people of Earth 3012 paid the tax to keep the peace, but not without comment."

"Years went by and eventually the younger people of Earth 3012 stopped paying the levy and soon all trade between Saturn Four and Earth 3012 ceased. Their relations completely broke down. This was not in King Nathaniel's plan; therefore he tried to take what he could not freely have.

The annihilation of Veloris Three was simply King Nathaniel getting back at King Tartan."

"What happened to Veloris Three?" Sarah asked.

"King Nathaniel, well, his daughter Manola, practiced magic and she disguised herself as the daughter of King Tartan. She visited Veloris Three and met King Ander's son. While there it is said she cursed Veloris Three and the young prince. When she left, Veloris Three exploded."

"So, King Tartan's daughter had no prince and Earth 3012 had no army." Sarah concluded.

"Yes. But there is no proof that Manola's alleged curse actually destroyed the planet. Some say it was over-mining."

Queen Zoë paused to clear her throat.

"It did not matter. Tartan was furious and blamed King Nathaniel."

"A war?" she asked.

Nodding slowly, Queen Zoë said, "Yes. They went to war and have been at war ever since."

"And Valek?"

Standing, Queen Zoë crept to the side entranceway, her bare feet stepping cautiously, taking each step gradually. "Come, this is no place to discuss such matters as him."

Sarah followed the Queen down the side entranceway that forked one path to the kitchen, the other up a close spiral staircase that lead to the second floor, then they walked down the short hallway and off to the right they arrived at the Queen's chambers. Three guards stood watch just outside her door.

"Good morning," The guards stated in unison.

"Good morning," Queen cheerfully responded. "Come, Sarah."

The guards did not seem to notice or question Sarah's presence with the Queen. They made no indication that they saw her at all. As tall as some of the evergreens growing in the forest, with thick tree trunk-like arms and bulky frames, the guards were identical in appearance from their dull brown eyes to their huge bare feet that had four toes on each foot and extended yellowing toenails.

They carried no weapons, beside their appearance and size; Sarah had no doubt that the three were some trick of magic and wondered where they came from.

Yet another question to ask the Queen.

Pulling back the silver wire embellished screen, Sarah entered the Queen's chambers, which was comprised of two rooms: a small sitting room and a larger bedroom. Sarah expected the Queen's room to at least have a door, not a screen to protect Veloris's most prized citizen and royal. Again, Sarah wondered if possible magic and sorcery had any place in Veloris and the Queen's castle. Was it the Queen that practiced magic or some other which Sarah had yet to meet?

Decorated in rich, warm tones of copper and brown, the sitting room had a few chairs and one rounded wooden bench. Here too, herbs of rosemary, leaves of evergreens and acacia trees were tossed about on the floor.

Miniature tapestries hung from the walls; one pictured a reproduction of Marion, although a much younger man in the tapestry and directly across was a mirroring tapestry of Kalah. In the middle, next to Marion's tapestry rested the

Minister Knights of Souls' banner embroiled with silver thread and made of a finer cloth. It had a far more regal appearance than the one hanging in the castle's foyer.

Cattycorner to the entrance was a fireplace, but no windows, the only illumination arriving through several torches that were mounted to the walls. Two shelves filled with jars of herbs, toadstool and other substances occupied a tiny space of the sitting room.

A petite anteroom adjoined the sitting room and Sarah could only speculate on the cloth, jewels and spices that might be stored there.

Sarah made her way to one of the elegant, high backed chairs, but Queen Zoë entered into the other room.

Sarah followed and entered the Queen's bedchamber, where an enormous bed with four electric blue posters and a soft bluish linen curtain hung. The curtain pulled back in the daytime and closed at night for privacy as well as protection from the bitter cold. The bed took up most of the room. Three fluffy feather pillows in varying shapes rested at the top of the bed and quilts and blankets were folded neatly along the width of the bed.

Taking a torch from the wall, Queen Zoë placed a few electric blue logs into the boxy fireplace to the right of the bed then tossed in the torch.

"It chases away the chill," Queen Zoë explained. "This planet is so cold."

Sarah remained standing as she looked over the Queen's room. To the left of the bed was a makeshift chest, made of the same wood as the bed. Homely, it had scars and dings. Not what one would expect a Queen's room to be like, although she had never been in a Queen's room before.

On the floor were crushed petals of every color and shape giving the room its perfumed smell of forest.

The two windows with creamy, almost clear glass offered views of the west side of the castle, which showed the rising sun and snippets of the Northern Forest. Sarah thought the view from her room was better.

"Where was I?" Queen Zoë asked as she climbed into her bed and under the covers. She leaned over, reached for the quilt, and unrolled it.

"Valek," Sarah said as she helped the weak Queen place the quilt over the bed.

"Oh, yes, Valek." Queen Zoë fingered the quilt's fringed ends. "Yes, well, Valek had been a smuggler of small shipments of spices, garments and supplies between Earth 3012 and Saturn Four. Although at war, certain people on both worlds had a desire for what the other planet offered And Valek made a business out of smuggling those items. A big business."

Queen Zoë concluded by sighing and lying back against the two fluffy pillows.

"So, what do the soul cages have to do with his business of smuggling clothes, spices and supplies between Saturn Four and Earth 3012?" Sarah asked.

Closing her eyes, Queen Zoë did not answer.

"Queen Zoë!" Sarah touched the Queen's slender shoulder feeling the bony frame beneath the thick robe.

"Yes?" Queen Zoë opened her eyes slowly.

"Valek and the soul cages?" Sarah urged as she stood up from the bed.

"Valek's soul cages and kidnapping of souls began about twenty rotations ago. He discovered this potion on a trip to someplace outside the Pixlis galaxy that allows him to read minds."

"Impossible!" Sarah gasped. The old Queen must have truly lost grip with reality.

"But true." Queen Zoë patted Sarah's hand. "Please, child, I must rest now."

"But." Sarah started then fell silent as she watched Queen Zoë close her eyes and her body relax into the comforting arms of sleep.

Bewildered, Sarah glanced outside the window, Veloris's shallow sun had rose just above the tops of the forest and shined down on the blinding white snow on the ground. The day had just begun, and the Queen was already sound asleep as evident by her snore that tenderly resounded through the bedroom.

Unsure, Sarah left the Queen's quarters with her head full of more questions than what she had when she entered.

Chapter Five

Sarah closed the screen and brushed past the three royal guards. They did not acknowledge her as she squeezed by them and walked down the spiral staircase.

With hopes dashed and engrossed in a whirlwind of questions, Sarah stepped off the bottom step and directly into a woman who happened to be crossing her path, causing the woman to drop the items she was carrying.

"Oh! I am terribly sorry." Sarah hurried to assist the woman who smelled of danker beast and forest.

Holding her nose, Sarah stepped back five paces from the young woman with the woman's garments extended out to her. "You dropped these."

Shorter than Sarah by only a couple of inches and sporting a short blonde wooly-hair Afro, the woman lowered her tinted glasses and smiled at Sarah.

"Hello," she said.

Surprised by the sultriness of the strange woman's voice, Sarah offered a quick "hello" and stepped back three paces more. The danker beast was strong and awful.

"Danker beast." The woman laughed revealing a set of tiny, even teeth that seemed to fit just perfectly in her mouth. Her lips were thin and her skin resembled the slick surface of Solis, midnight blue. Perhaps it was more an indigo color, and as the woman turned to the left, Sarah noticed a short, narrow scar just above her right eye.

The woman removed her tinted glasses and placed her dagger into a pocket within her velvet boots and said, "My name is Zykeiah."

"Sarah."

Zykeiah had amazingly bright eyes and as they remained rested on Sarah, Sarah started to squirm under the woman's intense glare. But Zykeiah did not seem to want to move and Sarah could not go around her due to the hallway's narrowness. The retched smell of danker beast had killed the remainder of Sarah's appetite and the only thing she wanted more than to escape to her room was for this woman to move from her path.

"I see you have met," Marion said as he appeared from around the corner to Zykeiah. "I did not know you were coming so soon today. I thought I would see you closer to dusk."

Zykeiah finally removed her gaze from Sarah and over to Marion whom seemed unabashed by her fierce glare. "There is much to tell."

"I am sure." He patted Zykeiah on the back and added, "But first things are first; your celebration and dubbing ceremony…"

"…is tomorrow," Zykeiah finished. "Yes, I know."

"Then you must meet with tailors, bathe and then see Queen Zoë"

He flicked Zykeiah's ear playfully, smirking at her.

"Yes, but first I must talk to the Queen." She glanced at Sarah then back to Marion.

"No, first you must bathe!" Marion quipped. "I will help you."

He winked at Zykeiah and playfully slapped her bottom.

Laughing, Zykeiah playfully punched him in the stomach and Sarah noticed her well-sculptured arms. This Zykeiah had little stock on her bones, her build, although not tall, was stout and solid, like a hard, rigid stone wall.

"Come on, Zykeiah." Marion teased all the more as the two of them wrestled.

Sarah watched with growing impatience at how comfortable they were with each other. Marion did not order this woman around or treat her like a child, the way he treated Sarah.

"Pardon," Sarah mumbled as she pushed past Zykeiah, who had Marion in a headlock, and rounded the corner leaving the two to discuss whatever 'celebration' they needed to. She had not been told of any celebration or dubbing. In fact, neither Marion nor Kalah had mentioned anything of the sort.

They continued to reiterate that she was not a prisoner, so why did they treat her as such? She could neither leave nor was she informed of news that surely everyone in the castle was aware of. It certainly felt more like she was a prisoner than a guest.

She passed through the foyer on her journey back toward the East Wing. As she walked through the groups of people, she noticed that one of the foyer's two hearths was ablaze and bright. Three servants carefully swept the floor then tossed the old herbs into the awaiting flame, while a fourth placed fresh herbs and crushed flowers onto the foyer floor where the old herbs had been removed.

As Sarah got closer to the East Wing Hall, the delightful smells of sweet cakes, rolls and eggs filled the air within the tight corridor hallway. The smell aroused her hunger and she quickened her pace to reach the Hall before the cook decided to shut down for morning meal. If she hurried she might be able to get a quick bite to eat, then perhaps she could venture outside to those smaller cottages she observed the night prior. Maybe there she could get some answers.

Servants were often thought of as a part of the castle's furnishings, often seen but not heard. Contrary to that belief, servants heard many, many things that royalty discussed and would no doubt some have information about the Minister Knights, this Zykeiah person and probably about Sarah herself.

Fighting down the temptation to run to the Hall, she marveled at the appetite she had developed. Stolen and taken to Solis as a young girl, Sarah could barely remember if she had such a large appetite before her trip to the cages. She enjoyed the meal Kalah made the prior night and that only made her anxious to try the morning portion of meals.

Finally the overpowering aromas of morning meal condensed at the entranceway to the East Wing Hall, which surprisingly was empty, this late in the morning.

Sarah entered and sat down at one of the wooden tables, not exactly knowing what to do. A servant girl, perhaps about ten years old carried out a plate, cup and fork. The girl placed the plate in front of Sarah, carefully, and without making eye contact.

The girl's hands were scruffy, red and almost covered by her elongated robe's sleeves; the hood hid most of her face. The robe did not disguise the girl's hefty frame and pudginess. Her wide body made it difficult to reach over Sarah, so the girl moved to the front of the table to finish setting out the bowls, cups and plates.

"Good morning," Sarah said to the girl.

The girl did not respond, but rather turned and fled to the kitchen, reappearing after several minutes with breads and hard-boiled eggs. The girl sneaked a peek at Sarah as she placed the bread on the table alongside the eggs, before hurrying back to the kitchen.

Shrugging, Sarah picked up one of the boiled eggs and immediately dropped it.

"Ouch!" She rubbed the angry red spot on her hand where the hot egg had burned her skin.

"Careful, those things are hot," Marion called to her as he entered the East Wing Hall.

He took a seat across from her and whistled for the servant girl. The young girl reappeared, this time with a small boy that carried a plate and cup.

Marion placed both elbows on the table as the young girl sat still more bread and eggs onto the table. The smaller boy struggled to place the plate and cup in front of Marion. He seemed caught between his duty and trying to get a good look at the Minister Knight.

Marion did not speak until the young girl and the smaller boy had returned to the kitchen.

Sarah cautiously picked up the egg. Feeling the hard cracked shell, she rolled the now slightly cooler egg around in her hand, noting its texture and shape. Rolling the shell away from the actual egg, she grimaced at the gooey slime that separated with the shell, leaving just the pinkish color of the egg's "flesh", the yolk was till to come.

Marion watched with interest as Sarah examined the now shell-less egg before slowly placing it into her mouth and biting.

"It is good," he remarked before rapidly removing the three eggs' shells and placing an entire egg, one at a time into his mouth.

"No?" he asked around a mouth full of egg before swallowing.

Sarah swallowed then felt the squishiness of the eggs and hardened yolk inside her mouth. "No."

Draining her cup of the bitter ale, Sarah decided she needed something that tasted better than eggs and reached for the sweet bread.

Glazed with an almost clear substance that was sticky and sugary sweet, the sweet bread lived up to its name. Liking her fingers again and again, Sarah ate three sweet bread rolls before she said another word to Marion.

Marion did not eat any of the sweet bread; he only ate the eggs and a few pieces of the flatbread. He tried not to stare at her, especially as she licked her lean, elegant fingers to free them of the sweet bread's stickiness. He should not be eating with her in the East Wing Hall; he should not be this close to her at all, except he could not help himself.

And if Queen Zoë found out, worse, if Zykeiah found out, his life in the castle might be made more difficult for many lengthy rotations to come.

"What are you doing here?" Sarah asked as she beckoned to the young servant girl that she was finished.

"Having morning meal," he answered before finishing his third cup of drink.

"You know what I mean. Queen Zoë told you and Kalah to have morning meal more than an hour ago."

Sarah stood and brushed the sweet breadcrumbs from her pants.

The young servant girl blushed beneath her hood and dropped an empty cup to the ground. Marion waited until the servant girl had left before reaching across the table and snatching Sarah's wrist and nearly dragging her across the table. He stood up.

"If you ever speak to me in such a tone in front of a servant again, it will be your neck. I do not care who the Queen thinks you are!"

Thrusting her backwards with a hard shove, Marion stalked out of the East Wing Hall. Cursing himself for coming to this end of the castle, he did not hear Sarah's calls to him until he reached the door to his chambers.

"Marion! Marion!" Sarah raced after him down the East Wing hallway towards the foyer. The same hallway, where just yesterday, Marion and Kalah were discussing Valek's threat and the Queen's health.

Out of breath, she stopped in front of a door labeled with a crossbow and a brass door handle. Marion placed his hand on the door handle, and then turned to look at her.

"What?" His eyes burned into hers. Anger forced his mouth to form a sneer.

"I-I am sorry," Sarah whispered.

Her fear of him returned for the first since she tried to escape from him on their way to the castle. With the fear was also the new fluttering of things that Sarah did not readily understand…an oozy warmth that burned inside her. It was almost pleasant, but she could not linger on that feeling because her fear quickly eroded it.

Marion's pale gray eyes continued to stare at her. They seemed to be searching and silently questioning her. Sarah did not flinch; she found herself unable to glance away and unable to speak. Her words were stolen from her before they escaped her lips.

"Fine," Marion finally replied as he turned the doorhandle.

"Wait!" Sarah reached out and placed her foot in the door's closing pathway. "Please, tell me what you meant in the Hall."

Opening the door wider, Marion grabbed her arm and pulled her into the room, slamming the door just as she was in.

"I should not have said anything," he mumbled as he wiped his head.

His chambers had only a bright red sleigh bed, a makeshift rocking chair and a woven basket of greenery. On the wall was one tapestry, an exact replica of the one hanging in Queen Zoë' s chambers. Like her room, this room only had one window that faced the castle's small courtyard that housed the central baths, the greenery and the supply rooms.

"Sit," Marion ordered.

Sarah slowly looked around the room for some place to sit before deciding to sit on the floor, which was covered with herbs of rosemary and thyme.

The room smelled of forest and smoke and Sarah noticed that beside the bed were swords, daggers and crossbows all shined and polished. Upon further inspection, she saw that despite their polished gloss, the swords had nicks, dings and outright damage to them as if they had been used heavily.

"You promised that Queen Zoë would tell me, but today she did not tell me anything of my purpose here."

"No?" He paced in front of his bed. "The Queen is quite ill, as you saw this morning with the coughing."

Nodding and wrestling with the idea of whether he should tell her or wait for the Queen, he soon fell silent as his pacing increased. Sarah watched, unsure of what to say or do. Should she leave? Stay?

Finally, he turned to her and said, "You must know before it is too late."

Marion sat down on his bed, removed his sword and placed his glasses on the bed. "Where do I begin?"

"I know of Valek's smuggling and his potion that allows people to read minds," she said softly, "but what does that have to do with me?"

"Then you know almost as much as we," Marion said as he sat down on his enormous bed. "But there is something that we believe Valek does not know."

"And that is?" Sarah inquired.

"According to the Antiqk scrolls, there would be one to arrive into the galaxy that would possess extraordinary powers of magic and sorcery. Her powers would be so fantastic, that she would free the souls from Solis, destroy Valek and cease the war between Earth 3012 and Saturn Four."

Marion glanced quickly at Sarah before continuing. "I know the Queen has waited since she was a child for this person to arrive on Velorios. Queen Zoë had researched, meditated and visited the Oracle of Antiqk for years, most of her life, in search of the signs that would lead us to know when to act."

"And let me guess," Sarah interrupted. "Queen Zoë believes that person is me?"

Without waiting for his answer, she laughed at the sheer ridiculousness of it. She stood, ready to leave Marion's close cozy chamber.

    "It is true," he said as he stood too and walked across to the door.

    "Look, I am grateful for my rescue, but my sister is still trapped on Solis." Sarah turned to leave. "And I must free her."

    "You do not believe-" he asked.

    "No! You can't expect me to just believe some prophesy..." she said

    Marion placed a hand on her shoulder and said, "Come, I will give you proof."

    She followed him out of his room and down a hallway toward the West Wing of the castle. Just before they reached the Great Hall, they entered an adjoining hallway that Sarah must have missed earlier that morning.

    It led to the stables.

    Once they arrived at the stables, Marion gave Sarah a heavy woolen cloak complete with a hood to protect her from the cold outside. As she wrapped it around her, she thought of Amana and the ugly green coat.

    A servant page saddled the danker beast for her; Marion required no saddle. He simply threw one huge leg over the beast. His size seemed to make the beast erupt in protest followed by a series of moans and onks.

    Marion said to the servant page, "Tell Kalah that Sarah and I have gone for an afternoon ride, we will return before evening meal."

    The boy nodded and went to lift the doors. They guided the danker beasts closer to the door and watched as the stable doors rose.

"Where are we going?" she asked as they were now out of earshot of the servants. She gathered that Marion did not like speaking in front of them.

"To the Antiqk Oracle," he answered flatly.

"Where is it?" Sarah felt the icy breeze slip through the hood's protective layer and into her ears. The weather was so cold, her nose burned. The rawness of the morning had not melted off under the afternoon's sun.

"Not far from here in the eastern section of the Northern Forest."

Marion, shirtless and wearing only his tinted glasses, black leather pants, and boots, did not acknowledge the frigidness of the weather. Again Sarah wondered about whom exactly were Marion and Kalah.

She knew they were brothers. Kalah had admitted that the night she and Marion arrived at the castle. They were both Minister Knights of Souls, but how did they arrive on Veloris? How did they become Ministers? Did Queen Zoë recruit them? If so, what planet did she find them? Why was there so few of them?

They were headed towards the Antiqk Oracle where the scrolls had prophesied her birth and her purpose. But Sarah knew nothing of magic and sorcery. No, she knew little regarding the mythical or the surreal. She only prayed that some how this would lead to Amana's freedom. She could play along with what they wanted.

"It is not much farther. See even from here you can see the glow." Marion pointed straight ahead where an almost orange color lit up an area of the forest in an eerie pulsating hypnotic rhythm. Why they had not seen it from the path last night, she did not know.

Sarah could feel the nerves in her stomach began to move about in protest to the fear that had crawled there. A sickening feeling also crept into her throat making her cough.

"Come." Marion commanded as he whipped his danker beast into a faster trot. "We must hurry, faster."

Sarah patted her danker beast and hurried after Marion towards the glimmering glow of the Antiqk Oracle.

As they hurried, Sarah felt an overwhelming familiarness tugging at her memory, a memory of being here before as she passed the various trails, trees and frozen lakes on the path to the Antiqk Oracle. Even the air held a certain smell: a mixture of rotting logs, crisp snow and dung that somehow felt like home.

Coaxing her danker beast ahead of Marion's, she followed the memory right to the opening cavern of the Antiqk Oracle that opened wide, eagerly waiting for its latest visitor. Red flecks of light, weathered stones, intermingled vines of various colors and odors dominated the Oracle's entranceway.

As soon as she reached the cavern's opening mouth, Sarah dismounted from the danker beast and again felt the overwhelming feeling that she had been here before. Her danker beast proceeded to back up from the cavern slowly, than faster, until it reached Marion.

"I know this place," she whispered.

Marion dismounted, too, and walked over to her. "Do you? I thought you had never been to Veloris."

"I have not," she answered before starting up the two stone steps towards the cavern.

Marion silently followed her, for it seemed Sarah was in a trance, she neither looked at him nor waited for him. She simply plowed ahead as if she had no will of her own. It called to her in soft whispers of promise and knowledge; a key to unlock her trunk of questions. He remained just outside the cavern of the Antiqk Oracle. The wind wrestled in the leaves at the mouth of the Oracle

According to legend, the Oracle only admitted one at a time; two would bring immediate death. Not to mention, the oracle prophesies were the business of the one entering the cavern and for no other.

Sarah entered into the cavern and walked directly to the glowing sphere of the Antiqk Oracle. About the size of a fully-grown melon, the Antiqk oracle resembled the blue spheres that Valek used to capture souls, except this one was six times as large and rested in the huge chiseled open palm of a great hand that rose from the ground. This Oracle was made of an orange glass substance and it hummed a rhythm to its pulsating glow over and over again without pause. It sounded like, "Come, come, come."

It seemed to call to her, to beckon her to touch it, to "come" into its atmosphere of unlimited knowledge of the past, the future and the unexplained. Come to know herself.

Come.

Sarah placed both her hands on the oracle and the sphere began to blink faster and faster, spinning all the while, spewing answers as instantaneously as she asked them. Some answers came before she even consciously acknowledged the question. Rapid fire like bullets of awareness resounded through her psyche and lodged in the orifice of her mind with such force and impact that after what felt like a few minutes, she physically collapsed to the unyielding floor.

Chapter Six

Zykeiah passed Marion's room and stopped at the door next to his room. There were three doorways in the hallway. This door, right next to Marion's, resembled the other two doors except this one had a silver door handle. Sighing, she turned the door handle and entered into her little room.

She tossed her garment bag onto the floor beside the blackened fireplace. The fireplace occupied the right wall her room that separated her room from Kalah's. Her room shared the left wall with Marion. Zykeiah often wondered if Queen Zoë found it amusing to have Zykeiah sandwiched between both Marion and Kalah.

Zykeiah did not find it amusing at all.

Using two stones of flint, she lit the logs in the fireplace and cautiously placed several more pink logs into the growing flame. The pink logs acted not only as a source of heat, but also as an air freshener, offering the floral scent of the potta trees, which were pink in color, into the air. The clinging scent of danker beast was still attached to her clothing and hair as she sat down on the wooden bench and removed her boots, but at least the smell would not stain the room.

    She removed her clothes and piled all of these items into the garment bag that was already filled with other garments. Putting on a robe made from rough but comfortable tarra, she opened her door and walked down the hallway between the Great Hall's kitchen and Marion's room to the central baths.

    Zykeiah watched as servants rushed to and fro with decorations and supplies. Some children carried their best dress outfits through the Hallway to the servants' homes, just cleaned from the wash. It was not often that the castle had something to celebrate, not since Kalah's birth, according to Queen Zoë, had there been much to celebrate on Veloris.

    Smoggy, humid, and thick, the air in the corridor to the central baths always made Zykeiah sweat as if she had run full speed up to the highest point of Stocklah Mountain, the highest mountain point in the Northern Forest and on the entire planet of Veloris. She knew Stocklah and the higher grounds of Veloris better than anyone; the area was ideal for meditation and rides.

    Making a sharp right into the central baths, she breathed a sigh of relief. There were no others at the baths today. Thankful she could be alone with her thoughts, and she had much to think about, she chose the triangular baths in the back of the bathroom itself, closer to the castle than the forest.

Book-ended by the Great Hall and the East Wing Hall, the central baths satisfied the needs for both kitchens by providing a centralized location for water. The main basin had a projecting trough that allowed servants to carry water to either of the kitchens. The baths themselves were sectioned off from the main basin and the Greenery by stonewalls on three sides with the back wall being the back section of the castle. A small stone courtyard separated the central baths from Kalah's, Zykeiah's and Marion's rooms. The room that housed the central baths was as long as all three rooms put together.

There were a total of five baths. The largest bath, which was closer to the forest, could hold approximately ten people; it was considered the community tub. The tubs themselves were wooden and most often protected by a canopy, except the Queen's bath, which resided in an elevated section of the room farthest away from the other wooden tubs and secluded by a heavy, iron screen that was dense with shapes and rosemary flowers. Each tub was lined with cloth to protect the skin from the wood.

The remainder of the tubs lined the back wall of the bath; three wooden tubs of equal length and depth could each hold two people if necessary. It was the first tub farthest away from the door that Zykeiah chose and often found the best spot for obtaining as much privacy as could be had in such a place.

The baths room was heated by an enormous open hearth towards the front of the room that was kept ablaze by the bath maid to the point of the room becoming a sauna.

Upon seeing Zykeiah enter the bath, the bath maid followed her in and went to the built-in basin that resided beside the hearth. Turning the bronze tap, she began to fill the bucket with hot water. She lifted a full bucket, she quickly placed an empty one under the tap to fill as she hurried and poured the water in to the bathtub.

"How hot would you like?"

"The same as always," Zykeiah answered.

She continued to fill her tub, running back and forth from the basin to the tub...careful not to slip on the slick flooring with his buckets.

After several trips back and forth, the tub water waited patiently for Zykeiah. Steam rose into the air as if offering itself to her. *Come, come, and cleanse yourself.*

The bath maid waited beside Zykeiah...out of breath and wiping his damp face.

"Yes?" Zykeiah asked as she held her robe closed.

"Would you like help with your bath?" The bath maid smiled exposing toothless gums and horrible offending breath.

"No," Zykeiah answered and a frown formed on her face.

Seeing the anger on her face, the bath maid abruptly bowed and offered, "My apologies, my lady." She raced out of the baths without looking back.

She thought she heard him mumble "witch" as she exited.

Digging into her robe's pocket, Zykeiah removed a sack of salt, hand-chopped by the souls of Solis that she had taken from her latest trip. She dropped a handful into the steaming water and watched them dissolve.

Next, she needed to regain her spiritual balance. This could be obtained by dropping leaves of clove, lotus, musk and wisteria into the steaming water.

She removed her robe and lowered herself slowly into the soothing waters of the bath. Zykeiah closed her eyes and thought of the one called Sarah.

She had more important things to think about, like her knighting in the next cycle, the results of her trip to Solis and much, much more; but for now, she only wanted to relax and think of pleasant things.

Zykeiah closed her eyes and thought of the woman's fabulous eyes that were the color of gosha, but still fantastically enchanting. Yes, Queen Zoë was right. She was the one.

Opening her eyes to stare at the ceiling, Zykeiah knew that that alone would complicate matters.

***

Marion waited patiently in the frigid afternoon at the mouth of the Antiqk Oracle in silence for as soon as the Wrangler birds entered the invisible sphere of the Antiqk realm their screeching fell silent.

"Come on Sarah," he whispered as he gazed up to the blushing sky. "It grows later."

Sarah appeared shaking and moving sluggishly from the cavern. She stumbled, slipped and fell. Running to her side, he picked her up an almost lifeless Sarah. Tossing her over her danker beast, he mounted his danker beast and made his way back to the castle with Sarah in tow. He hoped she would awaken before they reached the castle, Queen Zoë would be furious if she found out that he had jeopardized their plan for this. He could feel the Queen's disapproving scowl as he entered the castle with Sarah blackened out by the Oracle.

It was not uncommon for the Oracle to overpower a person, if that person required too much information. The Antiqk Oracle gave only as much as the person touching the oracle required. It required an excellent mastery of one's mind to query its wisdom and prophecy. Perhaps he should have warned her of that.

One such woman, who lived in the sphere surrounding the Antiqk Oracle, had scrawled the scrolls and derived wisdom of the Oracle for many rotations before Queen Zoë. She then had given them to Queen Zoë upon her deathbed. It was said that the woman was insane upon her death.

"I should not have brought you here," he said to Sarah, as she remained unconscious. "But you are supposed to be our savior."

As they moved further from the pulsating glow of the Antiqk, Sarah began to stir and moan, but she did not awaken.

"Be strong," Marion urged. "For the heavens, be strong."

***

"Where is Marion?" Kalah asked as he stalked in to the central baths.

Groaning softly at the interruption, Zykeiah answered, "I do not know and do not wish to know."

He raised one of his eyebrows, but his questioning look was lost on Zykeiah, who eyes remained closed as she relaxed in the tub.

Leaving the central baths, Kalah knocked on Marion's room door again, but no one answered. Searching between the two Halls, Kalah tried the baths, then back again.

Finally he made his way down to the stables, where the overwhelming stench of danker beasts almost made his eyes water.

"Have you seen Marion?" Kalah asked the servant page who smiled at the visit by the young knight. It was rare that the stables saw Kalah; he hardly left the castle.

"Yes. He and Sarah left mid-morning for a ride." The servant page then moved over to feed a handful of dark green leaves to a young danker calf.

"Thank you," Kalah responded promptly before fleeing for the sweeter air of the castle.

Slowly Kalah walked past the royal guards and into Queen Zoë's bedchamber where Queen Zoë reclined against her pillows. Propped up like a puppet, the Queen ate a bowl of roasted beef with crushed rosemary.

"Your face gives me the answer I have been looking for; you do not have to speak," she said firmly.

Kalah shrugged, "I cannot find him."

"He is not in the castle." Queen Zoë had not asked, but merely stated.

"No, Mother, he is not." Kalah answered half-heartedly as he stared out of the window.

Queen Zoë smiled. Kalah only called her mother within the cozy confines of her bedchamber. Marion did not call her mother at all once he had become a knight; the secret had to be maintained and kept to a small group.

"You do not approve, Kalah?" Queen Zoë could see her young son wrestle with the looming shadow that was Marion. The shadow was so much larger that it deflected any sunlight of recognition from Kalah.

"He is your brother." Queen Zoë pressed. "Not your rival."

The words burned into Kalah's ears, forcing his short temper to fester and boil over. "No, Mother! He is a knight and that woman is Veloris's and the whole Pixlis

Galaxy's hope of freedom. He can't just take her from the castle, tell no one but a stable page and…"

He turned and stalked out of the room.

"Oh, Kalah." Queen Zoë collapsed into her pillows and wept.

***

The aroma of fresh bread floated and filled the air of the castle as Kalah waited in the Great Hall for Marion's arrival. Marion and Sarah had been riding for the better part of the day. Where had he taken her? The weather outside was bitter and cold. How could Marion have taken Sarah for such a long time?

Zykeiah, refreshed and free of the danker beast smell, arrived at the Great Hall for evening meal in full knight attire, although her official knighting was still one full rotation away. Tight, burning pink leather pants, black leather boots complete with thigh dagger strap and a furry pink sleeveless sweater that exposed her sculpted arms, caused the female servants of the Great Hall to gasp and whisper to each other and overt their eyes when she passed.

Queen Zoë raised her hand to beckon Zykeiah to the front of the Great Hall. Though evening meal would not be served for another few minutes, the Hall was packed with the Queen's servants, the knights, and those vying for the knights' favor.

"Are you ready?" Queen Zoë asked Zykeiah once she reached her throne.

"Yes, my Queen," Zykeiah said.

Smiling, Queen Zoë slapped her leg lightly and said, "Your are like one of my children now."

"Yes, my Queen," Zykeiah answered, making the Queen roar in laughter and then into fits of coughing as the color quickly drained from her face.

"Are you all right?" She leaned down as the Queen pulled a spiny green leaf from her pocket, placed it in her mouth and started to chew it. The soothing juice from the leaf calmed the Queen's coughs, but did not cure them.

Zykeiah kissed the Queen's bony hand and went to sit next to Kalah at the table closest to the Queen. The Hall had filled up fast; there were not many more spaces in which to sit.

"Your concern wrinkles your face, Kalah," she said as she squeezed in between both of Kalah's girlfriends, Tate and Mary.

"He should have returned by now," Kalah grumbled. "Give us leave, Tate and Mary. Tonight dine in the East."

Sighing and pouting, both the twin sisters, Tate and Mary, barely more than sixteen years old, stood and left Kalah without question, but with many longing looks of lust and sadness that tonight he would not be with them.

Zykeiah laughed at Kalah's gross indulgences, from the two sisters to his collection of daggers; Kalah lived largely and with extravagance. He had to have the best. Even his red leather pants were derived from the hide of a kowlata, fierce tough creatures that resided primarily in the Southern Forest. Their skin held the coloring ink better than any other, and Kalah would not rest until he had several of their hides. Marion and Zykeiah's leather came from the kowlettas, which were in the same family as the kowlatas, but had been domesticated and bred for the purpose of using their skins and other things.

When Marion had suggested Kalah use the kowletta's hide, Kalah disagreed and left to go capture a few kowlatas, stating that the hides of kowletta were weak and not as protecting to the cold. Marion did not argue with the insistence of youth and even traveled with him to the Southern Forest. They returned with several kowlatas and Kalah returned with a hand that was nearly bitten off by one of the angered beasts.

Queen Zoë repaired it, and Marion thought his younger brother learned his lesson about appreciating what was available.

Kalah had not. He boasted in the Great Hall of his experience with the kowlatas and continued for months about his strength and courage displayed there. He even went so far as to challenge Marion's courage by stating that his brother feared and began to cower at the kowlatas' roar during their hunt.

This announcement received a hard punch in the face from Marion, just when Kalah actually thought he was big enough to step from his big brother's shadow. And what greater situation to defeat Marion than in front of a full audience at the Great Hall! But Marion returned him to second best, cloaking Kalah in his shadow, making sure that Kalah never thought of stepping out again.

But it did not end there. At every given opportunity, Kalah tried to circumvent Marion's authority, leadership and even his mother's affection. Over the years the stress to Queen Zoë wrecked the older woman's health. The aftermath of the arguments and debates was that the two brothers grew apart, each blaming the other for her sickness.

Only as of late have the two brothers tried to make amends.

It was prior to that when a weakened Queen Zoë called upon Zykeiah for help.

She remembered the day clearly as if it was today.

Outside a winter storm dropped inch after inch of soft snow onto the Northern Forest. The castle waited for the storm's fury to pass and prayed it hurry and move on. It continued for several full hours. The coldness entered through cracks, windows and even seeped in from the ground making the floor icy cold. This seemed only to exaggerate the widening gap between Marion and Kalah as the bitterness spread.

    Zykeiah was relaxing in her favorite tub in the baths when Queen Zoë came down the stairs and into the central baths with her advisor and servant, Octiva.

    Zykeiah watched as Octiva prepared the waiting bath water for cleansing. The tiny Queen coughed repeatedly as she crumpled fresh thymus into the bath. She lit several incenses that lay alongside her tub and she inhaled deeply.

    When Octiva departed; the Queen prepared to bathe privately without aid. The thick canopy hid her from view and all Zykeiah could make out was the Queen's shadow as it moved about the tub, then as it entered the water.

    "I know you have just arrived here," Queen Zoë said as the two women bathed alone in the central baths. "You are needed here. It is your destiny, child!"

    Zykeiah sloshed lukewarm water into her own face as she struggled to sit upright in her tub. "But, but, I am a slave."

    "You are the one who escaped from the cages," Queen Zoë said firmly. "From Valek, no?"

    Zykeiah's fear increased. She could hear her blood thundering in her ears as she tried to think of a way out of this. "Yes, but--"

    "Then here is what you must do…" Queen Zoë replied. "You must return to Solis."

***

"Where are you, Zykeiah?" Kalah interrupted Zykeiah's memory. "Not nervous about tomorrow?"

"Just thinking."

Kalah's eyes moved from her face to the Great Hall's entranceway. "He is never this late."

"Perhaps it is the girl," Zykeiah said, neglecting to mention Sarah's name; the Great Hall was far too crowded.

"Perhaps," Kalah grudging agreed. "He was like that with you. Once."

Turning away from Kalah's accusing stare, Zykeiah said, "He was never like that with me."

***

Marion and an unconscious Sarah reached the stables and by the position of the few stars visible, Marion knew evening meal was to be served within moments.

"Tell no one of the hour." Marion ordered as he slid from his danker beast smoothly placing the reigns into the open palm of the servant page. He lifted Sarah from her danker beast and tossed her over his shoulder with equal fluidly as if he had done it hundreds of times before.

"Yes, sir." The servant page quickly agreed as he herded the danker beasts into the stables.

Marion's heavy footsteps landed squarely as he carried Sarah up the stairs from the stables.

He peeked around the corner before scurrying down the Hallway to the Greenery. The hot, smoggy air from the central baths caused Marion to cough and sweat. No one heard for all had gathered in the respecting Halls for supper.

Placing Sarah on the floor, Marion quickly scanned the aisles of potted planted and sprouting herbs, spices, vegetables and fruit. The Greenery housed over sixty herbs and all of the food harvested for the castle; Veloris's climate demolished any herbs and most spices that grew outside the castle's walls. Only certain plants native to Veloris had adapted to withstand her arctic temperatures.

Queen Zoë favored other plants not native to Veloris and had educated both Marion and Kalah extensively and vigorously on the identification and use of herbs and spices.

"There!" He rushed to a yellow-spotted spiny plant called squalla. Ripping off a leaf he hurried back to Sarah and placed the leaf under her nose.

"Awake!" Marion commanded and gently blew on the leaf. Its spores flew into the air and into her nostrils.

"What happened?" Sarah asked as she awoke, her eyes fluttering rapidly as if still buzzing from the experience at the Oracle.

"Gently," Marion said. He could feel her trembling beneath the heavy sweater. "You must eat."

Almost relying exclusively on Marion's arm for support, Sarah hoisted herself to a standing position. They walked sluggishly down the Hallway to the Great Hall.

"Ah, there, see Kalah. I told you he was fine," Queen Zoë said quietly as she smiled at the sight of Marion and Sarah entering the Great Hall.

They reached the table closest to Queen Zoë, where Kalah and Zykeiah sat. Marion helped Sarah into the seat next to Zykeiah. She was still groggy, but awake.

"The ride went much better than expected," Marion said as he leaned down and kissed Queen Zoë's cheek bringing a wider smile to her aged face.

"I am sure," Queen Zoë said as she playfully swatted Marion's arm

"Where have you been?" Kalah inquired heatedly as soon as Marion sat

"We went out."

Marion winked at Zykeiah, who smirked then rolled her eyes.

Kalah grunted as the servants brought out the evening servings of crushed tanger-flavored henckens with tartberries. The meal was accompanied by ale. Sweetened berry juice was also served. Marion ate greedily as oily juices dripped from his chin and he said little despite the questioning stares from Kalah and Zykeiah.

"So, how was your ride today?" Zykeiah asked Sarah who ate very slowly.

Sarah shrugged as she chewed slowly.

"There are some great waterfalls higher up towards Stocklah; I could show you." Zykeiah offered. "If you are up for another ride."

"Sure," Sarah said anxiously and eager to have Zykeiah's gaze move to someone else, some place else. She hated the woman's intense stare. It made her skin crawl.

"You are a real lovely woman. That must have brought you many favors in the cages."

"The cages know no favors," Sarah curtly responded.

"Surely, you remembered that Zykeiah," Marion said. "It has not been so many years ago that you were there."

Zykeiah said softly, "No, it has not."

"You have been to Solis?" Sarah asked failing to hide her surprise.

"Yes, I was a slave in the Soul Cages." Zykeiah answered as she moved the food around her tin plate.

"You were rescued?" Sarah continued to question. She knew many of the slaves that resided in the cages, but had never seen Zykeiah before.

"No." Zykeiah took a deep breath. "I escaped."

"That is why she is to be knighted tomorrow," Kalah announced before guzzling his ale and signaling the servant for a second round.

"It was not just her escape from the cages," Marion added, "but her courage and unflinching bravery that she has demonstrated since arriving here."

The others at the neighboring tables stomped and clapped in agreement to Marion's declaration.

Zykeiah only grinned before saying to Sarah. "You will be there, right?"

"Yes." Sarah did not know what she had committed herself to but it did not matter as long as Zykeiah kept her penetrating gaze directed at everyone else.

As the Great Hall emptied, the Minister Knights, Sarah and Queen Zoë remained. They dismissed the servants and only those few in the kitchen remained to clean.

"Tomorrow will be crazy; try to sleep tonight," Queen Zoë suggested to Zykeiah." The time draws closer still."

"Evening all." Sarah excused herself. Before Marion or Kalah knew it, she was already out of the Great Hall with Zykeiah fast on her heels.

Just outside the Great Hall's entrance, Sarah turned and said, "What do you want of me? "

Tired and mental drained from the trip to the Oracle, Sarah just wanted to go to sleep.

"I just want to talk to you," Zykeiah said.

"I am tired. Can this not wait until tomorrow?" Sarah said softly.

"Yes. Of course, enjoy your sleep," Zykeiah smiled and turned back to the Great Hall.

Sarah started again for her chambers. Once she reached her door, she was out of breath due to the trot up the stairs. She pressed back against the door as if she was trying to blend into the door. She let out a sigh of relief and entered into the safety of her room.

Chapter Seven

Valek brushed his hair briskly with hard, even strokes as he stood naked in his bathing quarters. The tub of cool, dirty water remained stagnant in his wooden tub. Incenses burned lazily as he placed his brush onto his stand and dressed in his favorite soft leather cream-colored suit.

He quickly braided his hair into a thick plait and hurried from his private quarters through the heavy screen and into his office where General Ogroth waited.

"My dear General Ogroth." He extended his skinny hand. "Good to see you."

"Sure," General Ogroth grunted. "Can we get this over with?"

Just as Valek sat down in his chair, the plump General Ogroth slowly walked over to the gold desk and threw down ten silver coins.

Valek picked up one of the coins and closely studied it.

Several seconds passed as General Ogroth's foot tapped impatiently. Valek continued his close inspection of the coin.

"Valek, the SOLANCE! I am a busy man!"

"You idiot!" Valek threw the coin into General Ogroth's bushy beard. "You demand nothing from me!" Valek leapt from his chair and slammed his fist against his desk.

"Ten silver coins?" Valek whispered angrily through clinched teeth.

"What you ask is ridiculous!" General Ogroth yelled back. "We will not pay; it is robbery!"

Sighing noisily, Valek sat back down in his chair. "Then leave and allow Earth 3012 to obliterate and take over your pathetic Saturn Four."

Valek slowly extended his hand, but did not get up again. He said, "No more business. No more Solance."

General Ogroth said with a sneer, "You little piss."

Valek turned his chair so his back faced to General Ogroth before saying, "Good day, General Ogroth."

Silence as the General roughly stroked his bushy beard.

"All right, fine, Valek." General Ogroth dug deep into the scratchy pockets of his green pants. "Thirty silver coins."

The sack made a loud "thwack" as it landed on the desk.

"As agreed." Valek turned around to face the General, exposing his pointy teeth with his smile.

"I am glad to see you have agreed to the new price." He beckoned to Orono who waited back in the shadows of the room. He came further into the sparsely lit office.

"Take General Ogroth to the warehouse and allow him to transport back to his pathetic planet. Give him three cases of Solance. One on the house." Valek smiled with a wink at General Ogroth.

General Ogroth wiped his sweaty brow with a thick meaty hand and grunted again, this time causing cloudy streams of smoke to spew from his flared nostrils.

"Tsk, tsk, General Ogroth," Valek said. "Save your temper for your enemies."

Orono led General Ogroth from Valek's office into the drab hallway.

Once the two were out of earshot, General Ogroth asked, "Why are you insistent on working for him?" His voice sounded like a low roar. "Valek is obviously mad."

Orono hurried through the chilly corridor with urgency only utilized when Valek needed it. He knew the system of corridors and hallways better than anyone else at Valek's castle. Once he felt they were far enough away, he stopped short and quickly looked around before replying, "Do you not know?"

General Ogroth snorted and said, "What do you mean?"

"Do you not *use* the product you paid so much for?" Orono asked impatiently.

"No!" General Ogroth patted his head and said, "I do not need it. Intelligence is born, not sold."

Growling, Orono snatched away and resumed his pace in the direction of the dungeon. He hurried as fast as his legs could carry him. He wanted to be away from the General and soon. He had other business to take care of.

"Besides, Valek would kill me if I tried to read his mind. You should know it does not work on him." General

Ogroth mumbled as he, too, sped up his pace. "So what is it? Are you are a coward? A spineless, fat snake?"

Grabbing the torch from the wall, Orono led General Ogroth down the stairwell to the dungeon without comment. Orono pulled the lever to raise the creaky elevator that led even further down into the warehouse. The warehouse housed crates upon crates of packaged Solance. It occupied the area below the dungeon and the dungeon-quarters. Clients were not permitted to enter the warehouse, but Orono had already stacked Saturn Four's shipment outside the warehouse door.

Orono wheezed and sweated profusely as he lifted the boxes of Solance, the bottles clinking and clanking together uneasily inside. General Ogroth watched with fear prying into his stomach.

"Break them and the silver comes from your hide!" General Ogroth smoothly threatened. The decaying flesh smell that was condensed just outside the cool warehouse caused General Ogroth to place his hand over his mouth and nose. He had to take sips of air to breathe.

General Ogroth coughed and clawed for sweeter air, but was denied it. Orono put down the crates and opened the warehouse's door, slamming it quickly as he went in, leaving the General alone in the hallway.

Moments ticked by as the General continued to cough and gag. The smell was overwhelming, yet he could not leave until Orono came back to escort him to the circles. He would leave if he knew the way back to the circle.

Finally, Orono came out of the warehouse. He lifted the crates and started off without comment or explanation.

General Ogroth followed a sweaty Orono to the Circle of Solis, where several of his soldiers waited to transport to Saturn Four.

General Ogroth asked, "What does he make that stuff with?"

"I cannot tell you," Orono quickly replied. He lowered his voice so that only the General could hear and said, "But for a price the mysteries of the galaxy will be opened to you."

"It smelled like death in there." General Ogroth pulled on his too short jacket and wiped his face.

"There are many, many secrets that I am happy to tell you," Orono said as he smiled at General Ogroth.

"Ah, yes, depends on what you know." General Ogroth lifted a hairy eyebrow.

"I do not sell junk," Orono barked before turning away. "You know where to find me."

***

The cloak held a faint scent of danker beast like most things in the castle; yet, the rank smell also held brief spots of myrrh. It did not matter to Sarah; she only had to go a short distance. She tied the belt securely about her waist. She went to her window and gazed at the moon, then down to the trail that led from the East Wing kitchen to the servants' homes a short distance away. The moon illuminated the cluster of servant cottages nestled just off the east end of the castle.

"I must go," she whispered. It was tonight or never, she thought. Every day that passed put a greater distance between her and Amana. Sarah held her breath as she opened her door and crept quietly down the stairwell. At this late hour she hoped everyone would be in bed resting for the ceremony tomorrow.

She hurried into the East Wing Hall, past the abandoned tables, and into the kitchen. There was a doorway just past the fireplaces and stoves that led outside.

Sarah listened for footsteps or voices. She did not hear any, so quietly she slid back the door's wooden lock and stepped outside. Silence seemed to encourage her and she turned towards the direction of the servants' cottages. They seemed to call to her. It was almost like they were begging her to come to them.

"Come, come," the cottages seemed to plead.

The ground crunched beneath her feet. She stepped cautiously, but snow blanketed the ground. The brownish muddy dirt of Veloris could be seen just underneath the layer of snow. Along the trail, Sarah observed discarded bones, seeds, and other objects that failed to make it from the castle to the servants' homes.

The howling wind ripped through her cloak, blew it about her face, and temporarily obscured her view. Her ears burned and her feet ached as she hiked on. The distance looked so much shorter when she first saw it from her window. Maybe the distance between the castle and the servants' cottages was elongated by the biting cold of Veloris at night. It almost caused her to turn back, but the internal yearning to visit, to see what was there, tugged at her. She pressed on.

"Almost there," Sarah said quietly as the wind blew another gust of snow and ice into her face.

Thoughts of Amana came to her as she continued through the wet snowflakes that fell from the sky and the burning lashes of the wind. She thought about how miserable Amana must feel.

***

Amana felt no sleepiness, fatigue or drowsiness as she sat in her cage. The nothingness clung to her like a wet blanket, always following her as she went through the tunnels to the mines where she and dozens of other souls labored. The souls mined the slick, black Solis rocks for Valek's less than profitable business...rock salt. He sold rock salt to smaller planets that required the substance for fuel, beauty aids, and magic.

"Hello," said a young woman with eyes empty like the caves beneath the cages. Her hair was a shallow red color and it flickered as she entered Amana's cage.

"Who are you?" Amana asked as she rose from her seat. She tried to see around the new arrival to the place where MaxMion waited. She had seen the new arrival around the cages, and she was even in Amana's cage last night; however they had not spoken

MaxMion rubbed his hands anxiously together and whispered, "New arrival." He hissed as he retreated into the shadowy blackness and quickly vanished, as the midnight dark tunnels swallowed him up.

The new girl floated over to the corner of Amana's cage and started to cry softly. No tears fell for there was no body in which to produce them. They were souls trapped in a cage. She was bodiless, a soul without a home. The body was no more, but habits like eating, sleeping and crying did not immediately fade away.

The new soul peeked through her balled-up fists at Amana.

"Do not be afraid," Amana offered. "The shock will wear off soon. You'll get used to it here."

"I am Amana," Amana tried again to calm the new arrival.

Amana got up from her spot on the floor, crouched next to the shivering girl, and tenderly patted her arm. She said, "It will be all right."

To her surprise, the girl whimpered and gave her a tentative hug. It was a surprise. She didn' t feel the hug, but the gesture reminded her of her sister, Sarah.

"I am sure it will," the new girl said in a hoarse voice. "My name is Katelin."

***

MaxMion and Orono, partially hid by the shadows of the caverns, watched as the new arrival Katelin embraced Amana.

"Are you sure?" Orono asked for the third time.

"Yes, can you not smell her erotic scent?" MaxMion sniffed the air and then greedily rubbed his tummy. "If only she was flesh, I would roast her over the tender licking flame of the berry bushes."

"Patience, my dear friend." Orono pulled a small, opaque ball from his pocket. "Our time will come."

"Yes," MaxMion hissed excitedly. He jumped up and down in a hurried motion that caused Orono to smile…briefly.

"Come, we have much to do." Orono melted into the obscurity of the tunnels with MaxMion following close to his heels.

***

The wholesome home at the forefront of the servants' neighborhood windows was illuminated with candles, as if it was waiting for her to arrive.

The ground, solid and coarse, had been down trodden and worn by the daily pilgrimages between the servants' quarters and the Queen' s castle. Although tightly compacted, Sarah stumbled over occasional loose stones and rocks that had been unearthed from the path. Her eyes watered as the sharp wind sliced through her clothes, bring the piercing cold directly in contact with her skin.

The first house looked just like the others: a small home with a snow covered roof and windows that held curtains and flickering candles. She gravitated to the first house either out of a desire for refuge from the bitter night's frigid temperature or because the place seemed to call to her. Nevertheless, it attracted her.

The Antiqk Oracle had revealed much, although she did not remember all of it. She *did* remember that the information had come at a lightening speed. So quickly she could not match responses with the questions. In some cases, she had not formed the question before the oracle had answered them. The dizzying speed in which her questions were answered only left her head aching and her stomach uneasy. Yet, here she was before this home.

She stepped on the first narrow, cracked step that led to the door. She stepped up two more steps and reached the door when it opened revealing a woman. Long, straight, ash-blonde hair was scattered across her face, camouflaging her eyes, but it failed to hide the woman's knowing smile. She stepped back into the house as she beckoned Sarah in.

"Come in. It's freezing out," she said softly. Her voice was warm, inviting, and musical all at once.

Sarah followed the woman into her home. Once inside the quaint residence, the woman pointed to a makeshift bed on the floor close to the fireplace. It resembled a pile of blankets and quilts on the floor.

"Warm yourself by the fire," the woman suggested as she stepped over the makeshift bed to the fireplace. She added a few more logs and turned back to look at Sarah.

"Please make yourself comfortable," she said.

The tiny house seemed to have only one large room, a kitchen and maybe a back room; Sarah was unsure. The little kitchen had shelves stocked with jars of various herbs and other items that Sarah could not make out.

Eclectic and unusual, Sarah's heart swelled at the absolute simplistic beauty of it. There was nothing glamorous or divine about the home, but it held a certain charm. This is how she would like her own home to be — silent, comfortable and every available space filled with things that belonged to her. She had never possessed anything or had such a home. Her years on Earth, before the cages — from what she could recall — were spent traveling around to where there was food and safety from the government's soldiers.

The woman herself was eclectic and unusual in that her hair was bone straight, and it fell almost to her ankles. Her face seemed to be no older than a young servant girl; yet, her home indicated that only one person resided there. She obviously was old enough to care for herself, but her age remained elusive.

"I have not seen you at the castle before. Are you new to Veloris?" Sarah asked as she cautiously sat down on the pile of blankets near the fire.

"I am the Queen's personal servant. You are not supposed to see me," the woman said as she took bottles from the kitchen's shelves and placed them on the table. She then opened one of the bottles and poured a powdery substance into a mug.

Sarah said nothing. She had met the Queen that morning and did not see any indication of a servant. Although ill, the Queen still struck a powerful figure and a dominant one. She had assumed the Queen did things for herself.

"I am with her when she is at her weakest and to assist her with her baths, among other things," the woman said as she poured a blood red-colored fluid into the mug as if reading Sarah's mind.

"My name is Octiva," the woman continued. "I have been expecting you."

Octiva brought the mug from the kitchen and handed it to Sarah. "Drink."

Hesitantly, Sarah took the mug, peeked inside and then sipped a little. "There is no smell, what is it?"

"It is a drink mixed with crushed toadstools, thyme and feathers from the henckens, among other things," Octiva answered as she sat across from Sarah on the blankets. Her legs were long, but she seemed small to Sarah.

"What does it do?"

"It will chase the cold away and relax you," Octiva answered as she removed her sweater revealing thin arms and small breasts. The undershirt was almost transparent, and Sarah looked away.

Sarah sipped a tiny bit more, but felt no different than she had when she arrived. The mixture, smooth and fruity, tasted far better than the bitter ale from the dining Halls. Lifting the mug to her lips again, she eagerly drained the mug of its remaining contents.

"You like?" Octiva quipped. "That's good."

Sarah could only smile as she wiped her mouth with the back of her hand. There was an aftertaste of something metallic, but she could only swallow the taste and grimace.

"You said you were expecting me," Sarah started once the aftertaste had passed. "Why?"

"Yes, well, the scrolls stated the one would come here." Octiva tilted her head sideways as she watched Sarah. "You are the one. I know you do not believe it," she continued. "Despite what the Oracle told you today?"

"How did you know?" Sarah asked, shocked. "I - I don't remember what the Oracle said."

"I know everything that happens in the castle," she replied. "It is not because I am a servant that I know all. But you are not here to debate the value of servants, are you? And the Oracle, well, just wait a few moments."

Octiva folded her legs and placed her hands out in front of her with the palms facing Sarah. The room seemed to slant to the right and suddenly Sarah could see the pores on Octiva's face. They seemed large and close. Her perception tilted and the room slowly began to fade in and out as it became blurry. Shaking her head hard, she squeezed her eyes shut then opened them.

The room appeared bloated and much too warm. She took off her cloak and fanned her face. "What did you give me?" she asked Octiva who was now standing with her palms still facing Sarah as if pulling or pushing energy toward her.

"I have already answered that question," Octiva said as she helped lay Sarah down on the makeshift bed. "Now, what is it you really want to know?"

Octiva rubbed her hands together, "Why are you here?"

Sarah felt sick and the urge to vomit raced up her throat. But instead of throwing up, she coughed out, "I want to know who I am?"

The ceiling continued to languidly rotate around and around. "Marion said I was the one," Sarah added weakly.

Octiva pulled her hair back from her face. Sarah could now see her chestnut brown eyes. They suddenly glazed over and became a creamy white as she spoke in a monotone voice that soundly eerily like the buzzing chant of the Antiqk Oracle. Chills spread over Sarah's body despite the hot room temperature.

"You are the one named Sarah, whose birth has been foretold by the Oracle at Antiqk since the time before the Minister Knights and Zoë. You are the savior of the Pixlis Galaxy."

Sarah violently shook her head in denial. "No, no, it is not true. I am only a woman. I am only a woman!"

Octiva continued as if Sarah had said nothing. "You must save the Pixlis Galaxy from Valek or all is lost. All is lost. All is lost!"

"Stop it!" Sarah screamed. She wiped her damp hair away from her face. The dam inside her memory broke, and a flood of hidden images from the Antiqk Oracle commenced along with memories of her father, a high priest of the Antiqk council on Earth when she had only been a young child and of her sister Amana. The Antiqk Oracle had resurrected the memories, making her remember her father's violent death at the government soldiers' hands. It went on to replay how she and Amana were sold to Valek and taken to Solis where their souls were placed into the cages. She was no longer mentally in the room. Her mind had floated back into history and ancient lore.

Octiva tossed leaves of clove about Sarah's body as she thrashed about in a fitful sleep and alarming visions.

Her mother had been murdered as well, and Sarah had suppressed those memories. Instead she had replaced them with false memories of her father and mother being farmers when Valek arrived on Earth. She recalled now how she made the story up to ease her younger sister's pain, but over the decades, she had come to believe it, too.

Octiva tossed rose and tulip petals around the place where Sarah slept. Twigs of pine and evergreen had already been stuffed under the makeshift bed. Octiva next took a handful of bay leaves and scattered them over Sarah's wet face. Her eyes were open but she did not see the room's surroundings, only the vivid visions of the Oracle.

"Your destiny has already been written. Embrace it for you can not elude it." Octiva, now the smiling woman from a few moments before, patted her shoulder.

The visions had ceased as suddenly as they had begun. Wet with sweat, Sarah uncoiled herself from the tight ball in which she was in and breathed a sigh of relief.

"You are a very wise and brilliant sorceress," she said as she blinked repeatedly and stretched. The pale streams of the morning sun streaked through the windows and lit up the large room. The fire had burned down to almost nothing and Sarah shielded her face from the light.

"How much time has passed?" she asked, no longer seeing the darkness of night.

"It is morning," Octiva answered as she folded up her blankets and moved about the room picking up various leaves, twigs and flower petals.

"Morning!" Sarah shouted as she got up from the floor. She snatched on her cloak. Tying the belt tightly around her waist, she dashed from Octiva's home, started to sprint back to the castle when she stopped just a few paces from the door, turned and yelled, "Thank you!" before running down the trail. Octiva waved as she watched the savior of the Pixlis Galaxy hurry to the castle.

Just as Sarah was out of sight, Octiva returned to the large room where the reconciling of Sarah's memories had finally dissolved into the truth of her existence. Lifting both hands to the ceiling and whispering a spell of unraveling, Octiva's cute face melted into the very distinct older face of Queen Zoë. The Queen, now back in her own shape and appearance, called to the back room where the real Octiva stepped out and rushed to the ailing Queen's side.

"Madam, are you okay?" Octiva held Queen Zoë's arms as she half carried, half dragged her over to the fireplace.

"I must get back to the castle, to the central baths. I must replenish my strength," Queen Zoë whispered.

"Yes, at once," Octiva answered as she went to get the Queen's cloak and danker beast.

***

So concerned about the possibility of Marion or Kalah not finding her in her quarters, Sarah barely took notice of the cold. The sun had already chased the usual coldness of the night away with its morning rays; nevertheless, the temperature of Veloris was still frigid and chilly.

The early morning servants were already busy in the kitchen and were starting to prepare the morning meals when Sarah reached the backdoor. They pretended to take no notice of her as she hurried through the kitchen, through the empty East Wing Hall, and up the stairwell back to her room.

She took the stairs two at a time as she anxiously quickened her pace to get to her room before it was discovered she was missing. She reached the top step and let out a sigh of relief that no one was impatiently waiting for her there.

She slipped into her room, quickly took off her clothes, and crawled into bed, where exhausted, she slept.

Chapter Eight

The morning arrived too quickly for Zykeiah. She snuggled further under her warm blankets; the fireplace had long since died in the wee hours of the morning leaving nothing but the scent of floral petals in the air.

Heavy, loud knocks beckoned her from her cozy bed and into the brisk, chilly morning air, which did not put her in a good mood.

"What is it?" she barked as she wiped the remains of sleep from her eyes and opened the door. The refuge she sought in the bottoms of ale mugs last night did not seem a good an idea this morning. The throbbing at the base of her neck complained when she made sudden gestures.

"Mam, it is time to prepare for your knighting."

Groaning, Zykeiah opened the door wider to allow three girls to enter. Each carried an item. The three girls were known as the Ushers; they prepared all knight-aspirants and ushered the knights into the Ministry. No one knew exactly how long they had been around or how old they truly were despite their timeless youth. There was no doubt; they were far older than their looks indicated. Their beauty and sensuality must have been an added joy for the men who were knighted.

But Zykeiah wasn't interested in that.

While still in her favorite robe, Zykeiah was led down to the central baths by the first girl, named Iris. Iris's ice blue eyes, dark skin and hourglass frame caused a stir with the younger boys of the castle who were hanging banners, lighting candles, and sweeping. None dared to call to the Ushers. Their presence was sacred.

"Once we enter the central baths," Iris whispered to Zykeiah, "we must wash your hair and body to show your devotion to Veloris."

Zykeiah nodded, still sleepy and hungry. The rituals of the knights were kept secret, and she wished nothing more than to get it over with.

The two other Ushers set up for the continuing rituals once they entered the central baths.

Itala, the second young girl, had olive skin, slanted black eyes and straight jet black hair. She went to the trough, turned the tap, and filled two buckets with warm water.

The third Usher was named Iga, a bronze-colored girl with wooly hair and bright hazel eyes. She held the towels in her arms to dry off Zykeiah when she emerged from her hair washing and bath.

Iris dropped scented oils of lavender, frankincense and rosemary into one pail of steamy water. "This is for purity."

Zykeiah disrobed and climbed into the tub closest to the trough. While Iris used cups of water to wash and rinse Zykeiah's hair, Iga brought more water to fill the tub. Zykeiah waited for the hair washing to be completed with patience.

No one spoke as the tub was filled.

When the tub was filled almost to the point of running over, Iris said, "Zykeiah, this ritual is to cleanse you of illness, immoral habits, and negativity."

Iga placed several white candles that smelled of vanilla around Zykeiah's tub, and then lit each candle. Woody twigs of fresh rosemary were placed in the water, followed by more lavender that was dunked repeatedly before being removed.

Iris took gauze and filled it with chunks of salt from Earth 4016's dead seas. She dunked them seven times into the bath and said, "Concentrate on what you wish to be cleansed of. Water is purifying."

The three girls waited silently as Zykeiah meditated and tried to purge herself of the bitterness she had acquired while a slave in the soul cages. She lost track of how long she had been meditating when she heard Iris finally say, "Come, mam."

Iga and Itala, using white fluffy towels, dried Zykeiah off, taking extra care with each leg and arm, with each finger and toe, and with each breast. It felt very strange to be toweled dried like a Queen, Zykeiah thought. She was a former slave.

After being dried off, Zykeiah dressed in a white extended-sleeved tunic that fell to just above her tapered ankles. She followed the group to her room where her bed was stripped of its original coverings and replaced with a red covering that symbolized the willingness to shed blood for the Minister Knights of Souls.

Zykeiah was placed in the bed and covered with black blankets that symbolize her willingness to die for the Minister Knights.

Iris, Iga and Itala placed charcoal briquettes into the fireplace as Zykeiah rested in her bedchamber. As they finished, Iris sprinkled a pinkish powder made of bay leaves, cinnamon, blood wine and myrrh across the briquettes. Once the fire was lit, the charcoals burned the powder, creating a floral incense that radiated throughout Zykeiah's room, ridding it of evil and despair.

"Mam, this is a banishing incense that eliminates all unwelcome spirits and forces them from this room."

A drowsy Zykeiah nodded and fell asleep as the three Ushers prayed and meditated around her bed.

***

Sarah did not rest as she sat upright in the soft bed. Her stomach turned flips and rolled over again and again as she mentally replayed the scene in Octiva's quarters. It still made her nauseous.

Today was Zykeiah's knighting and Sarah's hands trembled despite the low fire and the three blankets that attempted to stave off the cold air. Sarah raised both hands with her palms pointing to the ceiling and focused on an image of a burning, intense fire.

At first nothing happened.

She felt foolish. What exactly did she think she was doing? She had seen how Octiva had commanded the elements of magic and earth to do her bidding, but Sarah knew she didn't have any power like Octiva.

Or did she?

She closed her eyes and urged the room to be warmer. She relaxed and soon the flames grew higher and brighter despite the absence of additional wood.

Satisfied and surprised, Sarah let out a yelp and then studied her hands as the fire continued to burn.

"Wow!" Sarah shouted to the empty room.

Strange, Sarah's hands had tiny markings on them that were not there moments before. A sharp burning sensation would occur, and then another tiny 'x' mark would appear, irritated and red. The markings were raised and turned purplish in color after a few moments.

Although tender, they did not hurt once they had surfaced. She would need to see the Queen today for some ointment to heal her hands. But how would she explain it?

The Antiqk Oracle had given her the basics of who she was, the rest she had found out last night at Octiva's home. It seemed like a dream, far away and surreal, as if it had happened to someone else. Sarah picked up her cloak and smelled it. It smelled of the exotic mixture of rosemary, flower petals, and fire.

If she went to the Queen, she would have to explain the markings. What would she tell Queen Zoë? Should she confess that she had been to the servants' homes? That she had been experimenting with powers she knew nothing about? Powers that the Oracle had shown her. What would Queen Zoë say?

Shouts and calls of excitement erupted outside and Sarah went to the window to investigate. A lengthy line of servants was walking from their quarters to the castle on the same trail Sarah had just walked a short time before. The servants laughed and carried supplies, which were mostly decorative items, such as ribbons, banners, and kegs of what could only be wine and ale.

"Oh, Zykeiah's knighting is today," she groaned as she watched the servants enter the East Wing kitchen. "And I promised I would be there."

She turned away from the window with a heavy heart. She could not afford to miss the knighting, for Zykeiah would most certainly be looking for her and who knows what Zykeiah would do if she found out Sarah did not attend. Zykeiah did not play by the rules; she was a rogue in a den of gentlemen.

Fear crept back in and gripped Sarah's heart at the memory of her meeting of Zykeiah yesterday. Zykeiah's intense and unnerving stare made her shudder. She pulled her gown closer as the sounds of celebration grew louder outside.

She knew that sleep would be delayed today as well as she balled her hands into fists and placed them in to her lap.

***

The drums heated to a fiery pace as Amana hurried to the mines. MaxMion rarely said anything harsh to the laboring souls except when they were late. He hated tardiness; they produced more when they were all present and working together.

The darkened caverns beneath the Solis's black, slick earth could be confusing and the winding tunnels that lead from this section to that section often were mistaken and souls would arrive late. MaxMion would then send them to the warehouse to be compressed into the Solance pulp, never again to regain life.

Compression into the Solance pulp was the only way in which a soul could die. Amana heard Orono telling MaxMion how the Solance was made He said that it was very similar to eating fruit. The flesh was the same as the outside of an orange, with the soul being the meaty inside of the fruit. Valek had devised a way to peel the flesh away, take the fruit's meaty inside and compress it into a juice. That juice was Solance.

Amana was not sure exactly what Solance was, but she knew it cost a great deal of coins. The mining the soul did was not as profitable to Valek. MaxMion had asked Orono why Valek kept the souls working the mines.

Orono did not know.

"Hurry, Katelin," Amana whispered as she quickly floated to the mines.

"Coming," Katelin called as she hurried behind Amana.

"We must hurry. Rule number one, don't make MaxMion angry." Amana advised the new arrival.

"I sure hope I don't." Katelin grinned. They passed laboring souls who, in silence, worked steadily, pounding the rocky caverns and placing chunks of rock into carts again and again.

Amana reached her spot and picked up her tool. She gestured to the new girl to follow her. Katelin picked up a tool and following Amana's example, worked laboriously in the blackness. No sweat, no fatigue, Amana and Katelin worked for hours along with the hundreds of slave souls.

"I hate this. How can you endure it?" Katelin asked as she dropped her tool to the ground with a clank.

"I do not know," Amana said as she continued smashing her tool into the hardened rock. "I think of my sister, Sarah, and feel hopeful that I, too, will be free."

"You have a sister?" Katelin inquired.

Amana glanced around before lowering her voice and saying, "Yes, she escaped."

"What!" Katelin's mouth dropped. "Really?"

"Shhh!" Amana said. "Well, actually, we had escaped together, but I was recaptured."

"No." Katelin shook her head in disbelief. "Really?"

"She escaped to another planet."

"That really happened," Katelin asked, "to your sister?"

"I believe so, yes."

Amana's memory of that night was fuzzy. "There may have been someone else there to help her escape."

"Who rescued her?" Katelin asked.

"I know not." Amana shook her head and continued chipping away at the rock. "I had been recaptured by the time she escaped."

***

Zykeiah awoke several rotations later and was led to the Great Hall by the Ushers. Queen Zoë, dressed in a white robe bearing the Minister Knights symbol, sat on her throne. On either side of her stood Marion and Kalah, dressed in matching white robes identical to hers.

Iris carried a sword; it was almost as big as she. She held it by its silver handle. She gave it to the Queen; her slender shoulders shook under its weight.

Taking the silver handle in her thin fragile hands, Queen Zoë opened a tiny vile of clear ota oil and poured it over the handle.

"This sword will guide you through your new life. A life that will be devoted to returning other people to theirs."

Zykeiah knelt before Queen Zoë; Sarah held her breath as she watched, amazed at the seriousness and splendor of it. The Great Hall, although filled with people, was quiet like a tomb.

"Will you give your soul for the souls of others?" Queen Zoë asked.

"Yes," Zykeiah answered around the hard lump in her throat. The Great Hall was packed and filled with people, mostly servants. All eyes were on her and she felt the weight of their expectations.

Queen Zoë lifted the heavy sword with trembling arms and tapped Zykeiah's shoulder once on the left and then once on the right.

"In the name of God, of Antiqk and the Lost Souls, I dub thee, knight. Be brave, ready and loyal." She quickly lowered the sword and then said, "Rise Zykeiah and take your place amongst the Minister Knights of Souls."

Zykeiah rose and took the sword from Queen Zoë. As Zykeiah placed her hand on the sword, the Great Hall erupted with outcries of joy and congratulations. She lifted the sword high into the air and cheered.

Marion was the first to embrace her with hugs and congratulations. While in his arms, Zykeiah searched for the one face she wanted to see. When her eyes landed on Sarah in the far back corner of the Hall, she smiled despite the loathe that seeped into her heart.

Their eyes met and Sarah quickly turned away.

"Welcome!" Marion bellowed as he continued to keep her in a tight hug.

Kalah rushed over and whipped Zykeiah from Marion's arms into his. "Congratulations!"

"Tomorrow, you must be ready for the branding!" Marion teased as he stepped back from Zykeiah for others to come and welcome the new knight.

"Yes," Zykeiah tossed back at Marion as she shook hands with various servants and received many kisses on the cheek from enthusiastic children. Kalah moved away and laughed at the scene.

"Come, Sarah! Greet our latest addition," Marion called to Sarah who had stayed a safe distance back from the crowd of people who meshed around Zykeiah.

Slowly, she hesitantly crept over to Zykeiah as some of the crowd dispersed to guzzle ale and to celebrate with dance. A trio of musicians had set up in the corner next to the hearth and had begun to play a lively tune.

As Sarah came closer to Zykeiah, Zykeiah gasped at the sight of her, for Sarah's hair, free from its confining braid was loose and flowing, each ringlet perfectly curled and springy. Sarah was simply radiant *How can she look that good?* Zykeiah thought bitterly.

Sarah extended her hand to Zykeiah to congratulate the new knight. Zykeiah grabbed Sarah's hand and pulled her close to her, then kissed Sarah hard on the mouth, while at the same moment locking her arms around Sarah in a hug. The kiss grew whistles, stares and outright cheers from some of the spectators in the Great Hall. Zykeiah wanted everyone to see how much she *liked* the new arrival.

Sarah's eyes grew large in embarrassment. She struggled to pull free from Zykeiah's iron clad embrace.

Marion felt a soft punch into his stomach as a sick feeling raced up his neck. He could not believe his own eyes; Zykeiah had just kissed Sarah and from where he stood, Sarah liked it.

It was customary for a new knight to choose a woman to hold his heart. Kalah, forever greedy, chose two, Tate and Mary. He had chosen Zykeiah.

And now, Zykeiah had chosen Sarah.

Chapter Nine

"Another Sir?" the wrinkled servant wench asked again.

"Yes," Marion slurred and rocked unsteadily on the bench, spilling some of his new ale onto the floor.

The Great Hall, now empty of boisterous laughs, congratulations, and celebration, waited as Marion continued to indulge his own private party.

He lifted the mug of ale to his lips and with one toss of his thick wrist; he guzzled the ale and slammed the empty mug to the table, drained.

His throat burned, his stomach churned, and his heart ached. An educated man, Marion had treated his own injuries since he was ten and even now the only thing he knew to numb heartache was to drown it. The side effects be damned.

The servant wench had been around since his youth and he knew her well. She would keep his blackened mood a secret from the others. As the oldest and unofficial leader of the Minister Knights of Souls, Marion couldn't show weakness. Weakness was not an emotion that should be shared or discussed. Marion knew all too well Kalah would enjoy it too much; so hungry was Kalah to replace him.

His younger brother both loved and despised him. It was no secret. Placing yet another watery mug of ale directly in front of him, the servant wench smiled beneath her aged skin and gooey eyes.

"Thank you, Chloe," Marion muttered.

"I am retiring for tonight," the servant wench announced without waiting for Marion's approval. She turned and headed back into the kitchen. "You should do the same, Sir."

Marion grunted and drained the mug of its contents yet again. Glancing around, he realized that finally he was alone. Even the kitchen servants and cooks had fled for the comforts of their beds and homes.

Marion staggered toward the Great Hall's entranceway where he slipped and fell. Just as he tried to reorient himself, he noticed that he was being watched.

Kalah leaned against one of the Great Hall's support columns and eyed his brother carefully.

"What do you want?" Marion tried to speak clearly but failed as he slurred the last part of the question.

"Drowning in ale again, brother?" Kalah asked as he walked further into the Great Hall.

He stopped as Marion jerkily stood up, using one of the tables as a stabilizer. "Tread lightly here, Kalah."

"Or what?" Kalah asked as he came closer and punched Marion in the stomach, knocking the breath out of him.

Marion collapsed to the floor and vomited shortly thereafter the countless mugs of ale.

Kalah applied a swift, hard kick into Marion's ribs, knocking him onto his back. He whispered angrily, "I think, Brother, your time has faded."

Marion rolled onto his stomach in agony. Kalah placed his palm under Marion's chin, pushed up and applied pressure causing Marion's head to be pulled backwards as if his neck was going to snap. "Leave this place, Marion, or name me leader…"

"Kalah, what are you doing?" Sarah inquired from the Great Hall's entranceway. The two knights were only three feet away from the Great Hall's entrance.

Quickly, Kalah leaned down to Marion and said, "My brother has had too much celebration tonight. I will help him to his quarters."

Unsure, Sarah crept into the Great Hall and swiftly smelled the strong, sour mixture of bile and alcohol.

"Whew!" She held her nose as she stepped over Marion. She studied his eyes that were partially closed and the blood that trickled from his mouth.

"He will be fine," Kalah coldly said as he lifted Marion to his feet. "Right, brother?"

"But he looks ill. Perhaps the Queen should treat him or at least see him." She suggested as she grabbed his hand. She pulled him closer to her away from Kalah.

"Leave me, Kalah," Marion grunted through clenched and bloodied teeth. "We will finish this later."

Kalah released him, causing Marion to almost slip back to the floor. He held tight to the table. Holding his ribs with his other hand, Marion wiped his mouth with the back of his hand. He watched Kalah stroll from the Great Hall.

"Do you need help getting back to your room?" Sarah asked as she inched closer to him. He seemed so small to her now. She recalled how at the Allerton Circle he seemed larger than life…a god almost. But now, he looked defeated.

He could smell the rosemary in her hair and feel the warmth of her body on his naked chest. He remembered how she looked when Zykeiah kissed her and it made him grimace.

"Does it hurt?" Sarah asked mistaking his grimace for pain.

"No, no, I am fine." Marion stepped away from the table and limped toward the entranceway, slow and deliberate.

"Are you sure?" Sarah asked again as she held his elbow, her soft fingers on his flesh.

"Yes," Marion answered stiffly.

Sarah glanced around the abandoned hall and said, "I saw Kalah strike you. I could see it from the hallway."

"Sibling disagreement," Marion said. "Nothing more."

"But he hurt you and had I not been here…" Sarah started.

"Nothing more!" Marion barked. "What were you doing watching us? Do you not need your beauty rest or something?"

Marion saw Sarah hesitate. Would she tell him that she came to see him? And when she found him not in his quarters at such a late hour that she was worried? Let this be her response, Marion secretly prayed.

Instead she said, "I, I came to see if I could get some warm milk." She pulled away from him. With her hand removed from his elbow, Marion felt as if a cool wind had blown in from the north, leaving him alone and cold.

"There is a kitchen in the East Wing," Marion responded as he limped along the hallway to his quarters.

Sarah smiled and then quickly dropped it.

"You do not have to tell me why, I know why you were in this part of the castle." Marion gripped his ribs again as he took an intake of air and he thought about Zykeiah and Sarah nestled in Zykeiah's quaint and cozy quarters surrounded by a warm fire, bottles of wine and probably the scent of floral logs.

"Do not flatter yourself," Sarah quipped, once again mistaking his meaning, before hurrying down the hallway towards her quarters. "Good night!"

***

Marion limped into his room and promptly collapsed onto his bed. He closed his eyes and tried to make the spinning in his head stop. The searing pain in his side made deep breathing difficult and it made taking sips of air equally painful.

But it was Sarah's last comment that caused the most pain.

Where, he asked himself as he disrobed, did he begin to admire her so? Why did it matter if she found favor with Zykeiah or Kalah?

Groaning, he leaned across his bed and put the sword amongst the many others. His boots plopped to the floor; first one than the other, followed by his pants.

She had only been here three cycles and already he had ruined any chance he might have had to be in her heart.

Or had he?

Zykeiah, too, must have been taken with Sarah, for she pounced on Sarah the very moment she laid eyes on her. He nodded to no one in particular as he mentally noted Zykeiah's offer last night of taking her riding to Stocklah. She failed to tell Sarah that he was the one who first took her there. How would Sarah feel if his past relationship with Zykeiah was known?

He couldn't blame Zykeiah for her interest in Sarah. He rolled onto his back and rubbed his tired and bruised face. His chilly room needed a fire, and he was too distracted to cover himself with any blankets. Inside, the pain still burned.

***

The tapping of Sarah's foot echoed as her anger escalated. Just who did Marion think he was? A prince? Some fantastic gift from the gods to women? Why was it so hard to say that she had saved him from being beaten to death? Did he think so little of her?

She roughly removed her sweater and threw it across the room, where it landed somewhere beside the chair. With the same jerky motion, she pulled her gown over her head and placed her arms through the sleeves. She quickly removed her boots and pants before the chilly night air could affect her. This night was unusually warmer despite the cool temperature of her room. Nevertheless, she piled on two additional blankets and crawled under the covers.

Then almost without thinking, she lifted one of her hands and directed it at the fireplace. The flames burned more intense at her direction. She had simply focused on the fire burning brighter and pointed. The fire willingly obeyed.

She searched her hands for any changes. Two purple markings now burned bright red and stung. The older markings from the morning had not faded. She had learned she had powers, but how strong? What else could she do?

What did it all mean?

***

"Yes, Richard, Solance will cost you 350 in silver coins." Valek smiled at the tella that loomed on his desk. The tella gave a watery image of Richard Agate, the ruler of Earth 4016. With his shrunken head and enormous nose, he bore a strong resemblance to a mouse.

"That is a lot to ask from a small, unfortunate kingdom like Earth 4016," Richard squeaked through the tella.

"Now, Richard, the reason it is such a small, unfortunate kingdom is because of Mars 2012. With Solance, you could change all the damage and pain they caused you. You could take back your family chest, your treasures and… your daughter."

Valek watched Richard hesitate. Richard rubbed his hands nervously together then looked about for his advisors. One appeared at his side and whispered eagerly in his ear.

"Richard, my time is quite precious…" Valek hissed.

"Yes, yes, Valek. I understand," Richard said and waved a hand at Valek nonchalantly, as if he did not understand.

If he were not attempting to expand Solance's market, Valek would have terminated the transmission and the deal. But he was asking a lot more than he received from either of the other planets combined.

"Consider it an investment," Valek offered as he continued to watch Richard's advisors cluster around him and flood Richard with answers and possible motives.

"And you are sure it will allow us to read minds?" Richard asked meekly above the head of an older advisor with big floppy ears.

"Yes," Valek answered for the third time. His patience was limited and Richard was eroding it.

"How do you know it works?" Richard inquired again.

He obviously was not a fool, Valek thought. Either that or he had good advisors. If he answered that he knew for a fact it worked, Richard would ask how he knew it. He didn't want to tell Richard he sold Solance to others. It would ruin the illusion that Richard was his sole client.

If Valek answered no, then Richard would demand the price be lowered or he might reject the deal all together. Too much silver was on the line to jeopardize for the sake of information. He would need to be watchful of Richard's advisors in the future.

"I know that it works because I have tested it," Valek answered coyly. His answer sent Richard's advisors into a frenzy of heated whispers.

Valek leaned forward in his chair and cooed, "Richard, I would not be offering this to you — believe me there are armies out there, and other kingdoms that would pay twice the amount that I am offering to you — but I believe in Earth 4016's cause and I feel terrible about the abduction of your daughter."

Some advisors were shaking their heads no, but Valek saw right through to Richard's heart. Advisors, no matter how good, were only advisors.

Richard was still king.

"Do we have a deal?" Valek leaned back in his chair.

Richard nervously looked around before saying, "Yes."

"Excellent." Valek smiled and said, "The details can be worked out later."

Valek did not wait for a response from Richard before terminating the tella transmission.

***

An expression of glee spread across Orono's face quickly as he backed away from the crack in Valek's door and hurried down the hall. Wait until MaxMion heard the latest news. Valek was expanding the Solance potion to the Earth 4016 planet.

Orono patted his stomach and grabbed the first torch from the wall before descending to the dungeon. He thought of an evening meal of roasted honey henckens and thick slices of bread.

Instead when he reached the lower half of the castle, MaxMion was hunched over parts of the latest human slave brought in. Beside him, on a tin plate, were decaying vegetables and plants he had picked out of the pit. That is where he had recovered his meal. The vegetables were for Orono.

The punch smell of decaying flesh and rubbish made Orono lose his appetite. He had tired of eating the discards from Valek's table. He longed to eat real, delicious food.

"MaxMion, you will not believe what I have learned," he said eagerly as he pushed his massive body into the tight room he shared with MaxMion.

MaxMion did not answer or even glance up; he was focused on his meal Whatever news Orono would wait until after dinner.

Clearing his throat, Orono tried again, "MaxMion, Valek plans to expand Solance sales to Earth 4016."

MaxMion shook his head anxiously, but did not stray from his meal as he ripped through the blackening flesh of what looked like an arm.

"This is extraordinary, MaxMion." Orono shifted his weight from one leg to the other. "This could be our escape. Our opportunity to leave this dismal existence."

MaxMion tore his eyes away from his chunk of meat briefly and gave Orono one final nod of his head, before returning again to his food.

Chapter Ten

The morning sun rose abruptly, or so it felt to Sarah as the rays burst through her window and illuminated the room. The bright room resonated with light.

Hurrying out of bed, Sarah put on her pants and discarded sweater. She plaited her hair into one single braid and left. She softly walked down the spiral staircase, but this time instead of going to the East Hall, she turned right and headed to the Great Hall.

She had decided that she was going to eat with the Minister Knights in the Great Hall, not ostracized like a prisoner.

She was almost to the entranceway, when she sneezed and brought both of her hands to cover her mouth. Seeing the purplish markings on her hands made her gasp. She thought they would have been gone as soon as she woke up. She had completely forgot about them. She could not allow the Ministers to see her markings. She fled back to the East Wing Hall for morning meal.

***

Once she was seated at a table in the East Wing Hall, Sarah laughed at her nervousness. A young girl, perhaps seven years-old, came from the kitchen trailed by a woman who looked like an older version of the girl. The girl set the plate and mug, while her mother put baskets of hot, sweet bread and boiled eggs on the table.

Sarah scooted the horrid eggs, with their strange mixed smell of danker beast and charcoal, to the end of her table. She picked up two sweet rolls and gingerly took a bite, savoring the sugary sweetness. The older servant retreated to the kitchen, but the girl did not. Instead she watched Sarah from a short distance away with curious eyes and a dirty mouth.

Around the East Wing Hall were other servants and their families eating morning meals. At the table next to her, a family of six, two adults and four young children ate their morning meals in remarkable silence.

Sarah noticed that they ate from brown, coarse bowls and fat wooden spoons. She watched, mesmerized, they ate a grayish paste-like substance. The youngest boy, no more than three Sarah would guess, grimaced with each spoonful and he would spit some of it out when his mother was not looking

When the servant woman returned to her table, Sarah asked, "Madam, what is it that family there is eating?"

The servant followed Sarah's finger to the adjacent table.

"They are eating gosha, Madam." The servant woman turned back to her and asked, "Would you like a bowl?"

Sarah's stomach turned over and she said, "No, no thank you."

Her answer received a weird expression from the servant woman, who made sure this time to grab her daughter's hand before heading back into the kitchen.

Sarah sighed before continuing to eat her pieces of bread.

"I thought I would find you here," Zykeiah called from the entranceway drawing stares from various people in the hall. Two Minister Knights in the same week coming to the East Wing Hall was highly unusual.

Sarah looked around to see whom Zykeiah was calling to, and then realized when Zykeiah sat down across from her, that Zykeiah was calling to her.

"Where else would I be?" Sarah responded as she placed both her hands out of view underneath the table.

"I am heading up to Stocklah for a short ride. I wanted to know if you were interested in going with me."

Zykeiah dropped a sizeable sack to the floor; the sack made a loud crash that once again interrupted the morning meals of those in the East Wing Hall.

"I - I…" Sarah stammered as she tried to think of a way to politely decline.

"Do come, Sarah. It is a beautiful place, besides, you and I have a great deal in common," Zykeiah smiled.

"Well, this morning, I have- " Sarah began to say.

"Nothing planned. I am not taking 'no' for an answer." She stood abruptly and said, "I will meet you in the stables in one rotation."

With that, she left and the East Wing Hall became extremely busy, buzzing with whispers.

Sarah stood and left the East Wing Hall shortly after Zykeiah. She headed in the direction toward the Great Hall, but she turned a sharp right toward the central baths.

Once she reached the central baths, she stopped at the outside trough and rinsed the stickiness of breakfast from her hands. She dried them with a large, coarse towel that hung beside the trough. There were few people about in the hallways. Most were probably sleeping in from last night's celebration.

Next, she continued on to the stables. At the early hour, the servant page was still somewhat asleep in the small front section of the stables. His bed consisted of a grassy mat.

The crisp air did nothing to eliminate the burning and horrid smell of the danker beasts. Sarah held her breath as she waited for Zykeiah. She stretched the sleeves of her sweater until they partial covered her hands. Only the tips of her fingers were visible.

"I thought you might need this," Zykeiah piped up from behind her, causing her to jump and yank down her sleeves.

Zykeiah handed a wooly coat to Sarah. "Put this on."

She put it on, making sure to tie the belt tight. The air would be cold — very, very cold — this early in the morning and she wanted to be warm.

Zykeiah wore a thick, insulated coat made from danker beast fur It had been dyed a flaming pink that matched her leather pants. On her feet, boots of smooth polished leather and her hair had been picked to a glowing, blonde Afro. Moving her tinted glasses down from her eyes, Zykeiah smiled at Sarah and said, "Let us be on our way."

She chose two small female danker beasts and gave one of the reigns to Sarah. "This one is Majaga. She will be kind to you."

"How long do you expect us to be away?" Sarah asked as she climbed on to Majaga.

"The better part of the day," Zykeiah answered as she secured her sack onto the danker beast before climbing on. "I brought food for us to eat later."

Without further comment, Sarah followed Zykeiah out of the stables and into Veloris's blistering cold morning.

***

General Ogroth's blurry face failed to stay still on the watery screen of Orono's tella despite his attempts to correct it. It did not matter; the General's words came through loud and clear.

"I have spoken to the committee and the King. We are willing to pay your price of seventy-five silver coins in exchange for what secrets of the Solance you are prepared to sell."

Orono smiled, making his flabby cheeks struggle and jiggle in the attempt. "I am glad to hear that."

"Do not be misled, Orono. The information had better be worth it or you will pay us with your life," General Ogroth threatened with a growl.

"It will be more than worth it," Orono replied coolly, his smile slipping from his face. He frowned at the watery visual of General Ogroth.

"We will be the judge of that," General Ogroth grunted again and terminated the transmission.

Orono swore as he left the tight dungeon quarters, being sure to pocket the black glass ball in which he had just spoken to General Ogroth. The plan was not going well. General Ogroth was a menace.

"What did he say?" MaxMion hovered just outside the lower entranceway to the castle.

"They accepted our price," Orono disclosed confidently as his eyes scanned the shadows for spies... or worse, Valek.

***

Katelin followed Amana back into their shared cage The next group of souls floated past them with dreary faces and sagging shoulders as if they bore the entire planet of Solis on their shoulders.

"Come, sit and rest," Amana said as she sat down on the sanded smooth, stone bench; the room had little else.

"I am not tired," Katelin remarked as she continued to stare as the hundreds of souls humbly floated by in remarkable silence. MaxMion stood at the forefront of the mines picking out those who had to work and those that had to die.

"I know. We never get physically tired," Amana replied.

"So why are we waiting here? Why does he not work us indefinitely?" Katelin asked.

"I believe it is because Valek needs refreshed souls for his Solance. Even though we do not need physical rest, I think we do need to rest our spirits."

Katelin did not respond, but she came over next to Amana and sat down. She laid her head onto Amana's shoulders and remained still. Amana could not feel Katelin's presence, but there was pressure from their souls intermingling.

Amana did not know what the role of being a big sister incurred, because she had always been the little sister to Sarah. She was learning with this new soul, Katelin. The more she learned, the more she realized what a burden she had been to Sarah.

Katelin demanded so much, many answers, protecting and explaining. Amana did as she remembered that Sarah had done for her when they first arrived at the cages. She found herself returning again and again to those memories as she tried to cushion and support Katelin. Despite this, Amana missed being the little sister and longed for her own big sister.

***

The area just northeast of the castle, some two hundred paces from the servants' cottages, sloped slightly as Sarah and Zykeiah made their way up the snaking trail, between cuts in the rock, and narrow passageways.

Neither spoke as the sun continued to rise as the morning melted into mid-day. The trail had been covered with a light, soft layer of snow from the night before It was quickly melting into water, and the trails of water stretched out like veins across the land.

"It is warmer than it has been," Sarah commented as she noticed sprigs of growing plants peeking between slushy piles of melting snow.

"The spring season is upon us now. Veloris will remain a frigid planet, despite the warming trend that comes with the spring, but it is nice see plants," Zykeiah answered.

Zykeiah's danker beast edged a little farther ahead than Sarah's did. Obviously, she was leading, for Sarah had no idea where Stocklah lay amongst the forests and mountains.

Sarah was amazed at how much warmer the day was as she rode beside Zykeiah, who had spoken very little. Odd, she thought, for Zykeiah seemed determined to have her go to Stocklah, but now that she was riding along with her, she behaved as if she was not there or like something was on her mind.

"How long were you in the cages?" Sarah asked.

"Too long," Zykeiah answered quickly. "Look there, a kowletta calf!"

Sarah looked to the east where some grayish shrubs and dense thicket of trees hid all but the black hooves of a kowletta calf. Its tiny hooves made a bright contrast to the white snow that blanketed the area.

"The mother is close by, no doubt," Zykeiah said. "Hidden."

The air started to thin as they ascended further north. The danker beasts moaned as they traveled through the dust-like snow. The slope grew steeper as they followed a narrow trail that had been cut through the Northern Forest centuries before.

"I am originally from Saturn Four," Zykeiah offered to disturb the silence between them.

"How did you become a slave?" Sarah asked. She had known Saturn Four to be a free colony.

"Valek sells Solance to Saturn Four," Zykeiah explained. "He would steal souls of the poor and sometimes, when Saturn Four could not make the full payment, they would offer the poor to Valek as part of the settlement."

"How horrid!" Sarah's own capture from Earth was an act of terror with traps set along the open, grassy fields. Valek's henchmen raced into the small towns, driving the people from their makeshift homes of cardboard, metal carts and shacks and into the open fields where the soul cages were set.

Valek's true interest was in the children. Their souls were the most pure; therefore, he had most of the adults killed on the spot, including parents.

"Yes." Zykeiah turned to look at Sarah. "But no different than any other soul in the cages."

"You speak the truth," Sarah said. She could just make out the green treetops a few paces away. "What is that ahead?"

Zykeiah peered ahead, then nodded. "Stocklah."

As if the mere mention of the name was an indicator, the danker beasts slowed to a crawl and eventually stopped.

"What is the matter with the dankers?" Sarah patted her danker beast on the head and in return, received a fresh expulsion of gas.

"They are tired," Zykeiah said as she glanced around for a spot to rest. She steered her danker beast to a patch of melting snow under a huge oak tree. Its skeletal limbs reached up toward the sky and tiny hints of green indicated a future blossoming of flowers.

Sarah looked behind her and saw that they had traveled a great distance up the mountain. She could see the entire roof of the castle and some of the surrounding land. The servants traveling from the castle to the quarter seemed tiny, like ants working in the snow.

Climbing down from her danker, Zykeiah gestured to Sarah to do the same. She led her danker beast to the tree and tied the reigns around the thick trunk. She watched as the animal began to graze on the vegetation hidden beneath the snow.

Sarah climbed down from her danker beast and led it over to the tree, where she tied it up with the other. The two beasts ate greedily, not stopping to lick the snowy ice from their nostrils.

The air was definitely warmer, so much warmer that Sarah was damp with perspiration. The sun's rays beamed down on the rocks and trees and even the snow retreated from the sun's intensity.

She loosened the belt and opened her coat. She wiped her face with the back of her hand and took in a deep breath of crisp, cool air. The shallow air did not help cool her off, but she felt somewhat refreshed all the same.

"Stocklah is an oasis buried between two mountains," Zykeiah said as she placed the sack onto her back and started hiking forward up the gradual sloping mountain. "We go on foot from here."

The two hiked to Stocklah at a brisk pace. Zykeiah led and Sarah followed, albeit further behind. Soon, she was out of breath and wheezing, but Zykeiah did not stop. She was so far ahead that she could not hear Sarah's complications or moans.

"Are we there yet?" Sarah panted loudly.

"Almost!" Zykeiah called back.

They had been hiking for nearly an hour, when unable to go further without water, Sarah collapsed to her knees. Her hands braced her from falling directly on to her face. Her throat burned and a sharp pain stabbed at her side.

"Are you all right?" Zykeiah ran back to the spot where Sarah collapsed.

"No," Sarah croaked.

"You maybe too hot. Remove your coat," Zykeiah suggested as she reached for Sarah's arm. "I promise it will be worth it."

"No!" Sarah snatched her arm away and immediately got to her feet.

Zykeiah slid her glasses cautiously to the top of her head and peered at Sarah. "Are you sure you are all right?"

"Yes. I was merely winded; let us continue." Sarah put both hands onto her hips and took several deep breaths. She couldn't let Zykeiah see the marks on her hands.

Without further comment, Zykeiah replaced her glasses and resumed the hike. Sarah followed.

The snow gradually gave way to healthy, muddy dirt and plants of greens and blues. After they reached the plateau, Zykeiah beckoned to Sarah to come and investigate.

"Come, you can see the Stocklah Oasis from here."

Zykeiah removed a smaller bag filled with water from her sack. She handed it to Sarah; then removed a second bag for herself.

Sarah guzzled the water, draining the small pouch of its contents with alarming speed. Then she looked around.

Just below where Zykeiah stood was a drop-off of some several hundred paces downward into a valley. Plush greens, blues and other colors Sarah had no words for grew with free abandon. The screeches, songs, and calls of several birds and animals provided a chorus of wild, untamed animalistic music. It was a tropical paradise surrounded by cold, snow-capped mountain peaks.

Directly to her left was a thundering waterfall that appeared to pour right into the oasis as it raced down the steep slope of the mountain and over the plateau and into the valley.

"It is beautiful." Sarah yelled above the waterfall's thundering. She finally tore her eyes away, but she found it even more difficult to choose where to look at next. It was fabulous; a totally different world from Solis's black emptiness and Veloris's frigid cold.

Zykeiah watched closely as Sarah stood paralyzed by the splendor and beauty of Stocklah. She recalled how she had the same expression of awe when Marion had brought her there for first time.

Zykeiah reached out and gently played with Sarah's hair.

"What are you doing?" Sarah slapped Zykeiah's hand away.

"I wanted to share this place with you." Zykeiah drew back a little and kissed the stinging spot on her hand. "A beautiful place for a beautiful lady."

"That is the second time you have mentioned your interest in my appearance." Sarah said as she rolled up the sleeves. "Keep your hands to yourself."

Zykeiah frowned then said, "When Marion mentions it, it bothers you not. So why can't I?"

"Marion is a gentleman and one whom I owe my life. What he says to me is no concern of yours," Sarah snapped back. Her temper was growing. She was tired of Zykeiah's games and she wanted to know what the woman wanted from her.

"No?" Zykeiah said softly. "Then you are as naïve as I would have hoped." She searched the dirt in front of her as Sarah balled her hands into fists.

Sarah had expected something deviant from Zykeiah or else why would she demand she come here? The woman must have thought Sarah a fool. "Do not come near me or I will think you are attacking me."

"Attack you?" Zykeiah smirked. "You thought I was going to hurt you?"

"Yes. What was that in the Great Hall last night but an attack?" Sarah placed both fists in front of her, ready to strike.

"I was not going to attack you," Zykeiah said as she looked out across the plateau.

"No?" Sarah gradually put down her fists.

"No." Zykeiah shook her head and said, "Come let us go down into the oasis."

Zykeiah started off without waiting for Sarah. As quickly as the fight erupted, she had simply dropped it. Sarah wondered what was going on.

She removed her coat and followed Zykeiah down the narrow trail to the Stocklah oasis.

***

"Sarah?" Marion knocked again on the door. He turned the knob and poked his head into her room. "Sarah?"

No response and he did not find her in the room. He wondered where she could be. He had searched in the East Wing Hall, the central baths and now her room without success.

He made his way back down the stairs and back to the East Wing Hall. Deserted except for those that cleaned the kitchen, Marion noted that Sarah still had not returned.

A servant woman scrubbing the tin plates by the open hearth said, "Sir, you are searching for something?"

Beside the woman sat a young boy who was playing with two wooden spoons, clanking them together over and over again in glee.

"I am searching for the woman called Sarah," Marion said.

"She left early morning with the knight Zykeiah," the servant woman said, her eyes cast downward.

"Thank you, woman for your observation." Marion smiled at the servant woman who blushed in return, but did not meet his gaze.

Marion left the East Wing Hall for his room. He knew the way to Stocklah, but thought it would be best to allow the two to be alone. He had made up his mind that if it was Zykeiah Sarah chose, then he must respect her choice.

He had not offered himself to her. Zykeiah beat him to it.

Does the kowlata complain when the wrangler bird swoops in and steals his meal? No, the kowlata continues on searching for other prey. Marion resolved himself to do the same.

Chapter Eleven

"This place was once considered holy by the people before," Zykeiah explained. Tiny handprints painted along the mountain's shiny orange rock were the only remaining indication of their existence. They walked single file along the thin path to the Stocklah oasis. Zykeiah added, "the people had vanished by the time Queen Zoe's people arrived."

"Vanished?" Sarah asked as she looked over and saw how far down the drop remained despite their extensive trek. One false step and she and Zykeiah could plummet to their deaths.

"Queen Zoë said that once her people arrived, there were no others here."

"Why are there so few Minister Knights?" Sarah asked. "I expected an army of knights…"

"The Minister Knights are relatively new. Queen Zoe's father was the first, and he had used the royal army to prepare to fight Valek. But he died before he ever found a way to stop Valek."

"So, the Minister Knights have never seen battle?" Sarah stopped abruptly. "There has never been any contact with Valek?" She could not believe it. There were stories and rumors of the furious battles between Valek and the knights.

Zykeiah looked back at Sarah and smiled. "Marion has been in many battles against Valek's henchmen. He has always been in disguise."

"Disguise? Why?" Sarah answered. "There were rumors in the cages about how the Minister Knights defeated Valek before and…"

"Slow down, Sarah," Zykeiah said calmly over her shoulder. "Let me explain."

She stopped talking and cautiously turned around to face Sarah. "When King William died, his wife took up the task of developing a group to stop Valek. An uneducated woman when it came to fighting, she journeyed to the Antiqk Oracle to learn what she must do. She never returned from the Oracle, leaving a young three year-old, Zoë, to sit on the throne of Veloris."

"But..." Sarah interjected.

"Wait," Zykeiah continued, "the advisors raised Queen Zoë and when she reached adulthood, she journeyed to the Antiqk Oracle to find her mother. Search parties had been sent years earlier but no trace was ever found of the woman."

"So," Zykeiah returned to walking the trail. "When Queen Zoë came back some time later, she had the scrolls. She spent many extended rotations reading them, translating them, etc. Her mother, under the direction of the Antiqk Oracle, wrote the scrolls in the ancient tongue. They foretell of a savior coming from another planet that will defeat Valek."

"What had become of Queen Zoe's mother?" Sarah asked.

"After she wrote the scrolls, she died. Her body was found deep inside the cavern at Antiqk. She was not found before because the search parties were too afraid to enter the Oracle."

"And the army of Minister Knights?" Sarah asked. She could smell the floral scents of the blooming flowers of the oasis. They were close to the bottom and she grew hotter the closer they got to the oasis.

"The original group of knights had died off over time. By the time Queen Zoë was ready to assimilate the knights, there were only boys or married men left on Veloris. The few single men did not constitute an army."

"So where did Queen Zoë find Marion and Kalah?" Sarah asked as she followed Zykeiah into the plush opening mouth of the Stocklah oasis. A rich canopy of vegetation hid the thriving ground from the sun's brilliant light. The waterfalls thundered, making it difficult for Sarah to hear Zykeiah's response.

The birds' screeches were louder and the waterfalls drowned out just about any other sounds that were not louder or shriller.

Zykeiah gestured to a cavern just to the right of the end of the trail and Sarah followed her in. It was remarkably quieter inside and the walls of the cave were lined with more pictures and handprints of the people before.

"Queen Zoë did not find Marion and Kalah; she gave birth to them." Zykeiah pushed her glasses up and smiled at Sarah.

"She's their mother?" Sarah's mouth dropped and she could not believe it. Yet it explained much.

"Yes." Zykeiah glanced around then added, "I am not sure you are suppose to know it; so do not disclose it to anyone."

Sarah stuck out her hand and said, "Deal."

Zykeiah's eyes grew wide as she leapt back from Sarah, making sure to whip her dagger from her thigh-holster. "What is that on your hands?"

Groaning Sarah lifted her hands up and noticed that the marking still had not faded. Laughing nervously, she said, "I have discovered I have powers."

Zykeiah slipped out of her sack, letting the heavy pack smack to the ground. She was not laughing and she still had her dagger drawn. She moved deliberately crouched as if ready to strike. "Powers?"

"Yes, powers," Sarah answered slowly, her eyes staring at the dagger

Sarah cupped her hands together and focused on the image of a sphere, like the sun, and fire combined.

Gradually an orange pale bubble-like sphere grew from her hands. Sarah spread out her hands and shaped the orange glowing substance into a circular sphere and pushed it toward Zykeiah. Sarah could feel the markings on her hands throb the more brilliant the sphere became.

Zykeiah's face was covered with sweat and fear as she leapt toward the large sphere and sliced it with her dagger. The sphere did not falter, nor did it burst when Sarah un-cupped her hands. The sphere was not as large as she and twice as wide. It threatened to outgrow the cavern.

The sphere pressed Zykeiah back against the hard cavern wall, threatening to suffocate her. Zykeiah swung the dagger with thrashing cuts and slices, but it did not falter.

Sarah closed her eyes and whispered, "Stop."

The sphere burst and disappeared leaving not a trace of the gummy like substance.

"Powers," Sarah said as Zykeiah wiped her face and replaced her dagger.

***

Amana had been trying to loosen this one section of rock for what seemed like eternity, but the rock would not budge. The drums had started again as Katelin worked along beside her with less enthusiasm.

"Katelin, if MaxMion finds you working like that, your number may be called soon," Amana warned.

"Tell me again about your sister's rescue," Katelin said. "It inspires me and takes my mind off this boring task."

Amana did not know why Katelin loved hearing of Sarah's escape. It was the same story over and over again.

"My sister and I had just arrived at the Allerton Circle when Orono stepped from the shadows..."

As Amana talked, Katelin's appearance slowly melted off and in her place Manola stood with a smirk.

"But I do not know who the rescuer was and there is much I do not remember." Amana concluded then turned back to look at Katelin.

"Perhaps I know someone who could help you remember?" She hissed.

"Who?" Amana asked as she turned back around to the spot where Katelin had been. "Who are you?"

Amana's tool fell loudly to the ground as she floated back from Manola and panicked. The stranger blocked her path.

Manola pulled a green sphere from her bosom and opened it.

"Come!" she called as Amana's soul was swept into the jade colored sphere.

"Thank you," Manola said, chuckling at her cleverness.

"What are you doing?" MaxMion grunted from the spot where Amana was moments before.

"Little man, I do not report to you," Manola spat as she placed the shiny sphere in between her ripe, full bosom. She started walking through the pitch-black tunnels that led from the caverns to Valek's castle, leaving MaxMion to ponder.

MaxMion watched the back and forth swish of her ample butt-cheeks and thought of how delicious they would taste sautéed with fresh berries

Laughing as he shuffled down the western cavern and making a left at the fork, he continued on towards the underground entranceway to Valek's castle.

Up ahead, he could just make out Manola's paleness in the bleak tunnel. His eyes squinted as he checked behind him to make sure he was not being followed. Manola could be tricking him with her excellent use of deception and disguise. If she found out Orono's plans, she would surely tell Valek. He knew he would pay with his life. Orono's death would follow his, for Valek' s temper knew no limits.

Shivering at the thought, he waited until he could no longer see Manola's red hair and white reflection on the mirroring surface of the rock, before hurrying to the castle's underground entranceway.

***

Orono was busy making Solance when MaxMion burst through the warehouse's door.

"What are you doing here?" Orono demanded as the last soul was compressed and deposited into the final batch of Solance.

MaxMion attempted to lick his stretched lips around his teeth but failed. "Manola kidnapped the soul, Amana, and brought her to the castle"

"What!" Orono barked. "Why?"

"I am not sure," he replied and braced himself for a whack from Orono. Valek forbade him to be in the Solance warehouse. The smell of flesh and death might be too much for him, Valek warned, and MaxMion might tamper with the inventory.

"Come, let us see what is going on." Orono pulled his cloak snuggly around his lumpy body as they made their way to Valek's office.

***

"Tell me who he is!" Valek roared spraying spittle and venom onto Amana who cowered into a tight ball on the floor of his office.

Manola chuckled. "She does not know."

Ignoring her, Valek demanded, "Now or you will be a part of the latest batch!"

Smashing his fist to the desk, Valek clinched his teeth in an open growl. Much time had passed since Manola released Amana from the green sphere and still the girl had no information, just the same tired response of ignorance.

"There were rumors of one called Marion," Manola offered. "A Minister Knight."

"Yes, Orono had mentioned that!" Valek snapped.

"My Lord, the souls say it was Marion who rescued the soul Sarah," Manola said unabashed by his anger. What else could he do to her; he had already killed her.

"How would they know?" Valek reached into his desk and removed the orange box.

"It is only rumor, but some of the older ones speak of an Oracle and one named Marion." She uncrossed her legs and walked behind Valek.

He stroked his dried mushrooms and herbs. She massaged his rail-thin shoulders as she shook her illustrious red hair free from the tangles of being braided.

"Amana," Valek called sweetly.

"Yes." Amana timidly uncoiled from her spot on the floor and peeked through the hands she held over her face.

"Stand up, dear child," he cooed as he, too, stood up from his desk.

Amana rose from her spot and glanced around her before cautiously turning her empty eyes to Valek.

It was a good thing that she could not feel for the temperature of the office fell steadily until the breath from Valek's mouth curled into thin whispers as it escaped his mouth.

Manola stepped back hesitantly from him until she was pinned against the wall for she knew from experience that a sweet, nice Valek was more terrifying than an enraged one. Sure he had killed her once, but why die twice?

"May I be dismissed?" Manola stuttered as she inched along the wall as far from him as possible, in her attempt to leave.

"No." Valek's eyes were glued to the frightened Amana, who, too, had inched further away from his desk.

Silence as his eyes penetrated hers, gauging her fear, feeding upon it, and reveling in it. Amana could not turn away and she dare not run; for where would she go that Valek would not be able to find her?

***

Evening approached and there was still no sight of Sarah and Zykeiah. Marion walked up the stairs and past the royal guards to Queen Zoë's quarters.

As he entered he called, "Mother."

"Marion?" Queen Zoë's call was barely above a whisper and her breathing was raspy and ragged. "Come, son."

He smiled weakly as his mother moved her legs from the lower section of her bed. She was propped up against her favorite pillows and was surrounded by rolled scrolls and the floral scents of rosemary and jasmine.

"What troubles you my son?" She put down the scroll she was reading and gently placed it on the floor beside her bed. "Marion?"

"She is with Zykeiah. Stocklah," he mumbled as he plopped down on the bed. "Not here with me learning the history of Veloris or tossing balled snow at one another."

"Would you like for her to be here with you?" she asked gently. He had been in love before, but this time it felt different.

"Yes." Marion glanced at his mother, then back at the coverings on her bed, his finger tracing the thread lines in circles.

"Why?"

"Because-" he started then stopped as he observed the smile that tugged at the corners of his mother's mouth. "Mother."

Queen Zoë patted her eldest son's head and said, "Did you tell her, Marion, how you feel about her?"

"I cannot; she is with Zykeiah," he said.

Queen Zoë sighed and repeated, "Have you not told her?"

"No!"

"You need to declare your love, Marion." Queen Zoë's voice had grown weaker and more faint. "Soon."

Standing he kissed his mother's cheek. "Good evening, Mother."

"Things are not always what they seem, son." Queen Zoë patted his hand before closing her eyes to rest.

"Yes, Mother." He left his mother to rest.

***

"How did you discover this power?" Zykeiah inquired.

"I was born with this gift," Sarah answered, "according to the Antiqk Oracle."

"You have been to the Oracle?" Zykeiah asked, angrily. "No one but knights are allowed there."

"I had a knight with me," she said sharply.

Sarah left the cavern and began feeling the soft plush petals of purplish flowers that sprouted next to the cavern's open mouth. "Tell me more about the knights."

Zykeiah swaggered out of the cavern and yelled, "What is it you want to know?"

"Anything, everything. They are so mysterious," Sarah said.

"The two brothers do not feel anything." Zykeiah hesitated before saying, "They are drones, nothing more."

That would explain Marion's standoffishness, Sarah thought.

Zykeiah smirked as Sarah continued on the trail toward the waterfalls. She put the sack on her back and followed behind Sarah.

Sarah, lost in her thoughts of Marion, made her way to the mouth of a large lake that received the volume of water that dumped from the Stocklah mountain's waterfall. *A drone, an unfeeling creature made without emotions was very much like a soul. How do you get close to someone who felt nothing at all?* Sarah asked herself as the crystal clear water of Stocklah's waterfall fed into the lake of Stocklah.

Why did she want to?

***

Valek was smiling as Amana cowered from his outstretched palm. She fluttered about all the more, because as he smiled he withdrew an oblong glass sphere similar to the one Orono used to capture souls.

"Please, whatever it is you are about to do, please," Amana begged as Valek pointed the sphere at her with the same grin of deranged joy etched into his face.

He uttered a string of untellable words and pointed the sphere at her, she fell silent as her soul turned to flesh and plopped to the castle's stony floor.

The olive skin stretched as it wiggled across her body and extended until it covered every inch. Her black hair cascaded to her lower back and the pink color returned to her ashen lips.

"Amana," Valek called again.

"Yes, lord," Amana answered, her mind no longer hers alone.

"You will go through the Allerton Circle and you will capture the one called Marion," he ordered. "Do not return without it."

"Yes, my lord," Amana answered in a flat monotone voice, not at all the comfortable, bubbly voice of Amana.

"Then return to me with his soul!" Valek extended a turquoise blue sphere that was tiny, almost the size of a silver coin, and placed it in her open hand.

"Yes, my lord," Amana repeated. She slipped the sphere into her pocket.

"Manola, take her to the circle." He clasped both hands together and collapsed back into his chair...satisfied with his genius.

Following Manola, Amana felt cold in the icy air of the Solis night. Nestled deep inside the zombie Amana, the true Amana screamed, at the thought of being forced to obey Valek's every whim. She tried to resist, to run away, but his will was stronger.

They reached the Allerton Circle and did not look back as she finally left Solis.

***

Zykeiah felt torn between the part of her who still desired Marion and the one that liked Sarah. She knew that lying to Sarah about Marion and Kalah was wrong. She was the one of which the scrolls prophesied, Zykeiah could not deny it any longer. Zykeiah knew it and hated it. The prophecy of the Antiqk scrolls did not hide the signs of the savior; they were well known.

The markings on Sarah's hands were undeniable and her power could not be explained away easily. She wondered if she was the only one who had witnessed the growing savior's new powers.

Zykeiah called to Sarah, "Come, it is time for the evening meal."

Sarah hurried back to the spot where Zykeiah waited. "So soon?" she asked.

"Yes."

Sarah tilted her head high exposing her elegant neck. She saw the position of the sun, and said, "Yes, you are correct."

The two began the slow climb to the plateau and neither spoke. They reached the top and started the rigorous hike back down the trail away from Stocklah. They stopped only to retrieve the danker beasts that napped under the retreating sun. There was certain sadness about leaving the plush, fragrant oasis for the frigid Veloris realm. But now that she knew the way, she could come whenever she wanted.

The warm day had cooled and soon the hairs on Zykeiah's neck were standing on end. As they reached the bottom of the mountain, Sarah shuddered and tied her coat tight around her waist.

Zykeiah was a knight and the low mumbling in her stomach had to do with the lie she had told Sarah; it was an internal protest. She had lied before, but this new pain had to be a result of her knighting and her recent placement amongst the Knights. She would just have to ignore it. *Being Marion's wife would be worth it,* she thought. But deep inside, she liked Sarah too.

"Are you okay?" Sarah's face wrinkled with concern and for some reason Zykeiah could not explain it pleased her tremendously.

"Yes," she said.

"You are quiet." Sarah guided her danker beast over to Zykeiah and touched her forehead, then her cheek as she searched for signs of illness.

Sarah said, "Come, friend, evening meals are being served."

Friend. Zykeiah's heart fluttered with enthusiasm at the very sound of the word. Friend could be the beginning of a relationship; that was more than Zykeiah had at the onset of the hike.

***

Sarah's peaceful ride down the twisting trail to the castle was not without incident. She had disturbed something inside her that had once been dormant. A knowing of sorts, but that did not accurately describe it. Zykeiah had said that Marion and Kalah were emotionless drones, but she had remembered, during her rescue at the Allerton Circle, Marion's anger, bravery, and intense desire to escape.

No emotions?

Sarah also remembered the morning after her first night in the castle when she woke to find him in her quarters. The expression on his face, she reflected now, could have been nothing but concern.

If Marion did not feel, than surely he would not have expressed concern for her or attempt to cover feelings he did not have.

And Kalah. His jealousy and outright disregard for his brother was not an unfeeling emotion.

She had been ready to accept Zykeiah's words as truth, but something had stirred inside her when Zykeiah mentioned that the knights were drones. She had lied, Sarah thought.

Why had Zykeiah lied to her about the Knights?

***

Unconcerned by the late hour, Sarah remained wide-awake as the chilly air filtered into her quarters bringing with it numbing cold and goosebumps.

She and Zykeiah had returned just in time for evening meals, but Marion did not join them in the Great Hall. When asked, Queen Zoë replied that Marion was ill and taking his evening meals in his quarters. The Queen herself looked terrible and quite sick.

Sarah stopped at his door on her way to the East Wing after the evening meal. He did not answer her numerous knocks and calls. The door remained locked.

Troubled, she returned to her quarters and the knowing within her crept around inside whispering into the far corners of her psyche. She tapped into the well of her powers; chilly, she cupped her hands together for the second time and concentrated on the fire that burned lazily and low in her fireplace. The fire grew more intense as she focused on it.

She needed answers and the beckoning within called for her to seek out those answers. Only one place could be trusted to tell the whole, unbiased truth. She took the steps down to the lower level two at a time before scurrying down the hallway to the stables.

Chapter Twelve

Cold, Sarah picked her now familiar danker beast; Majaga recognized her on sight and passed a chorus of gas in delight. She smiled wearily at Majaga and gave her thick fur a couple of strokes before they set out.

As they began alone in the wintry night, she noticed that Veloris at night was different than Veloris during the day. The absence of activity was not the only factor that separated the day from evening. Now the shadows seemed to reach out like dry brittle bones, threatening to grab and snatch her from her danker and into the dark, hidden crevices of the forest. The wrangler birds' screeching seemed eerie and foreign as did the owlers constant questioning of "who, who, who."

Once again, she cupped her hands together and concentrated on the sphere. A bubble-like sphere appeared that was full of light although clear Sarah could feel the markings burn on her hands as she increased the size of the sphere.

The sphere encased her and Majaga providing warmth and light as they made their way to the Antiqk Oracle.

Majaga grunted in surprise for now as they moved forward to the Oracle, the bubble went as well.

Satisfied, she opened her eyes and took up Majaga's reigns and encouraged her to accelerate. She had no desire to be out of the castle the entire night. Sarah had only gone a few paces when the shadows stirred, reminding her of Marion's initial comments on Veloris' nocturnal creatures and their appetite for humans.

The growling of a monstrous cat seeped in to the bleak air from a thatch of hairy vegetation growth to Sarah's right. Skinny with clumps of its coat ripped out along with a chunk of its ear, the cat growled, and then pounced.

Sarah flinched and closed her eyes tight as she waited for the agonizing pain of sharp teeth ripping through her flesh.

The animal ran in to the sphere and was catapulted back with as much force as he gave in its attack.

She opened her eyes and witnessed the cat shaking its head in disbelief and then watched as it whimpered off to the dim corners of the forest.

***

Marion tossed and turned about in his bed, throwing the covering and blankets to the floor. Sleep would not come to relieve his active mind.

He had deliberately missed evening meal to meditate and to realign his thoughts. The crushing blow to his heart and to his pride had to be repaired or else true sickness may set in.

He had remained seated on his danker rug, surrounded by the burning incense of spicy tellia and the musk scent of seabroaka for what seemed like hundreds of rotations following his meeting with Queen Zoë. The chaos within must be silenced. He had lost control of himself with Sarah; he must not allow that to happen again. For it was for Sarah to decide who would keep the keys to her heart.

Groaning, he turned over to his stomach.

"Bah!"

He could not allow her to be with another; the meditation had only caused him to focus on her *more*, her warmth and her smile and his need to possess her love for his own.

He climbed sluggishly from bed. He needed answers and direction. This usually came from Queen Zoë, but in her weakened condition, she was of little assurance or ideas, for this matter.

Pulling out his sword and placing it casually on the bed, Marion dressed in the twilight dusk of his quarters. He knew where had to go for answers.

The Antiqk Oracle.

***

The iciness of Veloris caused Amana to shudder and grimace. Dressed far better than her sister when she arrived rotations earlier, Amana's cloak and boots still left her ill prepared for the blizzard-like weather.

Searching around the blanketed white-covered forest, Amana saw glimpses of colorful vegetation, but little indication of a trail, road or anything that would point her in the direction of locating Marion.

Lifting her eyes toward the north, she squinted in the icy downfall as she made out the outline of what looked like furls of smoke. Where there was smoke, there was something that burned, so she started towards the north. She had to find Marion.

Amana marched on for what seemed like hours and she grew weaker and weaker. It had been eons since she was alive and in flesh. The numbing cold and her empty stomach did nothing to strengthen her hike up the rolling hills toward the swirls of smoke.

Her vision blurred and the back of her legs burned with each step she took. The gnawing ache in her back coupled with the tingling in her hands was further indication that she needed to find shelter and food.

Soon.

Amana hiked on for a few more miles before fainting into the fresh snowfall of the early morning hours.

***

Queen Zoë woke with a start in the undisturbed hours of the new morning. "Someone is here."

Tapped into the entire world network of Veloris, Queen Zoë climbed out of bed and stepped into her slippers. Snatching her robe from the bed, she wrapped her slender frame into the soft comfort of terra as she hurried down the stairs. She even knew that Sarah was on her way to the Antiqk Oracle.

Taking the steps from her quarters, she rounded the curb and like a blur she hurried on through the Great Hall and on to the cluster of Knights' quarters.

She wiped her now sweaty brow and huffing and puffing, knocked hard on Marion's door. He opened it immediately.

Surprised, he asked, "Mother?"

"Marion."

Marion quickly snatched his sword from his bed as he heard the fear in his mother's voice,

"What has happened?" Marion searched the worried folds of her face. "Sarah?"

"No. Someone has come through the circle," she panted.

Marion slammed his door and quickly hurried towards the stables The answers in which he sought would have to wait until he found the stranger that had come through the circle. He reached the stables and took out his danker beast. "Duty before love," he laughed as he sped off into the night.

***

Sarah clapped her hands together and the sphere dispersed. She gave Majaga a pat on the head, and she walked slowly to the opening mouth of the Antiqk Oracle.

She had not forgotten about the rapid-fire answers the Oracle gave when one did not have control of her mind. Unsteady, she entered the Antiqk Oracle and immediately the flashing orange glowing begged her to "come."

Hesitantly, she placed both hands onto the warm globe and the markings on her hands burned as if she had placed them directly into the flames of her fireplace.

Screaming she tried to pull her hands free, but they were plastered to the globe.

"Calm," the watery voice of the Antiqk Oracle commanded.

Sarah stopped immediately but looked around hysterically trying to locate the owner of the voice.

"I am the Antiqk Oracle, Sarah."

"What?" Sarah concentrated on cooling the burning sensation on her hands. "You are hurting me!"

"You can stop the pain; it is your power." The watery voice seemed amused, Sarah thought as she focused on the cooling water at the bottom of Stocklah waterfalls.

Sarah, breathing rapidly, felt her hands begin to cool.
"Why did you not speak to me the first time I was here?"
"You were not ready to hear," the voice again seemed to giggle at her.
"Tell me the truth of the Minister Knights," Sarah demanded as she tried in vain to extract her hands from the Oracle. She would not get to leave until the Oracle was ready to release her.
"The Minister Knights are the descendants of Zolla, whose daughter Zoë now sits on the throne of Veloris."
"Are they human?" Sarah gave up on leaving the Oracle; she came here for answers. Instead she focused on preparing to ask her questions.
"Yes, the Minister Knights are human."
"What is my purpose?"
The Oracle deepened into a rough, rogue color before continuing to speak. "You know of your destiny. Embrace it and listen to it."
"Answer me!" Sarah screamed at the Oracle.
"You have the answer you seek, listen and embrace, Sarah." the watery voice of the Oracle laughed at her, and it reminded her of Octiva. "Listen and embrace."
"Is this what you have beckoned me here for?" Sarah said exasperated, and started to cry. "Give me something; I am alone here."
"Here." The water voice stopped laughing and a vision emerged of a woman, a man and several children scattered about them in front of an open hearth. "You are not alone, Sarah. Remember to embrace and *listen*."
The Antiqk Oracle fell dim and Sarah had to peel her hands from its surface. The markings stung and throbbed in protest to the frying they received from the Oracle.

***

Marion encouraged his danker beast until it bled as he hurried to the circle. The early morning snowfall made it difficult to speed through the mounds of fresh coldness.

Her black hair was the only indication that something was different in the blanket of whiteness.

He jumped down from his danker beast, lifted the woman from the thin layer of snow that now covered her body and wrapped her in a blanket. He threw her body over the danker beast and started towards the castle with urgency.

He once again encouraged his danker beast to a breakneck pace. He had to get the girl to the warmth of the castle and he had to get her to the greenery for healing, for Marion had no idea how long the girl had been in the snowfall and frost. Veloris at night could be brutal.

He did not know how or why Amana had come through the circle, strange that someone had escaped the cages. It had been done before with Zykeiah's arrival, but not since. But he could not devote any more thought to the girl's arrival through the circle. All his attention must be toward reaching the castle as soon as possible. The girl was barely breathing and the tips of her fingers were blue.

He had to make it, for if she died Marion had no idea what Sarah would do.

***

Sarah wearily climbed onto Majaga and without much concentration summoned the protective sphere. She headed back to the castle, defeated and tired. The Antiqk Oracle had not answered any of her questions. Who was the woman in the vision? Who were the babes? More importantly, embrace and listen, the Oracle had said repeatedly. The instinct within her had to be what the Oracle had referred to.

The trip back to the castle dragged by as she fought to keep her eyes open. She had so much energy when she left for the Antiqk Oracle, and the Oracle had drained it with fiery precision, leaving her hollow and empty.

When she finally reached the castle, she tied up Majaga, fed her some grass, and dragged down the hall to the East Wing. She then went up the spiraling steps to the waiting comforts of her quarters.

Sarah did not remove any of her clothes, but dropped to the bed, exhausted.

***

Sarah had briefly closed her eyes when the pounding on her door made them flap open. Her eyes burned as she cracked the door.

"You need to come to the queen's quarters," Kalah calmly said as Sarah groggily yawned.

"At this hour?" She glanced at the position of the moon "Can it not wait until morning?" *Late morning,* Sarah thought.

"No," Kalah said before turning and leaving.

She shut the door and quickly hurried after Kalah. Kalah's deadpan expression and attitude indicated that something was going on.

Tired and still a little sleepy, she dragged as she made her way to the queen's quarters. Kalah did not ask why she was still fully dressed, but continued on ahead at full pace, until she could no longer see him.

The quietness of the wee hours was a double-edged sword, for it offered calm quiet, but that calmness also invited the madness that comes with constant thoughts. And Sarah had too many of the latter as of late.

The queen's guards were not in their traditional positions and the hallway leading to her quarters was dim and unlit.

"Hello?" Sarah called as she entered the Queen's quarters.

Kalah, Marion, Zykeiah and Queen Zoë were crowded in a tight circle; their conversation stopped as soon as she entered. The queen was not in her bed, but was seated in a chair. The others stood tightly around her in a semi-circle.

"What has happened?" Sarah asked as she stepped further into the quarters.

They turned to look at her, then nervously at each other before stepping back, revealing a woman who appeared to be sleeping. The way her head was leaning slightly to the side reminded Sarah of someone she knew, but this could not be her. Queen Zoë said that they could go back for her; the queen was not encouraged by the odds of her escaping.

On closer inspection, Sarah moved the spiraling black ringlets from the sleeping woman's face and gasped.

"Amana!" Sarah leapt forward and hugged her sister close, waking the sleeping woman.

Amana eyes opened slowly. "Sarah?"

"Yes, oh, yes!" Sarah gripped Amana tightly.

"Sarah," Marion gently called.

Ignoring him, she lifted her sister to a standing position. "Come, we have much to talk about."

Nodding, but not speaking, Amana followed Sarah out of Queen Zoë's quarters trailed by concerned stares.

Chapter Thirteen

"I cannot believe it!" Sarah gripped Amana's hand tightly as she led her younger sister through the scented hallways of the castle. She didn't keep her voice down, and she felt joy unlike she had felt since her escape from the cages.

Amana's eyes barely noticed the elaborate rugs and blazing hearths that lazily heated the castle in early morning hours. Her eyes never wavered from Sarah's as Sarah retold about the times they went about as children prior to their abduction from Earth.

"Amana, are you okay?" Sarah had reached the East Wing and hesitated before heading up the spiraling stairs to her quarters. She removed some strands of hair plastered to Amana's hot, moist face.

"Yes," Amana answered and gave a half-hearted smile that seemed to wane as soon as it started.

She tickled Amana behind her ear, but Amana did not smile or grin. Tickling, especially behind the ear, used to cause Amana to erupt in to fits of laughter that usually spilled over to her and the two would collapse to the floor.

But that was when they were younger and long before the cages. Perhaps now, after the grueling stench and abuse of the cages, the act of laughing and the joys of life might be lost forever in the blue spheres of Solis.

Shoving those questions aside, Sarah took the stairs two at a time and quickly turned back as she reached the top of the stairs to make sure Amana was behind her. All remnants of weariness had been chased away in light of fresh enthusiasm.

Amana, her sister, best friend and sole surviving family member was now right here in the flesh, in her quarters and sitting cautiously on her bed.

"Feel that Amana!" She pulled the blanket up and touched Amana's cheek. "Soft, Amana, soft. Remember?"

"Yes," Amana responded and gave yet another waning smile.

"Oh, Amana, let us go to sleep." She quickly pulled the covers back and beckoned for Amana to lie down as well.

Unsure of just how long Amana had been in her flesh, Sarah had no idea if she was aware that she was tired. Shortly after the soul was reincarnated into its body, the soul sometimes did not readily recognize that the new body grew weary. Sarah had only known one person to escape the cages and that was Zykeiah, but the older souls often told stories of when it suited Valek to do so, he would reincarnate souls back to the flesh.

At the time, she had dismissed them as the tales of overactive, long-abused imaginations of lost souls. Now, she found herself often referring back to those stories and tales for information and guidance. She wondered how the souls knew such detailed information when none of them had ever been to Veloris.

Listen... Sarah could hear the watery voice of the Antiqk Oracle warn. It was so compelling she had begun to feel the voice was in the same room with her and she was not alone.

She dismissed the ambiguous nature of the Antiqk Oracle's knowing voice. That night at the cottage, she had felt a deep knowing inside that moved and crawled around in her mind. The sharp, crisp images of the dreams had receded in recent hours, and in their place, bits and pieces still remained lost in a grayish fog of Veloris's early mornings.

She woke up and focused her attention on Amana sleeping beside her. Effortlessly, a smile came to her face. The cages may have spoiled her sister's understanding of joy, but it did not spoil her sister's beauty and youth.

The voice whispered from the hidden corners within her and she knew something was not right. The gnawing at the corners of her self-conscious mind did not cease as she returned to a fitful slumber. *Listen and embrace,* the clear watery voice of the Antiqk Oracle resounded as she slept.

***

"How did she come through the circle?" Marion asked as the first lights of the weakening Veloris sun kissed the frozen tundra of the icy planet.

Queen Zoë huddled beneath several thick blankets. A roaring fire and the three Minister Knights accompanied her. They had been in her private quarters since Sarah gleefully led Amana from the room earlier. The queen sat in her bed, and the knights had followed her into the bedchamber.

"I came through the circle without aid," Zykeiah answered from her spot near the fire.

"Yes, Zykeiah, but you should have seen Amana at the Circle," Marion began, "she had totally lost control; she was so frightened of Orono. She is not you; she would not have taken the chance to flee the cages alone."

Kalah remained silent as he watched Marion and Zykeiah search for an answer to Amana's miraculous arrival to Veloris, which he cared nothing about. Why complain that another beautiful woman had arrived on Veloris?

"Maybe her desire to be free eliminated her initial fear and she escaped."

Marion ignored Zykeiah as he paced, irritated, back and forth beside the queen's bed. His face was wrinkled with concern and thought.

Zykeiah mistook his silence to be an insult and said hotly, "Just because she is a *woman* does not mean she could not come through the circle on her own!"

"I know that!" Marion spat back.

"Stop it!" Queen Zoë said. "I want this to end right this moment. This must be settled, now."

The thin, fragile queen struggled to an upright position and pointed her long, elegant finger at Kalah.

"He is your family. She is your family. Veloris is your family and the caged, slaved souls of Solis are your responsibility. The time for which we have prepared is upon us. I can feel it in the wind. It whispers in the shadows of this castle and demands to be heard."

Kalah turned away. He had heard his mother's words before, and he was not in the mood for another lecture.

"Hear me, Kalah!" Queen Zoë fell into coughing fits and Zykeiah produced three green leaves of rosemary that the Queen quickly ate to soothe her coughs.

"You must come into the circle." Queen Zoë extended her arms to the ceiling and chanted the ancient prophecies of the Antiqk scrolls

Kalah clasped both hands over his ears and he fled from the queen's quarters, producing a different series of fits and cries from her in the foreign tongue of the ancients.

Marion looked to Zykeiah and the two watched as salty tears fell from his mother's eyes.

"Zykeiah, Marion, you must quench Kalah's jealousy if we are to defeat Valek."

"We will. I promise you, Mother," Marion said gently.

"Do not be so quick!" Queen Zoë wheezed. "You must settle the trembling within."

Marion released her hand and took his leave without further comment.

Zykeiah also turned to leave, but Queen Zoë was not finished with her demands that morning.

"You must also purify the aching desire that burns within you. You are knowledgeable of the scrolls; it will not fall favorably for you if you proceed on this course."

"I am aware, my queen," Zykeiah responded abruptly before turning yet again to leave.

"Zykeiah, she cannot love you. She is the chosen deliverer of the Pixlis Galaxy," Queen Zoë warned.

"Can she not?" Zykeiah asked before leaving.

"By the heavens, the scrolls must hold true." Queen Zoë snuggled against her pillows and gazed at the retreating clouds.

***

Amana and Sarah ate the afternoon meal of roasted henckens and fresh greens tossed with fruit juice, later than she expected. The rest of the castle went about its chores. The East Wing Hall had long since emptied the servants into the jubilant snow and chilly day.

Mechanically, Amana lifted the slick piece of henckens to her mouth and chewed in an unmotivated rhythm. Sarah could hear the watery voice of the Antiqk Oracle as it returned, refusing to be silenced. She attempted to enjoy her meal. She truly thought the act of eating was more enjoyable than any other act in which she had engaged since returning to flesh.

Again and again her eyes returned to Amana's face and the absence of the familiar brightness that was once frequent behind her eyes.

"Is it wonderful?" Sarah asked as she thought of her initial breakfast with Marion. The hot egg that she picked up without regard or any clear indication of its temperature burned her. The stinging sensation of the burn seemed to sear itself into her memory.

"Yes," Amana replied.

***

"I tell you, Zykeiah, the arrival of Amana *is* strange. Can you not sense it?" Marion said from the corner of his bed.

She noted the deep, dark circles underneath his eyes. His lips were white and cracked.

"Have you not eaten or slept today?" Zykeiah stood and went over to him.

"No," Marion grunted. He wiped his naked head and temporarily closed his eyes. They opened within moments and he said, "What if Valek sent her here?"

Zykeiah snorted. "Impossible. How would he know about you and the Minister Knights?"

"How did you?" Marion asked.

"It was rumored through the oldest souls that there were a group of rescuers called the Minister Knights..." she started to explain.

"That is all?" he asked, knowing there was more.

"No, the rumors were that the Knights resided on Veloris."

"Valek could have found that out. The rumors of the Knights could have reached him." He lay back onto his bed.

The afternoon sun's rays sprawled across his broad and hairless chest. Zykeiah could not take her eyes off it and she leaned over to rest her head against it, as she had done many times before.

He held his breath as she started to place gentle, soft kisses on the area just above his pants-tie and continued up until she reached his mouth.

"Zykeiah," Marion whispered. "This is not right-"

She leaned in to kiss his lips. But he grabbed her shoulders and slowly pushed her backwards until she was seated upright.

"It used to be like this, Marion. Say you miss me..." she pleaded softly.

"No, I do not miss you, Zykeiah," he said gently as he sat upright. He released her shoulders.

Zykeiah stood up and returned to her previous spot by the fireplace. "Then it is true, you love *her*."

"Zykeiah, I-I..." Marion stammered. "I cannot explain-"

"It is of no important matter," she said as she left his quarters leaving her floral scent behind.

***

Sarah and Amana sat on the hard stone floor of the foyer as the children played marbles and the mothers sat together in a semi-circle and knitted with various shades of yarn. They whispered and giggled amongst themselves, every once in a while casting a nervous glance towards the two new members of the castle.

Sarah thought that an afternoon relaxing with the children's laughter and the warm soothing flames of the two open hearths might provoke some emotional response from Amana. Perhaps by watching the children play, hearing their laughter and seeing the women's closeness would somehow help restore some of Amana's humanity and spirit.

"Do you see the children play? Do you remember when mother had given us a small bag of marbles and you placed them directly into your mouth?"

"Yes," Amana answered flatly.

Her eyes stared off into space. They were glassy and not directly focused on the robust environment around them.

Sarah leaned back against the wall and began to play with Amana's hair as the afternoon crept slowly into night. Kalah had rounded the corner and Amana's eyes lit up.

"Hello!" she said.

The loud greeting startled him as he had just placed his hand on the door handle to his quarters.

"Sarah, is that Marion?" she whispered anxiously.

"Hello, Amana." Kalah walked over to her and squatted down to her eye level. "My name is Kalah."

Amana blushed and giggled in a way that was short, nervous and shrill. But the excitement in her eyes had died.

Kalah continued to stare at her with growing interest and intensity. "Will you join me in the West Wing for evening meal?"

"Yes," she answered quickly as she traced his brand with her finger.

"We will both be there, Kalah," Sarah spoke up from beside her, "for evening meal."

Kalah flinched at the sound of Sarah's voice as if startled. He said, "Of course," before standing and returning to his quarters.

As if the sun had set into night, Amana fell silent and resumed her former staring into nothing as Kalah left to return to his quarters.

"Kalah is a Minster Knight like Marion," Sarah explained. "How did you know about Marion?"

"I have heard his name around," Amana said flatly.

***

The children's game of marbles had ceased and their mothers had taken them down to the East Wing Hall for evening meals. Sarah and Amana washed their hands in the water trough before returning to the Great Hall.

The Great Hall was significantly quieter than the previous evening, for there were no festive engagements arranged for Amana's arrival.

Kalah waited outside the Great Hall entranceway and upon seeing Amana, a wide smile spread across his face. The smile seemed strange, for Kalah was almost always sullen. Offering his hand, he escorted her into the Great Hall, leaving Sarah to enter on her own.

Sighing heavily, she entered the Great Hall alone as Kalah escorted Amana to the favorite spot of the knights. The smell of the evening meal scented the air and Sarah's stomach growled in anticipation.

Queen Zoë watched as Kalah walked the latest Veloris visitor to the table closest to her. The Great Hall fell eerily quiet as some of the servants received their first look at Sarah's sister.

As he sat down next to her, the whispers and conversations resumed but not without glances and sneaked peeks at Amana.

Queen Zoë walked over to the table and smiled at Amana. "Welcome to Veloris, Amana."

Sarah noticed Octiva hovering just behind the aging Queen; it was the first time she had seen the woman from the servants' cottages since her midnight trek there.

With nothing further, Queen Zoë left the Great Hall with her personal servant, Octiva, trailing behind her, no doubt eating her meal in her quarters.

The watery voice within spoke again, vibrant and forceful as Sarah turned to the Great Hall entranceway. Marion walked in with Zykeiah.

When Marion's eyes met hers, Sarah started trembling as if she had a serious case of the shudders.

She wasn't the only one affected by his arrival.

She ceased listening to Kalah's tales of bravery when Marion sat down across from her at the table. Her stare did not falter as she watched him smile and say, "Good evening, Amana. I am Marion."

She shook uncontrollably as she stumbled to stand.

Sarah turned to look at her sister, whose shivering was quite visible. "Amana, are you-"

The watery voice screamed inside her, piercing the balance between a deep knowing and quiet delusion. She placed both hands to her ears as she collapsed to her knees beside Marion's seat at the table.

Zykeiah raced over to her, "Sarah are you all right? What is the matter?"

The vision swirled in front of her as Sarah stared into open space. It obstructed her view of the surroundings inside the Great Hall. The vision showed Marion struggling and howling in agony in some dark cavern alone, dying. With each lash he received in the vision, she felt it.

"Marion!" Sarah sputtered as she reached out to him while attempting to fight off the vision and pain. She was blind; she could only see the horrific vision swirling in front of her. She had no control over her senses. The oracle was commanding her.

Marion stood slowly and leaned over to her. He listened to her screams with his back to Amana. He could see the pain etched across Sarah's face. "Yes, Sarah. What is the matter?"

Amana removed the small turquoise sphere and lifted it toward Marion's back.

Kalah yelled, "Amana, what are you doing?"

Marion, hearing Kalah's cries, turned to see what the yelling was about and saw Amana bring the sphere to her eye level.

Sarah screamed, "Marion!" and waved blindly trying to reach for him, but his attention was split between Amana and her.

Hearing the heart wrenching pain of Sarah's screams, Marion, whose interest was in Sarah and her well being, pulled his attention back to her, just as the pale bluish light of the sphere smashed into his back.

Sarah's vision ended just in time to watch his soul extraction. There were thundering screams as his soul was snatched from his body, causing a terrifying lump to form in her throat. "NO!"

His lifeless body fell hard to the ground, the eye sockets blackened and empty.

Jolted from fear, Kalah fled the Great Hall.

Zykeiah, instead of fleeing, pulled out her dagger, jumped onto the table and raced to Amana. As she reached the spot where Amana stood, Zykeiah drew back her dagger and without hesitation sliced Amana' s tender cheek, the pain piercing through the foggy cloud-like dream and awaking her from her trance.

"Oooh..." Amana howled with agony. "What am I..."

Sarah snatched Zykeiah wrist before she could strike again, "Wait!"

Zykeiah glanced back at Sarah and growled, "What?"

Just then Amana, holding her cheek, placed the sphere back into her pocket and disappeared. She vanished into the thin chilly air of the Great Hall, leaving in her wake stunned silence and confusion.

Chapter Fourteen

Zykeiah snatched her dagger and shoved it back into her thigh holster. "Now what Savior?"

Sarah flinched at her harsh words.

Zykeiah wiped her mouth and muttered as she paced the length of the table. The Great Hall had emptied except for her and Sarah.

"Were you brought here to assault Marion?" she demanded as tears welled in her eyes.

Sarah shook her head in disbelief; numbly she muttered, "I do not know what just happened."

Zykeiah balked and stalked over to her, smacked her hard across her cheek and quickly drew her dagger and pointed it at Sarah's throat. "Marion's soul has been extracted and it is because of you."

The hard knot in Sarah's throat grew larger as Zykeiah pushed the dagger's tip into her flesh.

"Zykeiah, Sarah, what has happened?" Queen Zoë wearily stepped in to the Great Hall followed by Octiva. "I no longer feel Marion's presence on Veloris."

Zykeiah cleared her throat and slowly removed the dagger from Sarah's exposed neck. She took a deep breath before turning to Queen Zoë.

"Queen Zoë, Marion's soul has been stolen," she announced firmly, keeping her voice from wavering.

A new wrinkled frown emerged on Queen Zoë's face as her burning pale gray eyes searched the deserted hall and then Zykeiah's face.

"Amana," Queen Zoë whispered as numerous tears spilled over and streamed down her face. As her eyes landed on Marion's discarded body, she broke down and wept.

"No!" she crumbled to the ground and stayed there as her grief escalated. Octiva remained by her side, trying in vain to comfort her. Zykeiah soon grew tired of the scene and left the Great Hall in a fit of frustration and rage. Her curses and cries echoed down the hall.

"Queen Zoë, surely we can rescue him." Sarah reached down and patted the Queen's shoulder. "Send the Knights to Solis."

She stopped her moans, briefly, as she looked up at Sarah. "Send the Knights?"

"Yes, they could rescue Marion's soul before it is too late."

"Sarah, Marion *was* the Minister Knights!" Queen Zoë gingerly stood. "Kalah has never seen true battle; Zykeiah has only been a knight for a short time," the queen said angrily.

Sarah recoiled from the fury in Queen Zoë's face and voice. She knew it wasn' t her fault, but she felt the anger and hostility directed at her.

"Sending them to rescue Marion would be sending them to their deaths!" she said.

"I mean no disrespect my queen, but isn't that the true purpose of the knights…to rescue souls?" Sarah asked softly.

She gave Sarah a puzzling look before Octiva guided her out of the Great Hall and to the kitchen. She stopped short and said to Sarah, "Come to see me later; we must talk."

Sarah nodded before leaving the Great Hall for the cleansing quiet of her quarters.

As she walked to her quarters, memories of Marion cropped up wherever she turned. The first night she arrived at the foyer; the morning in his quarters when he divulged her destiny and purpose for Veloris, and the evening when he carried her to the Great Hall after their trip to the Oracle. As she continued up the spiral steps, she recalled the look in his eyes when she awoke to find him in her quarters. She smiled at the memory and her heart was flooded with a warm feeling unlike she had ever felt before. She grabbed her chest and giggled.

"Where did that come from?" Sarah asked the empty hallway.

She remembered the look in his eyes, the concern. Sarah slowly realized that tonight in the Great Hall, Marion's eyes were filled with concern, that day in her bedroom they were not; he was feeling something else.

She opened the door to her quarters as the watery voice of the oracle whispered into her psyche the true orientation of the look in his eyes. The Antiqk Oracle's vision too became clear as her eyes were truly opened and the scales of ignorance were removed. She could now identify the people in the vision and she began to weep. "No, oh, no. I have been a fool!"

Sarah created a fire with the flick of her wrist and an unconscious thought for warmth. Her powers were growing rapidly, but it was little consolation to the emotional pain she was now feeling.

The echoes of Queen Zoe's cries filtered into her memory and she felt it was her fault. Amana would not have taken Marion's soul purposefully. She knew that there had to be more to her sister's arrival…a reason or a debt. She desperately wanted to believe she had nothing to do with it, but Amana would not have come to Veloris had she not been there.

Sarah lay on the soft blankets of her bed and continued to cry at the horror. She had lost her sister and her only friend, all in one day.

***

Zykeiah paced the length of her quarters as she twirled her dagger in her right hand, almost as an afterthought. Kalah had been a coward and Sarah an emotional menace. She would have had Amana sliced into chunks and Marion could have been freed had it not been for Sarah's interruption.

Savior?

Only if Amana was out of the way could Sarah be the true savior. But as long as she worked for Valek, Sarah would be useless to them. The stupid girl kept letting her feelings get in the way of doing business.

Zykeiah stopped pacing as a more sinister thought came to mind.

What if Sarah was working for Valek?

Marion had suspected Amana, but why not Sarah as well?

Sarah could have manufactured the markings on her hands. As for the powers she demonstrated at the Stocklah Oasis, Manola could have conjured those for show. Zykeiah knew of Manola's powers all to well. She also knew of Manola's skill at deception.

She quickly left her quarters and knocked on the neighboring door. "Kalah, open the door. It is Zykeiah."

"Leave me!" his strained voice boomed. His voice sounded strange as if it was filled with tears and something else.

Shame?

"Open now before I kick it in."

Heavy footsteps and then a small crack in the door as Zykeiah entered Kalah's quarters.

She had been in Marion's quarters many times, but she had never been in Kalah's. The outer room had two broad wooden chairs; both well cushioned by pillows and short stools reserved for the feet. A danker rug lay sprawled across the outer room and leaves had been scattered across the plush fur. A tiny open hearth burned thin logs of evergreens. The outer quarter smelled of fresh open forest and musk.

The fire provided the only source of illumination. Shadows danced across Kalah's face as he sat down in front of the fire. He placed his feet on the stool and leaned his head back over the chair.

Zykeiah rubbed her neck for the position looked awkward and painful. "Kalah, what if Sarah was sent to destroy the Minister Knights?"

He sat up and searched Zykeiah's face.

"I mean Amana obviously was sent here to kidnap Marion," she explained.

He groaned and shook his head. "Bah!"

"Think about it. Ever since her arrival, she has placed a wedge between us," she went on.

He rose and went to his bedchambers. He returned with a pitcher of bottled ale. It was warm and he grimaced as he took quick sips.

"Zykeiah, Queen Zoë said Sarah is the chosen." Kalah returned to his seat. "You know the scrolls."

The fire's embers danced in the paleness of Kalah's gray eyes.

"Yes, but she could be-"

"…and Marion and I were not exactly close. That had been established since his birth before mine and long before her arrival on Veloris."

"Damn you!" Zykeiah spat. "Do you not care for him? Are you merely a coward hiding behind his mother's skirt?"

Kalah stared into the fire. "I thought you would be glad to see your rival gone."

He turned to her and stared directly into her eyes. "No?"

"You are not worthy to be his brother," Zykeiah cursed as she left.

***

Kalah's ears stung as Zykeiah slammed his door.

He continued to sip his ale. He swallowed the bitterness with a mixture of pleasure and searing pain. He should be excited and joyous as the sole heir to the Veloris throne and the leader of the Minister Knights.

Since his youth he had waited for this day. He could almost feel the sunlight on his face as at last he could emerge from Marion's shadow. His desire for Marion to be gone and for him to be the favorite son had pushed him into doing the most ridiculous things to win his mother's affections, not to mention the most deceptive.

Now that the path had been cleared, and Marion was gone, he felt hollow. His victory was empty and his mother's grief would destroy her health and more than likely her life, making his accession to the throne a thing of the near future.

He stood groggily as he remembered Marion's drunken stupor in the Great Hall. He had swooped in to seize the opportunity to humiliate his brother and become the leader of the Minster Knights when Sarah arrived.

Marion's savior, Sarah. Did not the scrolls foretell of their love…their place in history already predicted by the ancients?

Kalah stumbled into his bed, knocking vials of dried herbs to the floor. They smashed into hundreds of tiny pieces of glass and leaves.

Marion would come for him had his soul been taken.

But would he do the same? Could he conjure the courage to try to save his brother from the soul cages?

He did not know.

***

Valek lifted his crystal glass and quickly gulped the wine. Peppery was the word that came to mind as he slowly observed Richard and several of his advisors.

Few candles were lit during evening meal as they dined in the modest dining hall in Valek's castle. He had few rooms that were accommodating for entertaining guests, but the client insisted. Orono had prepared a satisfactory meal of baked owlers stolen from Earth 3012 and decorated with orange and served with sweet bread.

Valek noted the savory meal and made a mental note to add cook to Orono's growing list of responsibilities.

"Valek, it is quite dim in here." One of the advisors leaned forward with his protruding nose and beady eyes. "You are not so poor as to not be able to afford more candles?"

The other advisors and Richard chuckled at the question.

A trick question, Valek smiled. Answer "yes" then they would make the comment that his love of money ruled him and they would pass on purchasing the Solance.

If he answered "no", they would think his price was too much and that he was trying to get rich from them.

Valek sipped his wine as several of the advisors held their breath and nervously looked at each other in anticipation of his answer.

"I am not proud of this, gentlemen, but the light hurts my eyes," he answered smoothly.

Yes, the wine was too peppery, he thought as Manola patted his hand like a good, dedicated wife, although she was no such thing.

Appearances mattered a great deal in the "selling" process and Earth 4016 was a small kingdom that embraced the theories of family and community. A slight amendment in his lifestyle to land the contract was worth the charades.

"Valek, it is rumored that you keep slaves. Is it true?" the same advisor asked yet another question.

Valek noted that he would have to get rid of that advisor; perhaps MaxMion would like him as a little after-meal treat.

"I do occasionally take slaves, but only for additional payment in lieu of silver. I do not make it common practice."

Some of the advisors shook their heads and smiled at his deceptiveness. Richard also smiled, nervously.

Pushing gently back from the table, Valek announced, "Now for some entertainment." He beckoned to Manola from the doorway.

Manola walked to the center of the dining hall.

"MaxMion get in here," he ordered.

MaxMion hurried in to the hall from the kitchen with a tambourine and a look of mischief.

"Play," he demanded as he sat back down. He watched from the corners of his eyes as the advisors whispered and gasped at MaxMion's appearance They would forget all about him once Manola started to dance.

MaxMion sat on the floor and began to play as Manola danced in her scantily clad black bodysuit. Several sections had been removed to reveal parts of her flesh.

Her fiery hair spun as she twirled and danced, mesmerizing the men in the makeshift hall and bringing a satisfying grin to one that was neither male nor female.

***

Valek was not the only one watched.

From the entranceway to the kitchen, Orono watched the evening meal as he ate cold gosha from a stool in the equally dim and filthy place.

He angrily stuffed yet another cold, gritty spoonful into his mouth as he remembered Valek's demand that he "take the role of *butler.* " Reduced to serving Valek's snotty new clients from Earth 4016 only fueled his desire for revenge. That witch Manola should be the one serving.

"Get the drinks, Orono," he mocked as he backed away from the entrance. "Cook the meal, Orono."

The bowl clanked as it made contact with the washing tin and gosha splattered against the wall. He picked up the remains of feathers, owler parts and leaves and he tossed them, too, into the washing tin.

"I will show you," he continued to mutter as he cleaned the tiny kitchen with the same apathetic attitude in which he performed all of Valek's commands.

Manola interrupted his mutterings as she slithered into the kitchen. She was not quiet enough; he quickly turned around to face her.

"What do you want?"

"Valek wants the celebratory bottle of wine," she said.

Orono blocked her path, "For what reason?"

Manola lifted her palm and blasted him in the stomach with a ray of green light. "You will have to ask him yourself."

Orono was knocked backwards to the washing tin and into the stone kitchen wall. His head tingled and a small cut appeared just above his floppy ears as he crashed to the floor.

Manola reached into the cupboard, withdrew the bottle and returned to the dining hall without looking back. Roars of laughter grew louder and more boisterous as the evening meal continued without any concern for his safety.

He unsteadily stood up and blinked repeatedly as he reached for the edge of the sink.

"Bitch." He swore again as he slowly made his way back to the entranceway. He knew all about their plans to expand Solance to Earth 4016. Nothing was secret in the castle, except what Orono wanted to keep secret, no matter what Valek believed.

Valek always overestimated himself.

Orono continued to watch as Manola began to dance again, this time to the strong musical voice of MaxMion. His voice was fantastic despite the leftover food and bones the advisors threw at him, which only made Valek laugh. The sadness swelled up in MaxMion's eyes, but he continued his song and play as if they were not there.

Then a smile so genuine and true spread across his face as he caught Orono's eyes watching him from the kitchen.

"Soon," Orono whispered, "very soon."

***

Amana's huge tears burned as they raced down her face and into the open cut on her cheek. She pressed her hand hard against her cheek, but it did not halt the bleeding.

She had arrived back through the Allerton Circle, yet she did not know how. The throb of the sphere in her pocket heated the spot on her leg as if it was demanding to be returned to Valek.

***

Valek clasped a hand to his ear as the evening meal drew to a close.

"Are you all right, Valek?" Richard asked. "Too much wine?"

"Yes," Valek replied coolly. "Excuse me."

But he was not all right. Amana had returned.

Chapter Fifteen

The morning came upon Veloris with the same ignorance and obliviousness to the pain and betrayal that had touched all in the castle the day before. It pulled them from the safe comforts of sleep and into the brilliant light of day to face again the plights that were abandoned the night prior.

Whispery and cool, the wind blew through the small cracks in the castle's walls, reducing the amount of warmth that filled each room, making Sarah burrow further under her blankets.

She finally gave up and sat up in bed. She had dreamed little the night before and slept even worse. Since her arrival on Veloris, she had received little sleep or rest. She thought the long shifts of the soul cages were rigorous, but this new life had proven that wrong.

Queen Zoë had taken her in, sent her own son to rescue her from the cages, and had fed her. She owed Queen Zoë a huge debt, not to mention it was her sister who stole Marion's soul and fled.

Zykeiah was not entirely wrong. Sarah was not sent to Veloris to kill Marion or to destroy the knights, but her presence on Veloris had done just that. Why else would Amana come to Veloris and steal Marion's soul? It had to do with her.

Octiva had asked Sarah to come and see her. Perhaps now was the time to go. She crawled out of bed and dressed. She went to the window and noted that the sun shined and the clouds had parted. There was no threat of snow, but she grabbed her cloak anyway.

She was hurrying down the stairs when she met Octiva coming down the hallway.

"Good morning, Octiva." She stepped down the last stair and went to meet Octiva.

"I was on my way to your quarters." Octiva's eyes were large with fear and her voice shook. "Come quickly to the Great Hall."

Sarah followed Octiva to the Great Hall that was amazingly empty. "Where is everyone?"

Octiva walked over to the spot where Marion's body still lay as it had the night before. "The servants are afraid to come in here. Many ate morning meals in the East Wing Hall."

She bent down and lifted Marion's head. "Help me with him."

Sarah grabbed Marion's feet and they lifted him onto the table. His black, empty sockets frightened her. "Now what?"

She glanced around quickly and said, "You must encase his body into one of your protective spheres."

Sarah obeyed and cupped her hands together. The sphere grew and she walked along the length of Marion's body, pulling the sphere as she walked.

"Why are we doing this?" she asked.

"We must protect his body. He is a Minister Knight and he is the son of Queen Zoë. His body is not the same as mine or yours."

Finished, Sarah clapped her hands together and the sphere remained intact. "Meaning what?"

"Meaning that if you and the other knights can save his soul, he must be reincarnated back into this body. You will not be able to recreate one for him. Your sphere will keep him from decomposing."

Octiva sprinkled some powders across the sphere as she watched Sarah "You must save him."

"Me?" Sarah asked, disbelieving her own ears.

"You are the gel, Sarah. You must convince Zykeiah and Kalah to assist you. You will need them both if you wish to save Marion and Amana and stop Valek."

"The three of us need more than that to do all that you ask." Sarah sat down, her pride deflated, on the bench in front of Marion's body. "Zykeiah believes I am a traitor."

Octiva moved from Marion's body and said, "Round up the knights and meet me back here in this Hall. I have much to tell you and them."

Sighing heavily, Sarah left the Great Hall and knocked hard on Zykeiah's door.

"Zykeiah, it is Sarah," she called.

No response.

"Come on, Zykeiah," she sighed. "Octiva wants to gather in the Great Hall."

The door to Zykeiah's quarters gradually opened to a mere crack from which Sarah could barely make out an eye, the rest was pitch black and cold.

"Go away," Zykeiah muttered coldly.

"Octiva said we must get together," she repeated.

Silence as the door opened wider. "For what reason?"

"I do not know," she concluded before moving over to Kalah's door. She raised her hand to knock before looking back to Zykeiah.

"You tell him," she said disgustedly. She was through with their judgments. Each of them had something to be ashamed of, why be so cold toward her mistake?

As she stalked into the Great Hall, the soft pulsating light of the sphere made the Hall seem eerily haunted. The Great Hall, totally devoid of people, did not seem so great. Sarah loomed sorrowfully in the entranceway despite the beautiful day springing to life outside the Great Hall. She did not want to go in, but she knew she must.

Octiva appeared like a pale apparition by the Queen's throne.

"Where are the others?" Octiva asked.

"Coming," she said although she wasn't sure they would come. She came into the hall and climbed into the seat across from Marion's encased body.

Within minutes, Zyekiah entered the Great Hall and said, "This had better be good."

Kalah trailed her and looked as though he had spent the night wrestling with demons and lost.

"No, Zykeiah, this is *not* good. This is tragic," Octiva said boldly.

Zykeiah halted her steps and frowned as she put her hand on her dagger. "Who are you to speak to me like that?"

Octiva said, "I am the queen's servant, as are you." She went on, "Queen Zoë has fallen into a coma."

"You did this!" Zykeiah reached for her dagger and stepped toward Sarah with a look of burning anger.

"Stop!" Octiva raised her hand. "Allow me to finish." Grudgingly, Zykeiah stepped back.

"This coma is because of Marion's soul extraction," Octiva declared.

"How?" Zykeiah asked heatedly.

"What?" Kalah asked, shocked.

"Quiet," Octiva pleaded. "This is extremely important."

The three remained quiet as Octiva continued. "You three must rescue Marion's soul and return it here or else both he and Queen Zoë will die."

Kalah snorted then laughed. "How do you know what will save them? You are nothing but a servant," he said.

"A servant yes, but also Queen Zoë's advisor and teacher." Octiva waved her hand across her face revealing an elderly woman.

"This is my true face." Octiva smiled beneath her layers of wrinkles and spots of age. "The Northern Forest was only a handful of seedlings when I was your age."

Kalah gasped and backed away from her, wildly waving his hand across his face as if trying to make sure his face was his own.

"You are one of the people from before!" Sarah shouted, unsure of how she knew that Octiva was one of the ancients; she just did.

With the wave of her hand, Octiva once again showed them her younger face, smooth and free of wrinkles. "Yes, I am the only one left. But all that I knew, I taught the queen."

Zykeiah had watched in silence. Sarah could not read her expression.

"Minister Knights, Veloris needs you." Octiva gathered her cloak to leave. "Your time is short, waste none of it."

***

Zykeiah turned to Sarah and said, "I guess that means you have to come with us, but that does not mean I trust you."

Sarah sighed. She did not argue. What good would it have done? She would just have to prove to Zykeiah that her devotion was to Veloris.

"Do we have a plan?" Kalah asked.

Zykeiah quickly turned her scorn to Kalah. "So does that mean you are coming with us?"

"Are you sure you want to risk it, being the next king of the castle," Sarah added.

Kalah coughed before shrugging. "She is my mother, too."

"Then I do have a plan." Zykeiah smiled for the first time since Marion's disappearance. "While I was on Solis just a few rotations prior, I learned that Valek is selling Solance to both Saturn Four and Earth 3012."

"Your plan, Zykeiah," Kalah said, bored already. He sat down next to Sarah on the bench. "Is to spread that knowledge to both planets?"

"Yes." She rolled her eyes in disgust at Kalah stealing her thunder.

"But why?" Sarah asked, still not sure about the plan.

"Because, we are only three. There is no way we are capable of defeating Valek alone. But with the help of both planets' Generals, we can rescue Marion. They can deal with Valek."

"We should rescue Amana, too," Kalah pitched in.

Sarah gasped and Zykeiah stared at him in disbelief.

"Why are you looking at me like that?" Kalah stared back at Zykeiah. "I saw her eyes. She was not in control. Her eyes were blank and dead like the bones in the burial grounds."

"I have one question." Sarah interrupted.

"You have had more questions than that," Kalah said.

She ignored him and asked. "How do we get there?"

***

"Where is that little spineless brat?" Valek spat as he spun around his desk.

"They are in the guest quarters." Manola licked her hand and rubbed angrily at the spot that had developed there.

"We do not have guest quarters," Valek roared.

"The group of rooms just before the stairs that led down to the dungeon is where we have placed them." She alternated between licking the spot on her hand and answering Valek.

"Those rooms had been used for slaughtering slaves." Valek placed his forehead onto the cool surface of his desk. "Idiot!"

She stopped her licking. "Sir?"

"Get out of here and find Amana!" he barked. "Do something useful for a change!"

She scurried out of his office faster than the first delivery batch of Solance. He sat back in his chair and turned to watch the slow descent of Solis's sun.

The situation with Earth 4016 and Richard was a done deal until Richard's advisors started coaching the king into requiring more evidence of Valek's claims.

"How about a tour?" Richard had asked.

Valek had drawn the line there. The contract be damned. There were other planets he could sell to. No one saw how Solance was made, no one.

Richard then asked for a tour of Valek's castle and evening meals instead. He reluctantly agreed. He had put too much time and money into wooing the kingdom; one more thing would not be so tragic.

He had been mistaken.

Richard would not leave until all of his advisors' questions and curiosities were answered. Now they were holed up in his castle; they threatened they wouldn' t leave for days. He hated spineless men; but the more spineless they were, the easier for him to manipulate, and the fatter his pockets would grow.

Grimacing, Valek stood up and went to the window. The blackening sky and the cool breeze of Solis swept pass his office with the smell of sulfur and death.

He had more important things to attend to then Richard's demands, like Amana's return with the soul of Marion. Yet, these things gained him no monetary benefit.

Satisfying Richard's advisors and appetite for knowledge would net him a nice hefty bag of silver.

Valek placed his thin fingertips to his temples and gently massaged. It was not that he was unaccustomed to changes or the everyday stress of managing a business. It was the little tiny nuisances that cropped up in droves and wasted resources and funds.

Those things angered him all the more.

He untied the top of his cloak and it collapsed to the floor in a hush just as Manola shoved Amana through the door of his office.

The girl's face had been sliced open and it was not a small nick, Valek thought as he walked to greet her.

"Manola, fix the girl's cheek," he ordered as he placed his hands on Amana's shivering shoulders and guided her to his desk.

Manola cupped her hands together and produced a chunky thatch of green paste in her hands.

Valek lifted Amana onto his desk, as if she was a child, and smiled.

Manola dipped two fingers into the paste and with her other hand held the flap of flesh up against Amana's cheek. Almost like glue, the green paste was applied to her cheek and immediately the skin rejoined and melted into smooth flesh. There was no scar or any indication her cheek was ever damaged.

"There," Manola said softly, almost motherly.

He lifted his hand and said, "You have something for me?"

The anxiousness within his heart pounded hard and fast, driving the rush through his veins until his entire body felt sensitive and alive.

Hopping down from Valek's desk, she dug deep into her pockets and removed the small turquoise sphere. "My Lord."

She dropped the sphere into Valek's outstretched hands without further comment.

Valek lifted the sphere to his eye level and peered inside. Marion's gray eyes turned to look at him and screamed what could only be insults and demands, but Valek could not hear it. Only the rapid movements of

Marion's mouth were any indication that the soul was speaking at all.

"So you are the one who dared to steal one of my souls?" he asked, although it was doubtful that Marion could hear him. He grinned and said, "Get MaxMion in here. Now!"

Manola sighed and left the office on yet another errand.

***

The day continued, undeterred by the undecided fate of Veloris, as Sarah sat alone in her quarters covered by the blanket Marion had given her on her arrival. It smelled faintly of danker beast, just as it had on her first night on Veloris, but the smell did not matter now.

Naked except for the blanket, she felt exposed and vulnerable. She imagined this was how Marion felt, nestled in the empty, drab soul cages. But she knew from experience that he probably felt nothing at all, which was all the more frightening.

She had to stay focused, for cradled in her hands was a tiny sphere the color of the Antiqk Oracle. This sphere was more pale and dimmer than her usual ones. This was how she would transport Marion's soul back to Veloris.

If they could rescue him in time.

Zykeiah's plan was almost perfect. They needed to find a way to get to Saturn Four. Marion knew Veloris like he seemed to know everything else, flawlessly and with precision. He would know what to do. But they did not have him.

Instead they had Kalah who did not know anything of his native planet. It would seem Kalah's attention and interests revolved around clothes, women, and strong drink.

It was as if Kalah became a Minister Knight by default, because his mother was the queen. She didn't understand what good his presence would do for them.

"Tell me, all knowing oracle. How do we reach Saturn Four?"

The quiet sphere grew more brilliant and the now familiar voice of the oracle spoke and this time Sarah listened.

"See Queen Zoë," it said.

The sphere returned to its unlit and silent state.

"You must be joking? That is all you have to say?" Sarah asked

The Queen lay unconscious in her bed, a prisoner of extreme grief and loss. What could she possibly find there?

She dissolved the sphere and climbed out of bed. She reached for a bronze colored shirt made of fresh cotta and black leather pants. Her sweater hung over the chair, but she could no longer wear it. A constant reminder of Marion, the sweater must remain behind. She would wear it at his homecoming celebration. She swore to it on the breast of her mother.

As Sarah made her way down the stairs and through the castle, children and servants moved about in slow motion. Or maybe it was she who moved in slow motion. They all seemed sullen and sad. Grief had truly blanketed the castle.

On her way to the Queen's quarters, a toddler boy ran into her as he fled from his older sister's make-believe monster.

It took Sarah several more steps before she realized the boy had become tangled in her legs. The sister had partially extracted him when she finally looked down. He had been screaming, yet his cries had fallen on deaf ears.

"Oh, little boy, I did not see you there," she said.

The boy's huge brown eyes looked up at her before welling up with tears. His mouth trembled, then opened to release a wail that shocked her.

The sister picked up her brother and ran off to the East Wing without looking back.

"What was all that about?" Sarah asked.

"They fear and blame you for Marion's capture," Zykeiah said from the opened door of her quarters.

"You told them lies, Zykeiah," she snapped.

"It was not I." Zykeiah smiled as she squatted to pick up a discarded marble. "Amana was your sister and you paraded around through the castle with her at your side."

Sarah resumed her walk to the Great Hall without another word to Zykeiah, whose attitude had changed dramatically since their trip to Stocklah. She wondered if it was the fact that Amana was her sister, or was there something more?

Then she remembered Marion and Zykeiah's friendliness in the hallway on her second rotation at the castle. Groaning as she found herself in that very same hallway, she thought that Zykeiah was trying to attack her at Stocklah and she had been right.

Zykeiah wanted to get rid of her rival.

As she made her way up the spiraling staircase to the Queen's quarters, she came face to face with the three royal guards and this time they took notice of her.

"Halt!" The guard on the right held up his thick, hairy hand.

"No one is permitted to see the queen," the third guard on the left finished as the middle guard grunted in affirmation.

"It is extremely important that I see her," she said.

"No one is permitted to see the queen," the third guard reiterated.

He reached out and grabbed Sarah's arm and lifted her into the air.

She put her hand on the guard's arm and pictured the fiery heat of an open hearth.

The pungent smell of burning flesh spiraled into the air as the guard screamed and removed his hand from her arm, causing her to fall to the floor. On fire, the guard screamed and raced past her down the steps.

Confused and a little exasperated, the middle guard tried to snatch Sarah's hair, but she had thrown one of her bubble-like spheres at him.

The sphere went splat against his chest then proceeded to grow and cover the middle guard. It grew until it restrained his every action and limb, causing him to fall to the floor. The more he wrestled with the gooey substance, the more it spread.

The guard on the right breathed fire at her, but she had already produced a shield that deflected the guard's fiery breath.

As the guard continued to assault her with his breath, she used the shield to protect herself with one hand and conjured up another throwing sphere with the other.

As soon as he heard the first guard take a breath, she lowered her shield and threw the sphere at him. The guard blew his breath of fire onto the sphere, but it did not dissolve.

Surprised, the first guard stopped for another intake of air when the sphere went splat against his mouth, sealing the guard's lips and making it difficult for the guard to growl or spit fire.

Like the middle guard, the more he wrestled, the more the gooey substance grew and soon the guard was covered from his head to his grotesque toes.

"Why are they attacking me?" Sarah said aloud.

"Bravo, well done." Octiva stood just outside the Queen's quarters. "Your powers are growing by leaps and bounds."

Winded, Sarah lowered her shield and stared at Octiva. "How long have you been standing there?"

"A little while. It was just a little practice. You wish to see the Queen?"

"Yes," she said, wiping her brow.

"Come!" Octiva snapped her fingers and the three royal guards were again in place and seemingly unaffected by Sarah's attack. There were no traces of her spheres' gooey film or any burn marks on the third guard's arm.

Puzzled, she stepped around them and they seemed not to notice her.

"So what are they?" she asked.

Octiva laughed and said, "Royal guards."

"But, but-" Sarah stammered.

"You came to see the Queen; here she is," Octiva said.

In the Queen's bedroom, Queen Zoe's body laid still and her breathing remained fragile as the sun's rays sprawled across her bed.

"Even the sun misses her," Octiva said.

Sarah did not hear, for the watery voice of the Oracle spoke once again and she needed to listen. She stepped closer to the Queen and a crunch resonated from her feet.

Looking down, she noticed several scrolls tossed about the floor.

"What are these?" she asked, turning to Octiva.

"Those are the Antiqk scrolls. The Queen studies them often for direction."

"Direction?" Sarah smiled as she dropped to her knees and began to unroll scrolls. "We need direction."

Octiva kneeled down on the other side of the Queen's bed and started unrolling the scrolls tossed about there. "What are we looking for?"

"A map," Sarah answered. The Antiqk scrolls were as old as Veloris; surely there was a map that listed the circles and their destinations.

Chapter Sixteen

The salty air blew across Orono' s nose and caused his eyes to water. The Labbia Ocean on the western coast of Saturn Four housed the most beautiful fish and aquatic animals in the entire Pixlis galaxy. The water held the same temperature through all rotations of fall, summer, and winter.

The temperature did not change much on Saturn Four; it kept a steady climate of tropical warm days and at night, cool comfortable winds from the oceans provided ideal sleeping weather.

Orono had never seen such a paradise of bright sunny weather backed against a crisp blue sky. He and MaxMion may retire to Saturn Four upon their departure from Valek.

"I meant what I said, Orono," General Ogroth growled as he snapped a pair of handcuffs onto Orono's wrists. "This had better be worth my time."

"What are these for? I have committed no crime," he said and within moments he had pulled the handcuffs apart.

General Ogroth's eyes grew with surprise, but then he muttered, "Bah! Come."

Flanked by heavily armed guards on both sides, he followed General Ogroth through the sandy blackened beach surroundings of the Aqua Circle and on to the flat forest that housed an entrance to the King's castle.

The area was absent of people, despite the great weather. The king's castle was nestled back against lush, rolling green hills and on either side was a small grouping of forest trees.

Saturn Four's king surely knew how to live, Orono thought. Hunting forest on both sides of the castle, a fantastic ocean as the front yard, and rolling hills perfect for horse or danker beast riding in his back yard.

As they reached the castle's gate, it was lowered to allow the General to enter. The gate itself was decorated with vegetation of every color. It glistened with moisture in the strong sunlight.

Orono secretly cursed himself for not asking for more payment.

"This way Orono. You are to remain in the guest quarters until further notice. I will come retrieve you when the king is ready to listen to you," General Ogroth said.

Orono smiled and patted his stomach. "That is all satisfactory. When will evening meals be served?"

"As if you had a choice," General Ogroth threw back his head and roared with laughter.

Orono remained silent, but he was beginning not to like the General. The sooner he got the business over with, the happier he'd be, he thought.

They arrived at a fork in the castle's hallway and took the hallway that veered to the left. Chandeliers of clear sparkling crystal hung every few paces and their thick ivory candles illuminated the hallways.

On the walls were hand-sewn tapestries depicting various rulers of Saturn Four. The tapestries alternated with heavy gold candelabras that were secured with what Orono could only make out as silver.

Servants passed by the entourage with cool indifference. He noticed that none of the servants looked up; they all walked about with their eyes downcast at the shiny floor.

The sweet smell of food filtrated into the hallway as they made their way past the kitchen. Orono's stomach growled at the thought of eating fresh, delicious foods that were heated and warm, not cold and gritty, like gosha.

He knew that if Valek discovered his absence, it might mean his life. It was an agreeable risk, for with money from Saturn Four, he and MaxMion could flee.

Besides, he thought as General Ogroth opened the door to one of the guest quarters, Valek has his hands full with Amana and Richard of Earth 4016.

"Here is where you'll rest until I come for you," said General Ogroth.

The guest quarter was three times the size of Orono's dungeon quarters on Solis. There was even a bed in it and the bed had blankets. He could hardly contain his glee. He may never leave this place.

Across from the bed resided a little wicker basket of fruit and a bottle of ale. On the floor, Orono noted the green leaves of alpine and oalka.

General Ogroth snorted, "Do not get too comfortable."

He sat down on the soft bed and General Ogroth slammed the door shut. He could hear the jiggle of keys in the lock.

***

"MaxMion take this slave down to the cages. Make sure his soul is not with any others." Valek dropped the sphere to the ground where it shattered to a thousand pieces and Marion's soul floated out.

MaxMion reached out and snatched Marion's soul by the arm. Powerless, he tried in vain to escape. Without a physical body, hitting or striking MaxMion was nearly impossible.

MaxMion was able to hold onto his souls by the little device planted into his arm that allowed him to cross the plane between physical and spiritual. "Come on now."

The tugging caused Marion to flutter to the ground defeated.

As MaxMion moved the soul out of the office, Valek called, "I want him in the very next batch!"

According to the moons, the next batch should be processed within one full rotation. By then, he vowed to have Richard and his advisors back on Earth 4016.

"Valek," Richard called as he poked his head into his office. "The advisors and I still have more questions, would now be a good time to discuss them?"

Inside, Valek tried to contain the rage that boiled almost to the point of spilling over. "The hour *is* late, Richard."

"Yes, yes of course, but we need answers." He entered the office and remained standing there with a look of disappointment on his face.

"Your answers will have to wait until morning, dear king," Valek answered, his voice growing colder with each word spoken.

Richard, feeling the drastic change in temperature, wrapped his coat tighter about him as he took notice of Manola, then Amana whose blood still stained her shirt and pants.

"I apologize Valek if I interrupted anything."

With nothing further the king fled the office for the smelly guest quarters.

"Wimp!" Valek barked. "Manola, take Amana to the dungeon and place her next to Orono's quarters. I am not quite ready to make her a slave again. Perhaps Richard or one of his advisors would like some entertainment or even a gift."

She yanked Amana's arm and led her from Valek's office. Neither of them heard Amana's whimpering.

***

"I got it!" Sarah whispered excitedly and held up the map for Octiva to see.

"The map of Veloris?" Octiva inquired from her spot on the opposite side of the Queen's bed.

"An old map, perhaps even the first map ever drawn," Sarah said, amazed.

"Come let us leave the queen. We have disturbed her long enough."

Sarah followed Octiva out of the Queen's bedchamber and into the hall where they could speak freely. There was no sight of the guards.

"This will show us how to get to Saturn Four," Sarah said excitedly, glad to be able to help.

Octiva nodded in agreement. "How soon before you leave?"

Sarah shrugged. She didn't know the time schedule. "Soon."

"Be sure not to waste time. Marion and Queen Zoë do not have much longer," she said, before turning and disappearing around the corner and in to the dark hall.

Sarah hurried down the stairs and on to Zykeiah's quarters. Urgency fluttered nervously in her stomach and her tongue felt swollen and heavy as if it was laid with sturdy lead.

"What is it?" Zykeiah growled at the knock on her door. She was dressed in her robe and her feet were bare.

"We must leave at once," Sarah said.

"How do we get there?" Zykeiah sighed.

"With this?" She held up the fragile scroll that unrolled into a detailed map of Veloris.

"And this is?"

"A map, an ancient map of Veloris. On it are destinations circles to other worlds."

"Wow!" she said.

"So we must leave soon." Sarah rushed over to Kalah's door and pounded hard until he opened it.

"What?" he barked as he opened his door.

"Get your gear, Kalah, we are leaving. Tonight."

Zykeiah's watched from her doorway, the map still in her hands.

"Tonight? Evening meals have not been served and the night air will be freezing-" Kalah scoffed and shuddered at the thought.

Sarah gave Zykeiah a nervous glance.

"Now!" Zykeiah demanded firmly as she handed the map to Sarah. "We leave within the hour."

Groaning, Kalah slammed his door.

"Come in, you can assist me," Zykeiah said to Sarah.

Her quarters were neat and orderly. Nothing was out of place, each dagger, flower and log was settled in its place.

To Sarah's surprise, Zykeiah bent down and pulled out a ratty sack made of cloth from beneath her bed. She then pulled out a second sack made of hide. She unrolled the leather one to reveal four glistening daggers similar to the one she wore on her thigh. They glowed in the warm reflection of the hearth. The points were coated in a glimmering, milky white coat that seemed wet.

She silently counted them with her lips barely moving. When done she rolled them up again and secured the leather belt tightly. She whisked them onto her back and secured them about her waist so that they would not fall or slide down during her ride.

Next, Zykeiah lifted the ratty, less polished sack to the bed. She piled vials of various herbs and rock salts along with socks and still more vials. She had almost emptied her chest of herbs.

"Will they not break during our journey?" Sarah asked.

"No," Zykeiah muttered before adding, "They are not glass."

"What are the vials for?"

"Valek and his witch, Manola." Zykeiah pulled the drawstrings tight with sharp, rigid precision. Sarah could hear the zing.

"Here," Zykeiah tossed the sack toward her. "You carry this one."

Extraordinarily light, Sarah slung the sack over her shoulder and hardly felt it at all.

She wandered out into the hallway and pondered whether she needed anything from her quarters. She was a guest, but Veloris had become more of a home than she ever had before. She was reluctant to leave it, yet she had to. Marion needed her.

She followed Zykeiah to the Great Hall, where they were to gather prior to their departure. The pulsating light still generated its eerie orange glow as Sarah dropped the sack to the table.

"Kalah was right; we must eat well before departing. We may not have another opportunity to do so," Zykeiah said before disappearing into the kitchen.

She had changed dramatically since Sarah's first encounter with her in the hallway. She rarely smelled of danker beast and smelled more often of fresh cut flowers and forest.

Suddenly, commotion erupted from the kitchen, laughter and a couple of shrieks, then more laughter.

Zykeiah's feminine scent was deceiving, for she was as tough as any male. Sarah thought back to the heated moment when Zykeiah sliced Amana's cheek without fear or hesitation. Kalah, the man of the group, had fled. Suspicious and direct, Zykeiah embodied a sea of contradictions: one, the soft tender woman who landed Marion's heart and within moments the dagger-slicing, second in command, leader of the Minister Knights.

And still Queen Zoë knighted her.

It was only now that Sarah could understand why. As she watched the commanding woman order with vigor the servants, Kalah and her, around with direct, firm commands; it became clear.

Zykeiah simply knew how to handle herself. She was a natural born warrior.

With two bowls steaming from heat, Zykeiah returned from the kitchen "I made the servants serve us a little early."

"Good, we need to eat," Kalah announced just as Sarah bit into her piping hot hencken.

She quickly spit it out and reached for her ale to cool her searing tongue.

"Too hot?" Zykeiah gingerly placed a torn piece cautiously in her mouth. "Good."

Kalah sat down between them. He peeked in to Zykeiah's bowl and said, "Good indeed, roasted henckens with peppers."

He slammed his fist onto the table causing the bowls to fly in to the air. "Food now!"

Sarah had to scoop the remainder of her meal from the table where her bowl had crashed, spilling its contents.

The older servant wench scurried out of the kitchen with a huge bowl in her two tiny hands. She placed it in front of Kalah with speed, just as another servant hurried to the table with a large mug of ale. They both retreated to the kitchen with equally quick speed.

He ate his meal and hurriedly devoured the small henckens. Sarah was only at the beginning of her hencken when he signaled for another two bowls.

"You may not want to eat too much, Kalah," Sarah warned as she recalled the dizzying power of the circles. Too much food on the stomach could make him very ill.

He briefly stopped chewing to glance at her with a scowl before resuming his meal.

"You would be wise to listen-" Zykeiah warned.

"What does she know?" he said hotly with a mouth full of hencken.

"She has seen a great deal more of Solis and Valek then you," Zykeiah concluded.

"You have been acting more and more like *you* are the commanding knight, Zykeiah. You are only a few days removed from your knighting." His voice lowered to a deep rumbling and his eyes darkened to a smothering gray, like the angry clouds of an approaching snowstorm.

Zykeiah's own electric eyes grew more intense as her hand crept toward her dagger. The air seemed to swell, thicken and then compress.

"Where were you great, daring Kalah, as Marion's soul was stripped from his body?" she asked.

His color drained from his face as if he had been slapped. Zykeiah's hand crept closer to her dagger.

The two continued to stare at each other as Sarah got up from the table and moved to the table across from them. They had to work this out themselves. The two servants and the servant wench had come from the kitchen into the Great Hall. They fell silent as the two knights verbally sparred.

Finally defeated, Kalah grumbled an "okay", forever scarred by his cowardliness.

Zykeiah smiled as she returned to her seat and meal. The kitchen servants smiled at each other and returned to the kitchen. The Great Hall itself seemed to breath a sigh of relief as Zykeiah announced," There will be no more questions as to who is leading this journey. I do not assume this lead out of arrogance or pride, but out of necessity. No one knows Solis better than I. Nor has either of you been to my native planet of Saturn Four."

Sarah secretly relished the explanation. Just the fact that she explained it to them demonstrated her growth as a knight in such a short period of time, since Marion's removal from Veloris.

"I trust you, Zykeiah. I will follow you until we recover Marion and I can wet his face with my tears of joy," Sarah declared then blushed as she wondered where such a strong statement had come from.

Kalah looked up and across to her, and then Zykeiah before agreeing. "Fine, but we go together from here on out. As a team."

"So it shall be," Zykeiah agreed, then fell silent as she finished her evening meal.

The servants solemnly removed the empty bowls and mugs as Kalah and Zykeiah gathered their belongings without comment. He had only brought two small sacks of goods made of smooth, slick leather that was free of stains or mutations. Somehow Sarah thought he would have brought more. He always wanted more, so she found it odd that he had brought along so few things. Did he not understand that they might not return?

Chapter Seventeen

"Come, it is time," General Ogroth ordered.

Orono could hear the hissing release of the heavy lock as it unfastened.

A frown nestled deep within the bushiness of General Ogroth's face as he greeted Orono, and the door swung open. He grunted in Orono's direction and two hefty guards the size of stone pillars cut from the Death Trunk Mountains flanked him.

General Ogroth disliked him; his every action and articulated speech betrayed his opinion. Yet, his desire to know the secrets of Solance outweighed his desire to strip the hairy, smelly skin from Orono's deceptive hide.

"What do you put in the pillows?" Orono grinned. "I slept like the dead."

"And yet you still awoke." General Ogroth pointed at the two guards. "See that this room is searched and cleaned. Double check to make sure all is accounted for."

The two walked down the illuminated hallway, Orono struggled to match pace with General Ogroth, who could hear Orono's wheezing.

The scent of honeysuckle gradually diminished, as an unidentifiable robust odor grew stronger.

Orono's head turned back and forth as he gazed upon the huge pillows of fat, cake candles that winked and at crystal bowls and vases decorated with pressed gold. He did not know what to look at first.

"Saturn Four has been blessed with not only light and victories, but also wealth." Orono rubbed his sweaty hands together. "No signs of a war-ravaged kingdom. It has faired well."

"Do not look too closely, Orono. You will not be here long enough to steal anything," General Ogroth said.

"Why would I steal when I have information to sell?"

"Your price will remain what we agreed." General Ogroth placed his hand on his sword.

"Only if I continue to agree!" Orono spat. " I have the information you seek, General. This information would benefit Valek, no?"

Orono smirked beneath his sickly folds and fleshy cheeks.

General Ogroth's bushy eyebrows rose in question then furrowed together in a furious scowl. He whirled around and pinned Orono against the stone wall. In a matter of seconds, he had unsheathed his sword and now had the glistening blade against Orono's bulging neck along with his thick, forearm that was pressed hard against Orono's windpipe.

"Understand this, you creepy piece of crud. This information you are selling us had better be all that you claim or it will be my extreme pleasure to painfully extract more information from you."

Streams of smoky swirls blew from General Ogroth's nose as he growled. "Agreed?"

Orono struggled against the slightly larger but surprisingly strong, General Ogroth. "No need for violence. It will be what we agreed," he sputtered and wheezed, but he dare not swallow the lump in his throat for he feared the lump would not make it over the sharp blade.

"Good." General Ogroth pressed the blade in and it bit into Orono's flesh, forcing a whimper of pain as a single line of blood trickled down and over his rolls of flesh.

"I do not like you," General Ogroth snarled. "Give me a reason to rid the Pixlis Galaxy of you and I shall do it."

Beads of sweat raced down Orono's face, mixing with the blood that pooled at the base of his neck.

"Now, follow me," said General Ogroth as he stepped back, releasing him. He quickly reached for his neck.

They turned eastward down a hallway that lacked the sweet scents and elaborate design of the others. The earthy scent of dust and mold scented the hallway and from hidden crevices ants and other small insects escaped into the obscure cracks of the castle walls. Thin, tapered candles were scattered infrequently down the hall, and the noises of the castle could not be heard.

They came to an old and weathered door. The smell of rotting earth grew stronger. It was the only door in the long hallway of dust and moist earth.

General Ogroth knocked twice and the door opened from the inside without aid.

No guards, servants or maids were about in this section of the castle. No music, food or elaborate celebration was being conducted. Orono searched for a sign of feast or life, but he only found eerie silence and emptiness.

"What is this place?" he asked.

"Enter," General Ogroth ordered.

Orono stepped cautiously into the room; the bare room had only one chair and several candles. Despite the early morning hour, the room remained shadowy and dim except for the candles' tiny, circular splashes of light. There were no windows.

Frozen by fear, Orono could not step forward. He had one foot in the room and the other in the hallway.

"Go on!" General Ogroth smashed his hand into his back, forcing him into the room, before entering in and slamming the door closed behind him.

A withered man draped in a ratty blanket sat in the room's sole chair. His bald-head occasionally caught the candlelight and Orono made out very little else. But the smell that filled the room was one that he needed no light to identify. Death.

"Your highness, Valek's henchman, Orono, has news hat may be useful to our cause."

The king raised his hand and beckoned Orono to come closer.

"Tell him, now." General Ogroth stepped back, giving Orono some room to approach the king.

Orono shuffled forward still holding his neck with one hand. "Good morning, your highness." He could not believe that this was Saturn Four's king. He was dressed like a servant.

"Get to the point," General Ogroth demanded.

"Yes, well, it would benefit you to know that Valek makes Solance from souls. For sanctuary on Saturn Four, I will show you how to make it yourselves."

"What!" General Ogroth sprung from his position and smacked Orono's head. "That is not what we agreed."

"Does he speak the truth?" The king's high-pitched voice startled Orono.

"No," General Ogroth said.

"Yes," Orono whimpered as he stroked his injured head. "I can prove it."

"General?" The king turned in General Ogroth's direction

"I do not believe him. Valek is known for deceitful trickery, and this one is no different."

"But, I--" Orono stampered.

"Forgive me, Your Highness, for wasting your time." General Ogroth snatched Orono by his cloak and dragged him from the tiny room, being sure to slam him into the unyielding wall.

"Guards!" General Ogroth barked.

The stone walls on either side of the door slid back, revealing hidden passageways. Three guards emerged and surrounded Orono.

"You have finally given me a reason to slaughter your pathetic hide!"

"I would not be so sure, General," Orono said softly.

Just as three of the palace guards rushed to tackle Orono, he reached into his pocket and threw a bright orange sphere to the floor where it shattered.

Billows of heady, thick smoke furrowed up throughout the hallway as one of the guards screamed.

"What happened? Where's Orono?" General Ogroth questioned as he fumbled in the smoke infested hallway. He could not see anything.

"My arm- it's been bitten off! Something bit-" the guard screamed.

General Ogroth caught a fleeting glimpse of Orono and a smaller person with large teeth running down the hallway to the north just as the smoke began to dissipate.

"There! He's fleeing down the hallway to the north!" General Ogroth shouted.

Silence.

"Guards!"

As the smoke cleared, his breath caught as he found himself standing in the center of three dead and mutilated guards.

***

"Excellent work and just in the nick of time." Orono patted MaxMion's head. "Did they miss me?"

"Doubtful. I told them I was going to eat and that you were covering the cages."

"That General Ogroth is an idiot. We will have to try something or someone else."

"King Richard is still at the castle," MaxMion said.

"How fortunate for us!" Orono laughed as he pulled the pink sphere from his cloak and elongated it to a portal just large enough for he and MaxMion. "Let us go home."

***

Kalah had been right. Veloris was frigid and terrible at night. The orange glow of Sarah's protective sphere shielded them from those harsh elements and strange nocturnal dangers.

Zykeiah said little as they journeyed towards the Southern Forest. She kept the map unrolled as she studied it by moonlight through her tinted glasses.

"How can you read that without any light?"

"The moon provides plenty of light, Kalah," she said.

Their voices echoed and penetrated the blackness of the night. The sounds of creatures and their own strange noises bounced back at them through the sphere. It caused them to jump and look over their shoulders

"How long before we reach the Southern Forest?"

"Not long if we travel throughout the night. We should reach the forest by mid-morning."

Zykeiah coiled the map and placed it into her sack.

"This would have been more difficult had it not been for Sarah's sphere. Let us be grateful for what we have."

"How do you do it?" Kalah slowed his danker beast so that Sarah could catch up to him.

"I do not know. I simply picture and think of what I need."

She hastened her danker beast and she passed Kalah. She did not want to talk to him. There were parts of her that did not trust him.

As Zykeiah and Sarah rode up front, Kalah covered the rear of the sphere.

"Not natural," Kalah remarked as he touched the sphere and sniffed.

"There are many things that are unnatural in the galaxy, Kalah," Zykeiah said.

She removed her tinted glasses revealing her glowing eyes to Kalah and Sarah.

Sarah screamed and for a few moments the sphere flickered and cool streams of the night air filtered in.

She replaced her tinted glasses, and smiled. "You have never seen my eyes at night, forgive me for startling you."

Sarah placed her attention back to the sphere and concentrated on maintaining it while her heart beat wildly I her chest.

"Speechless?" Zykeiah asked. "They were a gift from a friend."

"A gift?"

Kalah snorted. "You might as well tell her everything. We have more than enough time."

"Not everything." Zykeiah laughed. "It is enough to know this — my sight could not be restored when I was reincarnated back to flesh, so I received new eyes."

Sarah now understood her discomfort whenever Zykeiah turned her eyes and attention to her. Her eyes were unnatural, almost mechanical. Strange.

"I have never heard of such things," she whispered.

"They are not of this galaxy," Zykeiah said with a wink.

With that, Zykeiah fell silent as she quickened her danker beast slightly ahead of Sarah.

Removing a piece of leftover sweet bread from her sack, Sarah ate as the night wore on.

"The circle is called what?" Kalah, eager to disturb the silence, asked again. He was used to the thriving sounds of castle life, not the foreign noises of the forest.

"For the third time, Kalah, it is called the Circle of Elderon."

"The Circle of Elderon will take us to Saturn Four?"

"Yes!" Sarah and Zykeiah answered in unison.

***

The rank smell of animals, plants and snow seeped into the sphere forcing Sarah awake.

The sun's rays plunged through the trees in an attempt to lift up a new day.

She gazed around at Zykeiah, who was wide awake, too, as they continued to the Elderon Circle. A painful throb at the base of her neck protested to sudden movements and reminded her that sleeping while sitting upright was not a good idea. She longed for her bed back at the castle.

Kalah had fallen face forward into the coarse mane of his danker beast while still riding.

"How?"

"I do not know." Zykeiah shook her head. "The smell would wake me."

"Me too," Sarah agreed.

The two giggled as they rounded the bend of the trail that had gradually became more and more rugged. It was less apparent as to what was forest and what was trail.

The cries of the wrangler birds ceased and Sarah noticed that she did not hear the customary sounds of animals and branches breaking.

"It is quiet," she said.

"We must be getting close to the Circle," Zykeiah said. Suddenly she shouted, "Look there!"

Sarah eyes followed her finger to the blackening vegetation to the southwest.

"The Southern Forest?"

"Yes," Zykeiah turned to Kalah. "Wake, Kalah!"

"See there how the decay spreads and the tangled older trees are warped and gnarled? The Southern Forest is more than just the southern half of Veloris's Great Forest. It houses all of the major transport circles according to the map. This is both a privilege and a curse for the transport circles use the planet's energy. The more the circle is used, the more the circle destroys."

"How?" Sarah asked, in awe of the circle's destructive power.

"The circles use the energy of life around it. That is why the ground is blackened and dead. The more you use the circle, the farther out it has to expand to reach fresh life sources."

"Then why did it not kill us when we came through the circle?"

"I do not know everything." Zykeiah laughed.

"Well, how did you know that about the circles?" Sarah asked.

"It is a Minister Knight's duty to know Veloris's history and geology. Marion taught me," Zykeiah said quietly.

"History was his favorite," Kalah replied dryly.

"The Circle of Elderon should be to the left, just pass those hills."

"Great." Kalah licked his lips and rubbed his head over and over again... nervously.

Sarah's stomach knotted into small stones of fear. The slick black earth shimmered, indicating the Circle's presence, reminding her of Solis.

Smaller than the Allerton Circle, the Elderon Circle, from its appearance, did not get much use.

"Smaller than I thought." Kalah climbed down from his danker beast, pulled off his two sacks and crept closer to the Circle.

"Yes, but we only need it for this one time," Zykeiah said.

Sarah collapsed the sphere and climbed down from her danker beast. She grimaced at the cold air.

"We will have to leave the dankers!" Zykeiah yelled over the wind as she, too, climbed down from her danker beast. She removed her sack. "Into the Circle."

Sarah joined hands with Zykeiah and Kalah as they entered the tickling warmth of the Elderon Circle.

"Hold on!" Sarah screamed as the Circle began to spin.

The speed picked up and soon the faces of Zykeiah and Kalah were a blur of colors as she fought the urge to collapse. She was thankful her last meal was so long ago, for her stomach burned in protest to the constant spinning.

Finally, the spinning stopped and the three were dropped to the ground.

As Sarah sat up and checked for broken bones, she noticed that Zykeiah, who landed several paces away, did not sit up or move. Neither did Kalah, who had landed perpendicular to Zykeiah.

The salty air caused Sarah to cough as she made her way over to Zykeiah. Although not from Saturn Four, she knew by the warm gentle breezes and the lush green grass that they were not on Veloris anymore.

"Wake, Zykeiah. We are here," Sarah called out.

Zykeiah woke and sat upright in the grass. She looked around, sniffed the air, and then said, "Home."

"Then we are here? Saturn Four?" Kalah asked as he, too, sat upright and rubbed the back of his neck.

"That there is the Labbia Ocean. We are on the western coast of Saturn Four. The castle should be close by."

Sarah stood and dusted her hands to free them from the clinging wet dirt. Kalah joined them and they started towards the castle.

"There are beaches to the left of us, just before you reach the ocean." Zykeiah pointed to the west. "These are castle grounds, so be wary of palace guards."

"Do we have a plan for getting past them or into the castle?" Kalah asked briskly.

"No," she said.

"No?" he repeated in disbelief. "We've come here without a plan? Are we then just going to go to the castle and ask to see the king?" His voice grew hard.

"I think that will be best," she said.

"Kalah, do you have a better plan?" Sarah asked from her spot near the trail's edge.

"Well, no, but... are we just going to the castle, knock on the door, tell them who we are and what we want?" He shook his head in disbelief. "They will kill us on the spot."

"They can try," Zykeiah muttered as she pulled out her dagger. "But we have news I think they'll want to hear."

"Like Valek selling Solance to Earth 3012," Sarah said.

"Yes, Sarah. Exactly."

Chapter Eighteen

"Stop!" The gruff voice seemed to come from the dense thicket of trees to the east of Sarah.

"Raise your hands where we can see them!"

Sarah raised her hands up to the sky; Kalah did the same as he met her eyes. His eyes reflected the same level of fear that she had seen in the Great Hall. Yet a complete calm had settled over her and she was not afraid.

Zykeiah's hands hovered around her faithful dagger. She was perfectly still, waiting, watching for the person behind the voice to emerge Then she would attack.

"Now! You in the front!" The bushes rustled as a solid, square-shouldered man dressed in shiny blue armor stood up from the thicket. As he marched closer to them, Sarah could make out the small design of the Circle Clax bird stamped on the upper right of the man's armor. She had seen one long ago in a picture book. He also had a blue matching cape attached to the back of his armor and it flapped in the gentle ocean breeze.

Sarah noticed three more guards had emerged from the surrounding forest trees and discovered they all wore tinted glasses similar to Zykeiah's. They also had the same darkened skin and bushy, tightly coiled hair.

"Palace guards," Zykeiah whispered to Sarah and Kalah as she raised her hands to the aqua painted sky. "Do nothing."

Sarah could make out the edges of a smile on Zykeiah's face as the four palace guards made their way to the Minister Knights.

"Excellent."

Kalah exchanged a worried expression with Sarah as one of the Palace guards approached and began to search him. He grimaced as the guard's hands moved over his thighs and up between his legs.

"What is this?" The guard pulled Kalah's sword from its sheathe and held it high for the others to see. "See here, this one carries a sword."

The guards gestured for the three Minister Knights to get in a tight circle and then surrounded them. Sarah felt small amongst the four equally massive guards.

They had armor that gleamed in the mid-day sun. These guards had never seen battle, Sarah surmised as she thought back to Marion's assortment of swords that despite their polish, still showed signs of heavy use. *What would Marion do in this situation,* she wondered as she watched the four guards.

"Search them all!" ordered the palace guard who seemed to be the leader. His armor was different from the others. The others guards obeyed his orders without question.

Their sacks were taken and Zykeiah's daggers were seized, as well as Kalah's smaller one.

"You are not spies from Earth 3012," the leader said.

"No, we are not," Zykeiah confirmed as her eyes stared straight ahead at the gentle slopes of Saturn Four's Marria Mountains just behind the palace guard.

The lead palace guard examined one of the daggers, rotating it over and over again, admiring the craftsmanship as the polished silver caught the sun's rays. "What does this "M" stand for?"

Zykeiah did not answer.

"This piece is not of anything I have ever seen in the Pixlis galaxy." The lead guard raised his tinted glasses revealing blue eyes that seemed to be scooped from the heavens and dropped into his sockets. "And they belong to a woman."

He shook his head in disbelief and chuckled. He called to his fellow guards, "A woman."

The other guards joined in the joke that was not entirely lost on Zykeiah. Her own mother had slaved in the silver mines outside the castle grounds and after a sharp kick from one of the overseeing guards, became disabled. She could no longer work at the mines. She spent her remaining days at a brothel house for guards and workers not far from the mines.

Zykeiah would have met a similar fate, the silver mines or the brothel houses, except for Valek's raid on the poor camps where she lived, that took her to Solis.

At first she thought that she had merely traded one slave mine for another. Then she began to meet other women from kingdoms outside Saturn Four that told her stories of women who could do as much as a man and where women ruled alone.

So intrigued and convinced of their validity, Zykeiah vowed that if she ever escaped the cages, she would never be submissive again. Not to anyone. She would rule her fate.

"Take them to the dungeons," the lead palace guard ordered as he placed Zykeiah's daggers into his open bag.

Zykeiah met Sarah's eyes and shook her head, "Do nothing."

At her request, Sarah and Kalah obeyed completely, but doubt coupled with fear marked Kalah's face.

"To the castle. General Ogroth must be notified at once."

Zykeiah turned to Sarah and winked.

***

The day had held much promise for Valek. For it was his favorite day of the month, the third day. On the third day, Valek collected his payments and counted his Solance inventory. The souls learned to hate this day each month, yet he delighted in ordering new batches of Solance and getting paid. But this third of the month was extra fun for the defiant Minister Knight had been captured, Orono and MaxMion were working outside the castle and the temperamental King Richard and his troublesome advisors had announced they would be leaving Solis at first light.

"Perhaps today things will get back to normal," Valek hoped as he braided his hair.

Richard's arrival had taken his attention from his other businesses, but today he wanted closure and payments. All customers were to have paid him by the third of each month for batches already delivered.

Amana waited in the corner of his bedchamber dressed only in a sheer ivory gown and bare feet. Her hands were clasped in front of her and her eyes cast downward.

Her appeal did nothing for him, and her presence in his bedchamber was not for him.

The telltale click of heels on stone made his smile broaden.

"Manola."

She stopped abruptly as he came toward her with arms wide open and a bright smile on his face.

Her eyes flickered for an escape path, for a smiling Valek was a dangerous one. She had not expected him to be awake. Realizing she was trapped, she smiled back at him. He could smell her mounting fear.

"Are you well?"

"Yes, of course." He dropped his arms and instead slid back the wire screen to his office. "Today is payment day." He waited a beat and then said, "Your payment, dear Manola, is in the corner."

"The third day of the month. Yes, of course." Manola smiled and scanned Valek's partly lit room.

"Amana." Manola raced over to Amana and yanked her into the sunlight. "Valek, I am-"

"I am done with her. Do as you wish." He said nothing further as the unusual nice gesture had already been forgotten.

He closed the screen and waltzed to his desk. He collapsed into his chair and removed his orange sphere. He rubbed his hands together vigorously as he pressed sections associated with Earth 3012.

General Cullen's watery visual soon filtered in. The General's harried expression could only mean one thing.

"General Cullen, where is my payment for shipment 3476?"

"We are raising the funds as we speak." General Cullen shifted in his seat and wiped his brow. "It should be there tomorrow."

"Did we agree on tomorrow?" Valek asked coolly.

"Well, no, but we do not have it in full today-"

"Then not only will you pay the price but a 70% late payment charge."

"But, Valek, it is just one day later."

"Yes, but we agreed that payment for that shipment would be made by today," he said.

"Yes, but-" General Cullen said hotly.

"And you failed to meet that deadline! I gave you that shipment on 'credit' for you did not have the full payment last month — something I never do. Did I not explain that?"

"Yes, Valek." General Cullen leaned in closer to the sphere. "You were extremely kind to do that, but you increased the price. It has been difficult to meet the new price. But thanks to you, we whipped Saturn Four yesterday."

Valek leaned back further in his chair. He loved it when they tried to flatter him. His ego devoured such comments and suffering.

"Nevertheless, you failed to pay me," he said coolly.

General Cullen's face, wet with sweat, loomed in a fit of panic Valek had never seen the General so wrought with fear.

"Yes."

"Good. Then it is agreed that you will pay my fee in full plus the late payment charge tomorrow?"

"Yes, Valek," General Cullen said weakly.

"Tomorrow or I will pay Earth 3012 a personal visit."

Valek terminated the transmission.

Adrenaline surged through his body as he threw back his head and laughed. *Profit plus late charges equated to more profit. It was far better than sex* , Valek thought as he leapt from his seat, tightened his belt and left the office. As if he knew anything about sex, he headed for the dungeon. Why delay his second most enjoyable part of the day?

As he made his way down the drafty and dreary hallway, he came to the guestrooms where Richard and his advisors ate fresh fruit conjured by Manola.

"Valek, come here." Richard called as soon as he saw Valek's robe float past the open door.

All hopes of disappearing without seeing Richard quickly dissolved. Valek resolved himself to smile and applied effort to extinguish the burning anger that threatened to singe through his chest and on through his robe. Today was the third; the warehouse could wait a few more minutes. Especially if it meant he could rid himself of Richard.

"What may I do for you, Richard?"

The weasel grinned at his advisors as if Valek had fulfilled a hidden joke.

He watched the advisors withdraw behind Richard still smiling; only their teeth were visible from the shadows.

"Valek, we were discussing the foul odor that comes from the hallway by the dungeon-"

"Go on," Valek said slowly.

"We think it would be best if we knew what Solance was made of. A sort of ingredient list."

No, what he really wanted to know was how he could make his own version of Solance, Valek mumbled to himself as he turned his slender back to Richard. His mood had become sullen and drab, as he pondered how best to respond.

He had similar questions before from both Earth 3012 and Saturn Four during their initial purchases. It seemed to be the natural order of business. Once the customers were reassured that Solance worked and they were comfortable the product was worth the price, then the questions would turn to Solance's composition.

Idiots! Valek had brushed their inquiries aside with the explanation of business protocols and confidentiality clauses The two planets' plights were so severe that they accepted his explanations without argument.

But Richard and his advisors had already disregarded Valek's standing rule not to entertain guests. They may not accept a simple 'no'.

He would have to risk it.

Valek turned back to Richard.

"Speechless Valek?" Richard clasped his hands together and stole a glance back at his advisors. "Just the ingredients is all we ask. Surely you know them."

"No, no dear Richard." Valek secretly clenched his teeth before continuing. "The ingredients in Solance are strictly confidential. Only my staff and I know it. That is how it shall remain."

"You cannot expect us to drink it without knowing what is in it," one of the advisors said coolly as he slithered forward before smoothly melting back behind Richard.

"It is your decision to make." Valek shrugged. "I assure you it is safe."

Richard twisted his thin lips into a pout before he swirled around to his faithful advisors. "Now what?"

Valek counted the number of fat bulges protruding from several advisors as he cooled his temper. He was in no mood to have Richard completely ruin his delicious day.

"I am sure you can see your way out," Valek called as he faded from the room and met the overbearing smell of flesh as he started down the spiraling stairs to the dungeon.

He could see the wisps of his breath as the temperature steadily dropped a few degrees in the already chilly castle.

He passed Orono's quarters as he continued his trek down past the dungeon cells to the elevator and down to the warehouse, where he knocked hard on the door. He waited three minutes before shoving the door open.

Candles lapped at the air as Valek sped down the many aisles in the dim warehouse. The death smell, intense and thick, filled the room. Hundreds of bottles filled with the creamy white liquid, Solance stretched back to the rear warehouse wall. Three shelves held thirty bottles. Each row contained 23 shelves.

In the front of the warehouse were wooden crates filled with bottles, stacked for shipment. A sheet of paper held markings of which kingdom had received a shipment and how many bottles per crate.

Orono usually kept up with the entire process of packaging the order, charging the order, and delivering the order. Valek usually joined him to take the payments, but as of late, Orono had to go it alone. For the most part, payments were sent to Solis Orono and Valek rarely left Solis anymore.

The process for making souls into Solance was confined to a tiny room in the rear of the warehouse.

The warehouse, despite the early day, remained quiet except for Valek's footsteps.

"Orono."

No answer as he reached the rear section of the warehouse. The third day was Orono's only day free of the warehouse.

From a stained thick crystal jar with a silver plated lid, Marion's soul gazed back at Valek. Then grimaced as Valek laughed.

"Left unattended? Were you hoping I was someone else?"

Valek picked up the jar and peered closer. "Try to impose on my business, steal my souls... tsk... tsk."

Carefully, he replaced the jar and announced. "I cannot wait to extinguish your soul in the next series of batches. I may even charge more for that batch."

He pondered this new idea as he retreated down the many warehouse rows, counting his prized inventory and reveling in the immense smell of death.

***

Manola's nails scraped Amana's skin as they made a trail along her back sending chills racing up to the base of her neck and making her hair stand tall.

Naked, cold and hungry, Amana kept one hand over her stomach and the other over her private area as Manola kissed and scratched her back in some sort of ceremony.

With each wet, cool kiss, Amana cringed.

"How warm your skin feels," Manola cooed.

Amana whimpered in return.

"Do not be afraid of me. I healed you."

Amana wanted to run, but it felt as if iron clasps had been attached to the control sections of her mind.

Valek's smell lingered in her nostrils and her hair. Amana patted her empty stomach as it rumbled aloud, echoing through Valek's quarters.

"Hungry?" Manola asked between kisses and nips.

Shaking her head "yes", Amana could not open her mouth to speak for her throat was dry. It felt as if she had swallowed a coarse wool blanket.

"Here." Manola lifted her hands before Amana and from them arose a bright red plum. "Eat."

Manola sat inches from Amana as she bit into the tangy plum. The first bite was a small one, but with the next one Amana greedily devoured the entire fruit.

"More?" Manola's breath was like ice on Amana's cheek.

She spread her palms open and a bunch of plums sprouted from them. So many that they spilled over Manola's outstretched hands.

The fruit juice, red and sticky, smelled strangely of roses Amana thought as she snatched the plums from her.

She stuffed as many as she could into her mouth. The juice spilled over and raced down her chin where Manola licked with greed.

"I enjoyed your company so much when we were in the cages. It made me think of another one such as you."

Amana's ears perked up and her heart increased its beat at Manola's words. The words were warm and affectionate.

"A gift from Valek she was." Manola produced more plums as she spoke, which Amana ate slower than the last. "I do miss her."

"What happened to her?" Amana inquired softly around her mouthful of plums.

"So, you can speak." Manola's fingernail traced an invisible path from Amana's ear to the corner of her mouth. "I thought as much. My other one escaped and is lost to me."

She patted her lap; Amana placed her head there. "I will not allow the same fate to befall you, my precious."

Amana's heart sank as her hope of rejoining Sarah floated into despair.

***

"Where did you get this?"

General Ogroth's breath, cool and spicy, smelled of pepper-roasted henckens. Zykeiah attempted to twist her face away, but the pain of the ropes cutting into her face forced her to stare straight ahead at the searing light. The chair was hard and she had been tied up for hours.

The blinding rays of the sun obscured General Ogroth's face except when he leaned in to ask her questions.

"I am a Minister Knight sent by Queen Zoë of Veloris."

"Yes, yes, you are a knight. A Minister Knight at that!"

General Ogroth leaned in close to her again. "And a female!"

The General pounded his fist into the palm. "Do not lie to me. No one could have journeyed here from Veloris, the ice planet."

"Our mission is most urgent." Zykeiah closed her eyes tight and waited for the blow. He had already struck her.

"What mission?" General Ogroth chuckled.

"It involves Valek and Solance."

"Stop!" General Ogroth walked over to the window and closed the shutters. He pointed to the two palace guards. "Leave me."

"Yes, at once," they uttered in unison and marched from the room. But not before Zykeiah saw the confused expression the two men exchanged.

She blinked repeatedly and she longed to rub her dry puffy eyes The salt water they had dropped into her eyes and the blaring sunlight had made Zykeiah's eyes burn.

Although he dismissed the guards, he did not untie her.

Zykeiah sighed but said nothing as the General paced back and forth in front of her.

"Tell me about your mission."

"Untie me." Zykeiah shot back. "I am a knight, and I deserve to be treated as such."

"You are not able to demand things of me, woman," General Ogroth sneered.

She waited. Like any male, General Ogroth's ego needed constant stroking and she had not done that. In fact, she had injured it by demanding to be freed. Her patience had run thin. She could see Marion shaking his head in disappointment at her loss of temper.

"Tell me!"

"Yes, General." Zykeiah struggled to get more comfortable in a chair designed to be uncomfortable. "Our Queen has sent us on a mission to rescue our fellow knight whose soul Valek has stolen."

"Stolen? A soul stolen?" General Ogroth's eyebrows knitted themselves together as he frowned. "Rubbish."

"It is truth. He steals souls to make Solance, which he then sells to you." Zykeiah took in a deep breath before adding, "and Earth 3012"

Silence, then an eruption of laughter as General Ogroth stalked over to Zykeiah and began slicing through her ropes with her very own dagger.

Breathing a sigh of relief, Zykeiah rubbed her injured face and wrists.

"Come, I will free your friends and send you on your way. Tell Orono that his gag has failed, but nice try."

"What?" Zykeiah stood up.

"Good joke. Valek using souls..." General Ogroth could not continue for he was caught in a fit of laughter. He wiped a tear from his eye "You almost had me."

Zykeiah lowered her voice. "General, this is no joke. Valek is double-crossing you."

"Yes, yes." General Ogroth reached into his pocket and retrieved his keys. He opened Sarah's and Kalah's cells and called in the guards. "Now, go back to Veloris. Or wherever Orono hired you from."

Sarah looked to Zykeiah. "So he agreed to help us."

"No, he believes it is a joke."

"And that is what it is for sure." General Ogroth emerged between them. "Now leave Saturn Four before I change my mind."

The three rushed to gather their sacks and reholstered their swords and daggers.

"General," Sarah called, "is there no way we can assure you that what we speak is the truth?"

"No," General Ogroth barked. "I have more important things to do. Go!"

***

He watched them march single file out of the side door of the lower dungeons.

"A woman knight," he said to the fire that burned in his office quarters.

Saturn Four had won a series of battles in the last week, except yesterday. The idea of Earth 3012 also using Solance would explain some strange happenings he had noticed.

The soldiers of Earth 3012 had not lost the battles just by Saturn Four's soldiers being able to read minds; they had lost because Saturn Four had more men. Brute strength had won the last series of battles, nothing more.

Saturn Four had suffered more deaths yesterday and in the last few weeks than in the history of the battles between the two planets.

General Ogroth stroked his beard as he recalled how his last son had died, just four days earlier. The solider for Earth 3012 seemed to know exactly what move Ollie was about to make and countered.

Reaching into his desk, he pulled the orange sphere from its home. He touched the sphere in the sections Orono had noted that would reach him directly.

"What is it?" Orono barked as he searched over his shoulder. "I have no more to say to you."

"Orono, we had a misunderstanding during your last visit. Can we talk now of repairing that?"

Orono peered into the sphere. "It will cost much more than before and I have other news you could use."

"I am willing to pay it. But I want the information now. And no more talk of souls and such."

Orono hissed and glanced behind him again before turning back to the sphere. "Valek plans to sell Solance to Earth 4016."

"Why do I care about Earth 4016 having Solance?"

"Because General Ogroth, Earth 4016 could plan to attack Saturn Four. I am only the messenger. Now about the price for this information.." Orono licked his lips and panted.

"Yes, name your price and we will pay it." General Ogroth had no intentions on paying Orono. He simply needed to know the truth. Strange, that he had to come to Orono to get it, but if the three strangers were telling the truth, he needed to know for sure. "But not for that information. It is useless to me."

Orono peeked quickly over his shoulder. "Curse you General Ogroth. You have received two sensitive pieces of information, yet you do not pay. Do not contact me again. And next we meet it will be your last."

"Orono, no need to go away mad. Just tell me this one thing, and I will be happy to pay you three fold."

"What!" Orono spat. "Speak quickly you toad!"

"Does Earth 3012 receive shipments of Solance?"

"Yes!" Orono shouted back. "Now about my payment."

"Can't talk right now, Orono. Thank you for the information."

"I will be in touch about my price..."

"Yes, of course."

General Ogroth terminated the transmission and slammed his fist against the table. They were being double-crossed. Just like those three strangers said. "Guards!"

Two of the night guards raced into his office. "Sir?"

"Find me the three strangers that were found in the forest this afternoon and bring them back here. Now!"

"Yes sir!"

He replaced the sphere and left his office. The king would be asleep but this information could not wait.

Chapter Nineteen

"So now what do we do?" Kalah asked as soon as they had crossed the small clearing from the castle back to the forest that housed the Elderon Circle.

"We must try Earth 3012," Zykeiah answered as she scanned the trees for more palace guards.

"How do we get to Earth 3012? We don't have a map for this planet," he asked.

Sarah watched as the two Minister Knights debated what steps to take next.

"How do the soldiers from Earth 3012 and Saturn Four fight?" Sarah asked.

"That's it!" Zykeiah smacked her back. "The war is fought just over those mountains in the Marria plateau. There must be a Circle there that leads to Earth 3012!"

Sarah followed Zykeiah's finger to the purplish mountain range just beyond the forest. The peaks stretched towards Saturn Four's magnificent blue sky.

"We might as well get started, it's quite a hike." Zykeiah readjusted her sack, took in a deep breath and started walking.

Kalah sighed noisily and muttered, "What I wouldn't give for a danker beast right now."

Sarah laughed as she fell in step behind Zykeiah for she knew how long Zykeiah's stride was from their hike to Stocklah. "You can wish until the sun goes down, Kalah. Let's go."

He grimaced and started behind Sarah. They walked single-file through the thick trees. The crack of twigs and the howls of various animals provided the only sounds as the Minister Knights remained quiet.

Zykeiah's pace was quick and consistent as they made their way down the forest trail. The trail had obviously been used for several years, for it was worn down to the earth and alongside the trail were discarded shoes, broken pieces of knives and swords and rotting food.

Sarah thought back to General Ogroth's warning. If he found them still on Saturn Four and on their way to the Earth 3012, he would believe them to be spies. She shuddered to think what he would do to them. Zykeiah's face still bore angry purple bruises where the ropes had rubbed and burned her face.

The cool breeze from the ocean sliced between the forest trees and blew the smell of salt, earth and feces through the air. Sarah could smell, amongst the other odors, the enticing aroma of baked breads and roasting meat from the castle's kitchens. Her stomach grumbled to the lack of attention it had received, but Sarah dare not stop hiking to pull out her other half of sweet bread. Instead, she wiped the sweat from her face and focused on the task at hand, getting to the Marria plateau without detection.

Red maples and golden okas lined the edges of the trails and the dense forest extended far to the east and west as they made their way north. The thickly wooded vegetation blocked much of the sun's rays from reaching the ground; thus, various fungi and mushrooms had sprouted in abundance as well.

"Can't she slow down just a little?" Kalah asked.

"No." Sarah puffed, as the incline grew steeper. "This… this is how she does it."

They had reached the higher grounds, for the trail sloped upward and Sarah could feel her thighs burn from the brisk pace at which Zykeiah was hiking; yet she understood the need for urgency.

Zykeiah had remained silent, and Sarah wondered what she was thinking. Could she be thinking of Marion? Or was she thinking of their next move?

The day receded to dusk and they continued to hike without rest. Sarah noticed that their pace had slowed, but they had not stopped. Kalah no longer asked for rest, for he too must sense the urgency that fluttered around them.

Twilight crept slowly towards them and Saturn Four's rings glistened and shimmered, barely visible in the sky. Sarah had never before seen such a thing and she wondered why she had not noticed them during the day. It was as if the twilight kiss made the sky blush.

The slope continued to grow steeper until it seemed as if Sarah was walking straight up to the sky.

Her legs wobbled and she could not longer stand.

"Rest!" she coughed before collapsing to the ground.

Kalah panted and fell beside her without a word. He greedily reached into his sack and removed his sack of water. Dousing himself with it, he managed to get some into his mouth before draining the sack of its contents.

Zykeiah had hiked on a few more paces before turning back to them. Puzzlement spread across her face then wrinkled in confusion. She hiked over to them and asked, "Tired?"

"Must rest." Sarah coughed and closed her eyes.

"Why didn't you say so? Let's camp for the night."

Kalah groaned and Sarah could not believe that Zykeiah was not even breathing hard.

Zykeiah lay beside them on the trail and closed her eyes. Her snores joined the other nocturnal sounds of the forest and Sarah once again longed for her own bed back on Veloris.

***

The smell of death and the unmistakable aroma of burning flesh snatched Sarah from the cozy warmth of sleep. As she opened her eyes, she heard shouts and screams and immediately sat up.

"Shhhh." Zykeiah, who was crouched on her knees, placed her finger to her lips and gestured for Sarah to come over.

Zykeiah was wide awake and Kalah was as well. He was crouched beside her. "Come."

Sarah rolled over on to her knees and felt the hard stones and dirt of the trail grind into her knees. She winced and crawled over to the Minister Knights.

"I believe a battle has begun. We must be close," Zykeiah whispered, as the screams grew louder then became silent as the booming crash of some unknown weapon landed.

The impact smashed close to them, for it sent dirt flying across them, spraying them. "I'd say we were pretty close."

They remained low to the ground as the sun's rays crept closer to the edge of the forest. The light of the new day lit the end of the forest, and Sarah noticed that some of the trees were bent in half while other trees had been demolished as a result of the blasts gone astray.

There were no sounds of animals or birds as they continued to move closer to the forest's end. The smell of death and burning flesh grew stronger still.

"Into the bush, now!" Zykeiah ordered.

Sarah leapt into the bush and Kalah followed her. Zykeiah rolled over into the bush on the opposite side of the trail. The galloping hooves of what could only be horses, for they smelled of musk and moistened earth, raced past carrying several guards and others who could only be described as prisoners.

They had barely missed being trampled.

As the posse retreated, Sarah raised her head and scanned the area before saying to Kalah, who still had his head burrowed beneath his hands,"I think the coast is clear."

"Zykeiah?"

"I think it's clear again," Zykeiah said.

Sarah and Kalah waddled out of the entangled bushes and back to the trail where Zykeiah shrugged. "I heard them coming."

"Let's keep to the edge of the trail so we can move out of the way if necessary."

"Those were horses, right?" Sarah had only seen horses as a small child and her memory was foggy in regards to what they looked like, but she would never forget how they smelled.

"Yes, I believe so. Horses are from Earth 3012. They are not native to Saturn Four. It was one of the things we used to trade when the planets were still friends."

They inched along the trail that leveled out the closer the got to the forest end.

The raging sounds of guns and agonizing screams failed to cease as they finally reached the end of the forest. The sun's bright rays stung Sarah's eyes as she blinked repeatedly in the light.

The forest ended at the mouth of Marria plateau, which dropped several paces down to a wide field or plain that was littered with dead bodies And where a battle continued on.

Directly across the field lay the circle. Sarah squinted in the light, but could make out the glowing of the circle and the arrival of more soldiers from Earth 3012.

Below where the Minister Knights stood were several dead men and women, not to mention horses.

"We've got to cross the battlefield to get to the circle." Sarah pointed at the illuminated circle that lay on the other side of the battlefield.

"It looks like that's our plan." Zykeiah placed her hands on her daggers.

Kalah pulled his sword and stretched. "Might as well be ready."

It seemed that the soldiers of both planets were too busy to take any interest in them.

"Ready, we're going to run across. Hopefully, no one will take notice of us."

"Watch out for fire cannons and arrows!" Kalah called as Zykeiah started jogging.

He followed her and Sarah joined them as they ran onto the blood-soaked battlefield.

All about them the booming blasts of fire cannons caused the land to tremble. The moans, screams, and shouts of death and those dying were drowned out by the infrequent blasts. The air was saturated with the smell of death and Sarah was reminded of the soul cages.

She jumped over dead and falling bodies, sidestepped two men engaged in hand to hand combat, and tripped over the head of someone who had lost his.

"Watch out!" Kalah called as he ran alongside her.

A horse sped past them and Sarah turned to look. As she turned her attention back to the field, she ran smack into a massive soldier.

He turned to her and without hesitation lifted his sword and swung it at her. Kalah intercepted the soldier's blade with his own.

The soldier struggled to overpower Kalah, but Kalah's sword didn't falter. The soldier's sword reeled backward and snapped into pieces.

Angered, the soldier reached for Kalah.

Sarah threw a sphere at the soldier and he became entrapped in the sticky orange substance. The more he fought, the more the sphere expanded until the soldier was wrapped in a tight cocoon.

"Let's go! It-" Zykeiah called as she was almost to the Circle.

The booming roar of the fire cannon drowned the last of her sentence, but the look of displeasure on her face meant she was not happy.

"Thanks!" Sarah shouted at Kalah. She was unsure he heard; he was a few paces ahead of her as they raced toward the circle. She would thank him later.

Several other soldiers had taken notice of their fallen comrade and chased them.

"Hurry!"

Sarah noticed that Zykeiah had reached the mouth of the Circle, and was at the moment dueling with a soldier, sword to daggers. The soldier appeared to be losing for his cheeks were sliced open and he had cuts sprawled across his chest.

"Watch out!" Sarah screamed as an arrow whisked past Kalah's face.

"Thanks!" he responded.

Again the fire cannon's roar announced yet another batch of balled flames as it streaked through the air. It landed to the east of Kalah and the impact sent him flying into the air.

He landed with a loud thud a few feet ahead of Sarah. He did not get up or move.

A soldier dressed like the palace guards from earlier stepped on Kalah's chest and lifted his sword to stab him.

Sarah's shouts died as fear gripped her heart. She raised her hands and threw an orange sphere at the soldier.

He plunged the sword downward, but not before the splat of the sphere sent the soldier flying backward onto the ground.

Sarah's attention was swept to the mouth of the Circle, where Zykeiah waived for her to hurry. The soldier she had been dueling with had lost with horrible consequences.

Sarah reached Kalah and lifted him to a sitting position. Blood trickled down from his mouth and he shook his head. A blackening bruise just above his temple darkened as he touched it.

"Come, me must hurry. We're almost there."

The real enemy had interrupted the soldiers who chased them and they were engaged in hand-to-hand combat that kept them occupied.

Kalah groggily stood and picked up his sword.

Together, Kalah and Sarah limped towards the Circle.

As they reached the blackened land, Zykeiah came to aid Sarah. Kalah relied heavily on the two of them, for he had not regained full use of his legs, and he stumbled in his speech.

"What took you so long?" Zykeiah asked as they lifted Kalah to the Circle's entranceway that was evaluated slightly above the battlefield.

"Oh, fire cannons, soldiers and swinging swords," Sarah remarked as she struggled to regain her breath.

She glanced down at the soldier that Zykeiah had dueled with. Hardly more than a heap of parts, the soldier had lost his hands, his ears, nose and cheeks. She could not identify any of the other parts.

"Shall we?" Zykeiah asked as she wiped her daggers on the soldier's cape.

"Okay."

"Kalah?"

"I'm okay, just got this horrible ringing in my head."

They entered the warm tickling glow of the circle and the swirling motion soon began.

Kalah's eyes were shut tight and his lips were barely more than a thin white line as the circle continued to accelerate.

Sarah winced at the pain he must be in.

Chapter Twenty

The whirling of the circle stopped and the Minister Knights emptied out onto the dry, barren land of Earth 3012.

The smell of death had not changed, and Sarah remarked how much hotter the air had become. The intense smell of rotting flesh filled her nostrils and she coughed.

"Put your hands up!" ordered an angered, feminine voice.

Sarah opened her eyes and rubbed the spot of her back that had cushioned the brunt of her fall.

"Now!" the voice demanded.

She raised her hands and her eyes until they landed on the woman who barked the orders.

The soldier was definitely female, and her long, straight black hair flapped in the wind. She pointed a gun at Sarah and gestured for her to stand. The female soldier wore little more than a tunic, a scarf that hid most of her face and boots that had been held together with twine.

    Sarah stood up, but kept her hands held high. She searched around and noticed that Kalah and Zykeiah were being herded into a pile of prisoners in the middle of the field. The female soldier snatched Sarah's sack from her and then rammed the gun into her already sore and bruised back.

    "Go. Now!" the female soldier said and she moved to the center of the field. She joined Zykeiah and Kalah in the outer edges of the group. Most of the people in the field wore Saturn Four uniforms, and some had blue capes indicating they were of higher levels in the army. There were no more than thirty prisoners, and there were fifty or so Earth 3012 soldiers.

    "This looks familiar," Kalah whispered as the soldiers shouted for them to start walking. The Earth 3012 soldiers' skin was darker than Zykeiah's.

    "Here we go again." Zykeiah smiled.

    "Did they take your sack?" Sarah asked.

    "Yes."

    "Mine too."

    They marched across the soft battlefield, a huddled group of banged, bruised and dying people. Sarah noticed that she and Zykeiah were the only women in the group.

    "You there!" The female soldier pointed to Sarah. "Stop."

    She stopped and two of the male soldiers who had the same straight, black hair and dusty brown skin grabbed Zykeiah and Kalah from the group. The Minister Knights and Sarah had been segregated from the prisoners of war.

    "You are not from Saturn Four." The male soldier lifted Zykeiah's sack and shook it.

"No," Zykeiah answered.

The female soldier looked at the male soldier and shrugged.

"This is not of Earth 3012, either. Where are you from and what are you doing here?"

"I can only speak of my mission to the General or the King per my orders from my queen."

Again the male soldier turned to the female solider for answers, and again the woman simply shrugged. "Follow me, we'll take you to see General Cullen."

The soldiers did not return their belongings.

***

General Cullen rested the bulky bag of silver coins on the table of his study. Valek needed to be paid or else he would cut off their supply of Solance. That simply wouldn't do, for Saturn Four had seemingly unlimited resources and Earth 3012 did not.

He had decided to deliver the payment to Valek personally to assure him that he meant to keep good on his promises.

Hard knocks on his quarter's door roused the General from his thoughts of how to deal with Valek.

"Who is it?" he snapped, already tired and weary.

"Sir, we have returned with more prisoners from Saturn Four."

General Cullen swung open his door. "Why are you bothering me with such mundane matters? I am busy."

The soldier cowered and stuttered, "B-but sir, three of the prisoners are not from Saturn Four."

"What?" General Cullen stepped into the hallway and shut his door. "Where are they from?"

"T-they refused to say. They asked for you." The soldier recoiled from the General and scooted back against the wall. Slender, but forceful, General Cullen inspired fear in each of his soldiers. The General's torture tactics were legendary on Earth 3012.

"Where are they now?" General Cullen bellowed.

"In... in the dungeon."

General Cullen dismissed the soldier and walked back into his study. He picked up the bag of silver and placed it in his desk.

Who could be visiting Earth 3012? Valek would have contacted him before coming and the king's daughter and sons had been killed long ago, so it was not a suitor.

General Cullen hurried through the drafty hallways of the king's castle. The smell of moss and fungi saturated the hallway's stale air. He continued down the hall that led from the General's quarters to the dungeon, which was south of the kitchen. The king's quarters and the servant quarters were located there.

General Cullen did not mind being close to the dungeon. Sometimes to remove the stress of the day, he would visit the dungeon and play with the soldiers of Saturn Four. They provided plenty of entertainment. After which, he'd climb the stairs back to his quarters and fall right to sleep.

He could smell the urine and decay as it floated up from the dungeon The cries and screams of the new arrivals as they were branded also greeted him at the top of the stairs.

Smiling, the General continued on to the dungeons.
***
Kalah sat on the slab of red-colored rock and rubbed his head.

"Still aching?"

"Yeah, but it's waning."

"I have some herbs in my sack. If we get it back, I should be able to heal the ailment," Zykeiah whispered.

"Thanks, Zykeiah."

She stood by the cell's door. It was made of wood, and if necessary, Sarah's sphere could be used to collapse it. Sarah had suggested it several times already.

"We need to meet with the General," Zykeiah said flatly, indicating the end of the discussion.

"How long does it take to go and get him?" Sarah's internal voice was alive and muttering that something wasn't right. "Something isn't right I can feel it."

"Settle down." Zykeiah patted Sarah's shoulder as she paced by the cell's back wall. "Stop pacing, everything's alright."

"No." Sarah leaned back against the wall and tried to concentrate on the mutterings inside.

They heard frequent yelps and shouts of men being tortured. To the left of where Kalah sat was a pool of dried blood and across from their cell was a young man who had been badly beaten and stabbed. He was chained to the wall and his blood pooled beneath him. Fat, hairy rats scurried about across the man's face and they tracked bloodied footprints across his cell.

"Which cell are they in?"

Sarah heard the voice and knew instantly that it belonged to General Cullen.

"Last one on the right, sir."

His boots made little noise on the hard surface floor. His bony face seemed haggard and malnourished as he stopped in front of their cell and smiled.

"Do we know each other?" he asked.

"No, but we were sent here by Queen Zoë of Veloris," Zykeiah answered as she stepped back from the cell's door.

She didn't trust him and neither did Sarah. Kalah had stood up and he remained standing behind Zykeiah.

"Veloris? The ice planet?" General Cullen's smile faltered a little. "You are far from home. What does your Queen want with Earth 3012?"

"It concerns Valek and Solance," Zykeiah said softly.

If General Cullen knew what Solance was, he did not show it on his face. He merely glanced down the dungeon's hallway and called to one of the soldiers, "You are dismissed."

"Now tell me, strangers, what it is you want," he said, directing his attention back to them.

"Sir, my Queen wants your aid in rescuing our fellow knight from Valek's prison," Zykeiah said.

"Why would I want to do that?" General Cullen sneered.

"Sir, Valek is selling Solance to both you and Saturn Four."

"What? Impossible!" General Cullen spat spittle across the distance between him and their cell.

All resolve General Cullen had tried to maintain was lost as his face grew red and his tone held a smoldering wrath. "What kind of sham is this?"

"It is the truth!" Zykeiah spat back. "He is double-crossing you. Now, assist us in defeating him."

General Cullen ignored her as he spun around on his heels and stalked away.

"That did not go well," Kalah said.

"We've got to get out of here." Sarah clasped both her hands together, generating a small sphere.

"I don't think he believes us either." Zykeiah moved back against the wall. "Okay Sarah, do your thing."

Sarah raised her hand and threw the compact sphere against the wooden door. She then raised her hands and the sphere burst into flames.

The crackle of the wood as it burned sent small bellows of smoke into the air, forcing Zykeiah and Kalah to place their hands over their mouths. As a hole appeared in the cell's door, Sarah put out the fire with yet another sphere and kicked the damaged wood until it collapsed.

As the door crumbled, they raced into the dungeon's hallway.

"Now what?" Sarah asked.

Zykeiah shrugged "I need my daggers. The General went this way."

General Cullen had dismissed his soldiers, but he failed to order them back to the dungeon in his haste to leave. Sarah and the Minister Knights quickly moved down the dungeon hallway and reached the stairs that lead up to the castle. They noticed their belongings thrown on top of a huge basket of what looked like trash.

"Idiots!" Zykeiah smiled as she lifted her sack and felt around inside for her daggers.

Kalah retrieved his sack as well and his sword that had been carelessly thrown aside.

Sarah reached down and picked up her sack, too. They were fully armed again thanks to the temper of General Cullen.

"Someone's coming!" Zykeiah whispered and they hid to the right of the staircase.

The female soldier from the field walked past them. Her attention was focused on something else.

"Shella!" the General's nasal voice boomed.

"Sir?"

"I am going off to Solis. Listen, watch those three strangers from Veloris. They are not to be fed anything until I return."

"Yes, sir!" she said and departed. The General's footsteps could be heard climbing the stairs.

"Guess where we're going?" Zykeiah announced as soon as the coast was clear.

"Solis?" Sarah asked.

"Yes, Sarah. Come on, we've got to catch up with the General."

They swiftly raced up the stair and stopped short as General Cullen emerged from his study with a bulky sack and two palace guards.

The shadows of the damp hallways hid them as General Cullen passed by.

They followed about a mile behind the General, utilizing the shadows and the mournful gloom of the dimly lit castle to disguise their trail. General Cullen was so full of confidence and so sure that they were imprisoned that he didn't look behind him.

As General Cullen left the castle, two guards escorted him to the clearing to the west of the castle's grounds. Earth 3012's climate was too hot during the day for daylight travel. The earth had been scorched and fires were frequent amongst the little vegetation that grew.

Across the clearing the land melted from dusky browns and reds to pitch black. The ground became soft and moist despite the dryness of the surrounding area, which indicated the destruction of a transporting Circle.

Sarah watched from the shadows of the scraggily scrub brush beside Zykeiah and Kalah as General Cullen walked into the Circle and vanished. The two guards argued with each other but stayed outside the Circle with their guns positioned beside them.

"Aren't we going too?" Kalah asked.

"No. We need to prepare and plan." Zykeiah inched back from the brush. She said softly, "We will stay here for the night."

She removed her sack and dug around. She pulled out a tiny vial of brownish-colored leaves. "Here Kalah, this will aid the pain in your head."

He took the vial and poured the leaves into his hand. He stuffed them into his mouth and grimaced. "They taste awful."

"Yes, but they will help."

"Tomorrow we will get rid of the two guards and go to Solis," Kalah said.

"Yes." Zykeiah nodded her head. "Once we get to Solis, follow me through the tunnels to the castle. We'll try to locate Marion. He might be in the dungeon. Or the warehouse."

"Why wouldn't he be in the cages?" Kalah asked.

"Because Valek wouldn't want Marion giving the other souls ideas about escaping. He would be isolated."

Sarah watched as the guards, tired of standing, sat down on the ground. The wind howled, blowing sand and black dirt across the clearing. The guards could not hear them.

"We will need to split up to find Marion. If you find him, leave Solis as quickly as possible."

"Leave the others behind?" Kalah shook his head. "No."

"Marion and the queen are the most important thing. Marion is strong enough to destroy Valek. Nothing is more important." Zykeiah's eyes watered, but no tears fell. "Save him."

"The Antiqk Oracle states that the Minister Knights will rid the galaxy of Valek, not the knight," Sarah said softly. "We will leave together"

"Enough. You have your orders, both of you. Let's get some sleep. Tomorrow will be long." Zykeiah curled herself around her sack and closed her eyes.

Chapter Twenty-One

"Valek, be a dear and answer a few more questions," Richard pleaded as Valek again tried to sneak past the king's guestroom to the warehouse. There was still plenty of inventory that needed to be counted, and Orono had disappeared.

Valek had hoped this day would be different and somehow make up the loss of time he had wasted on Richard and his advisors.

He wasn't any closer to signing a contract with Earth 4016 then he was before the king arrived.

With that in mind, he sighed and walked into the room. "Yes, Richard?"

The advisor with the beady eyes and overlapping stomach stepped forward and said, "We want a sample of Solance."

Valek could not believe his ears. He did not give out samples and Richard had been advised of that during their initial conversations. Nothing wasted product more than free samples.

"No, I do not give out samples of Solance," he said calmly, despite his rising temper.

"Valek, we insist. We have an opportunity to try it. You refused to give us the ingredients, and now you refuse to give us a sample. How do we know you're not a magnificent trick master?"

A trick master? Valek felt his temper boil over and he squinted his eyes at the pudgy advisor. "What did you call me?"

"Valek, he didn't call you anything. Arthur is simply saying-" Richard started to explain, but before Richard could finish his sentence, Valek had unsheathed his sword and with a swish had severed Arthur's head from his body.

The head made a "thud" sound as it landed on the floor and Arthur's body collapsed on top of his severed head. The advisors behind Arthur were sprayed with blood and Valek bent over to clean his sword on Arthur's robe.

"How's that for trickery?" he snapped.

Richard's mouth remained gaping open, frozen with shock.

"MaxMion! Get in here!" Valek roared.

MaxMion, who had been sleeping downstairs in the dungeon, hurried up the stairs and into the guestroom.

"Here is your breakfast." He pointed with his sword at the robust advisor.

MaxMion cackled and pounced on the heap. He ate with big, chopping bites.

Richard and the remaining advisors drew back in disgust. Several of the advisors had lost their breakfast and were busy wiping their mouths.

"I suggest, Richard, you make up your mind before the end of the day I have given you all the information necessary to form an opinion."

Valek turned and stalked out of the guestroom leaving Richard to stare in horror.

***

"The mind control should have disappeared, yet you still do not speak," Manola said as she braided Amana's hair. "You are mine; do not be afraid."

Amana's heart, already eclipsed by loss and loneliness, burrowed further into despair.

"My precious little one, you look so sad." Manola maneuvered Amana's tear-stained face so that its direction was pointed at her. "Are you not happy with me?"

Amana stared back at Manola as her lips formed the word 'no', but no sound was made.

Manola's eyes grew wide and her mouth fell open to a round 'O'. "Why not? I care for you. I wash and feed you."

Tears and gloom filled Amana's eyes as she simply continued to stare at Manola. Inside she wanted to reach out with both hands and strangle the life out of Manola until she could hear her gurgle. But for now, she merely looked back at Manola and refused to answer

Amana knew that Valek's mind control had vanished, for she could think on her own without pain. The heavy fog that had surrounded her mind had lifted and the world was once again smothered with Solis' s darkness. Yet within that darkness, she had noticed that she could make her own decisions.

But Manola watched her each and every moment. When Manola was not with her, she was chained, hands and ankles, in Valek's bedchamber. Manola often stripped her of any clothing and she was left naked and barefoot.

When they were together, Manola led her around in nothing more than a sheer gown made of worm-spun silk. She seemed to be in a constant state of arousal and insisted that Amana be ready to kiss her and love her whenever she demanded it.

The first time had been a few nights prior and Amana had scoffed at the idea of loving a woman. But her mind was still partially controlled by Valek, so her will was easily bent to whatever Manola wanted.

Insatiable, Manola stayed awake for hours, one orgasm after another until sometime near the arrival of the next day's sun, when she finally allowed Amana to sleep.

"I know you miss her." Manola patted Amana's head. "She is probably dead by now."

Amana's lips started to quiver and the shaking trickled down to her toes. "No! She is NOT dead!"

Manola recoiled as if slapped. She stepped back quickly from Amana then squinted at her with disdain, despite the smile that tugged at her lips.

"There is more spirit there than you have led me to believe."

The candles flickered as Amana's ragged breathing tickled the flames She did not respond to Manola's taps and caresses. Anger pulsated through her and she fought down the urge to snatch Manola by her lustrous, red hair and smash her face into the rocky floor. Her sister was alive.

"How much spirit?" Manola questioned as she pulled out the chains to lock her up. "I must think about this more. Come."

No response from Amana; she felt low, burden down and resentful. Sarah survived. She knew that no matter the situation, her sister was alive and would come for her. She stretched out her hands and allowed Manola to clasp on the now familiar chains to her wrists.

Then she remained still as Manola put the chains around her ankles. She could smell the fleshy scent of the cages, for the night's wind had turned toward the castle. She remembered the cages and how Sarah had watched out for her when they first arrived.

Amana thought back to how she had once tried to assist a newcomer named Katelin who had been Manola in disguise. Now that same person she had tried to help had her chained to the bedchamber wall of the master, Valek, as her love slave.

She fought back burning, angry tears, but they spilled over anyway landing silently in Manola's hair as she struggled to lock the chains to the wall.

"There, you will be fine until I return." Manola stood and kissed Amana's hot wet cheek. "Tears? Again?"

With nothing further, she left the room leaving Amana standing and chained in the cold, bleak bedchamber.

***

General Cullen arrived in the dusky night of Solis. He emerged from the Circle of Gahana, located almost fifty paces from Valek's castle. The trail to Valek's castle was rocky, difficult and filled with traps. General Cullen knew he should have called prior to dropping off Valek's money, but he did not want to anger the short-tempered businessman any further.

The war had drained most of Earth 3012's treasure. Yet, the war had also brought about some seized treasure, which had been used to purchase Solance and materials for weapons. Valek's decision to raise the price of Solance came at a poor time. It put them in a serious crunch for silver coins.

The king's two sons had been killed in the war, so it had been impossible to offer them for a martial arrangement with another kingdom for allies and money.

The king and the queen had tried to produce more sons, but they had a total of eight daughters. Their looks borrowed heavily from the king, and their tongues had the stinging sharpness of their mother, which made them quite unattractive to men.

The king of Earth 3012 had pawned each daughter off to various kingdoms over the years, even providing a substantial dowry for the oldest three just to be rid of them.

In a word, Earth 3012 was close to being poor.

General Cullen stepped gingerly around the moist, black earth surrounding the circle. The bulky bag of coins felt awkward as he stepped. He could smell the strange scent of death on the air, and he spat for the chalky taste of the flying black dust had landed in his mouth.

Just as he had cleared the Circle's boundaries, he heard footsteps behind him. He should have brought the guards, but he could not spare any extras. The last series of battles had left Earth 3012 remarkably short for men. They had been forced to recruit women. It was disgraceful, but it had to be done. It seemed as if Saturn Four knew exactly what they were going to do before they did it on the battlefield.

Sure, the Solance that Earth 3012 used had notified them of the very moves that Saturn Four soldiers were about to make, but they had suffered heavy causalities.

General Cullen slid the bag to his left hand and placed his right hand on his sword. Gravel crunched and the sound resonated throughout the valley and echoed.

With speed and without hesitation, General Cullen withdrew his sword and swung around. "Stop where you are!"

The soldier shuddered and stood frozen in step. "Sir, I have an urgent message for you."

General Cullen let out a slow breath of air before replacing his sword. "Why didn't you say anything! I almost took off your head!"

"I-I apologize, sir. The message came from General Ogroth of Saturn Four."

General Cullen gasped as if he had been hit in the stomach. "What?" He had only met the General once and that was across the battlefield on Earth 3012's side of the Circle.

"Sir, shortly after you left, a message arrived from General Ogroth. It was highly urgent, but you had already left." The soldier stepped back a few paces from General Cullen. "Are you all right, sir?"

General Cullen's mouth had gone dry. Could it be possible that the General had decided to call a truce? Had the great and legendary General Ogroth decided that he had enough of Earth 3012? Could it be?

"What is the message?" General Cullen licked his lips anxiously.

"He did not disclose it, but said that he will only discuss it with you and you only at a secure sight neither on Saturn Four or Earth 3012."

"Does the king know of this message?" General Cullen asked.

"No, sir. I am the one who received the message and I brought it straight to you."

"And you told no others?" he continued his questioning.

"No, sir."

General Cullen thought it could be a trap. Why would General Ogroth want to meet at an alternate kingdom?

"General Ogroth stated that the information is quite sensitive."

"Fine," General Cullen grumbled. He hated to be rushed and the more the young soldier spoke, the more he felt hurried. He would simply have to deliver the money to Valek later that evening. General Ogroth had better not take too long. Besides, if it is a surrender that General Ogroth wants to discuss, then it could mean trade between the two kingdoms could resume. Earth 3012's economy would increase and they would be able to pay Valek his money plus his late fees several fold.

General Cullen followed the soldier into the warmth of the circle along with the sack of silver coins still firmly lodged in the nook of his left arm.

***

"Something's happening," Sarah called to Zykeiah, rousing the sleeping knight from her much needed slumber.

Zykeiah rubbed her tired eyes and sat up. Then quietly, she crawled over to the spot of parched earth where Sarah sat, partially hidden by brush, to see what she meant.

"See there, there is only one guard on duty. Another came from the castle's trail and spoke quickly to the other guard. Then he went into the circle."

Zykeiah scanned the area around them and pressed her lips tightly together. "What happened to the other guard?"

"He ran back down the castle's path. He seemed happy for he was smiling as he ran."

Kalah slept silently a little ways in the tall, brown grass. Sarah and Zykeiah's discussion fell on his deaf ears as he continued to sleep.

Zykeiah nodded as if confirming a debate she was having with herself "This is not right."

"Shhh-" Sarah crouched down in the grass. "Someone's coming."

Zykeiah parted the grass as she watched the circle's glow increase and vibrate.

The lone guard leapt from his spot. He stood taller with his heels together and quickly wiped the remnants of sleep from his eyes.

General Cullen stepped through the Circle and handed the sack of coins to the soldier. As he emerged, another soldier stepped out of the Circle and remained standing as General Cullen stalked down the path back to the castle.

"Hurry up!" General Cullen barked at the soldier holding the sack.

The soldier quickened his pace as the two made their way down the pathway to the castle.

Sarah and Zykeiah watched with mounting curiosity.

"Why is he back so soon?" Sarah wondered aloud after the General and his soldier had passed their hiding spot.

"Why indeed. It has only been a few hours. He did not look very happy." Zykeiah confirmed as she crawled back to her spot further away from Sarah.

Sarah followed, being sure to move slowly as to not arouse suspicion The dusty earth sent puffs of reddish grit into the air as she crawled. She held her breath to try to minimize how much she inhaled for her mouth seemed full of it.

"We must take action. Time is running short for both Marion and Queen Zoë." Sarah could hear the rumblings in her mind. The time was winding down. They had to act. "We cannot wait."

"Agreed," Zykeiah answered and shook Kalah's shoulder gently. "Wake, Kalah."

He coughed as he sat up on his elbows. "Is it light already?"

"No, we need to move. The air has changed and so have our plans."

He balked at the idea, but he did not argue for he noticed the seriousness of Zykeiah's face in the pale light of the moon. The chorus of the crickets seemed strange amongst the dusty and empty night.

"We must go through the circle and on to Solis. From there you will follow me through the caverns and tunnels to Valek's castle. Once there, we need to split up to look for Marion."

"And what of Amana?" Kalah asked as he pulled some hard but still sweet bread from his sack.

Zykeiah watched Sarah before saying, "If there is time and she is not under Valek's spell, then we shall try for her as well."

"Marion is our most important reason for being there," Sarah said. Her voice caught as she continued. "We must save him for all is lost without him."

The three shook hands and patted each other on the back for encouragement silently as they pulled on their sacks and prepared for the trip to Solis.

Sarah's stomach was remarkably calm despite the mounting danger and possible death. The thought of going back to Solis when she had worked so hard to leave it almost made her want to run back to Veloris. She knew she could not return without Marion, regardless of the threat that she may be imprisoned in the cages. She owed him one, and she planned to pay him back in full.

Chapter Twenty-Two

The moons were round, swollen, and full as the three stumbled out of the circle and into Solis's narrow valley of rocks and cellac. The air had been cooled as winter had approached and the lack of light gave Solis a sinister atmosphere. The feeling of gloom spread quickly to Sarah.

She noticed that there were no sounds. No animals remained on Solis, only the ones who lived and were protected behind Valek's castle walls.

The castle loomed large and magnificent above the valley on top of the hill, surrounded by rocky sculptures and the heavens knew of what else

The stench of flesh and death was faint but still prevalent amongst the Solis air. Her breath rushed out as her eyes adjusted to the low amount of light.

"I can't say it's good to be back," she said as she stepped through the wet, spongy land around the circle.

"No, it is not good to be back here," Zykeiah said, her voice hollow and surprisingly shaky as she followed Sarah across the decaying land surrounding the circle to the hardened surface just a few paces away.

Kalah stood mesmerized as he stared in wonderment. "This is Solis?"

"Yes, can't you smell the scent of death on the air?"

He sniffed then grimaced as he held his nose with his forefinger and thumb. "Whew! It smells like the carving stations out amongst the servants' cottages."

"That would be death, Kalah," Sarah remarked coolly.

"Come, let's get this over with," Zykeiah said as she brushed past Sarah and started up the trail through the valley that led to Valek's castle.

"You heard her. Let's go." Sarah glanced back at Kalah before starting behind Zykeiah.

Kalah took in a breath of air. "Here goes everything."

Sarah glanced back to make sure Kalah was with them. Zykeiah walked at her usual brisk pace as she struggled to keep up. Sarah tried not to think about what lay in wait for them on the other side of the valley's trail and inside Valek's castle. Orono would be there as well as MaxMion. A shudder went down her back and she swallowed hard.

She was not alone. Zykeiah and Kalah were with her and they knew how to handle themselves as was proven by their bravery displayed as they made their way here. Kalah even saved her life on the battlefield.

Although she was returning to Solis, she knew that she was not the same woman who left the cages. She had changed and her powers had matured.

"Is it always this dismal?" Kalah asked as he huffed and puffed up the trail.

"Yes," Sarah and Zykeiah answered in unison.

"The trail forks up ahead, we will go to the left," Zykeiah called over her shoulder.

"Left?" Sarah asked, for the right fork led directly up around the various hills to Valek's front door. The left fork veered downward and into what Sarah could barely make out as caves of some sort.

"Left," Zykeiah echoed.

She said nothing further. When they reached the fork, Zykeiah veered left and the two followed.

***

"How can you stand the stench?" Kalah asked.

"When you are a soul you can not smell, taste, or feel," Zykeiah answered.

The moons illuminated the path as it leveled out and then as it started to dip downward. The stench intensified the closer they came to the cave's entrance.

"Zykeiah, where are we going?" Kalah asked yet another question

She stopped short just a few paces from the cave's mouth. Its mouth was black and hidden from the moons' light.

Zykeiah waited until they caught up and the three came close together in a group.

Out of breath and sweating profusely despite the chilly night air, Kalah and Sarah placed both hands on their hips and tried not to take deep breaths, for the air was saturated with the smell of flesh.

"This is one of the tunnels that leads to the soul cages," Zykeiah explained quietly. "The other trail is filled with traps, pits and other nasty things that would have killed us."

She lowered a discerning eye at each of them and said, "This is the true test of character and bravery. I won't tell you that we will all leave here together, but remember to get Marion out!"

Sarah nodded and wiped her face.

Kalah pulled out his sword and nodded at Zykeiah. "Lead on."

Zykeiah smiled wearily, removed her dagger and inched into the cave's open mouth.

Sarah shuddered as Zykeiah entered the black mouth of the cave; it seemed to devour her.

Kalah placed his hand on her shoulder, then entered the cave slowly. He glanced back at her and smiled. At that moment she thought, *how much he now looks like Marion.*

Sarah searched the area around her and then she, too, entered the cave's gaping orifice.

The heavy sullen atmosphere reminded her of the moment of extraction — the last seconds when she could feel, and then that cold, bleak moment when her fingers could not touch anything except nothingness.

Zykeiah and Kalah waited for her to reach them on the inside of the tunnel. There were torches lit and secured against the solid walls every few paces, just enough to mark the trail. Shadows played on the ceiling and Sarah's eyes flickered around.

Kalah appeared to be holding his breath. Indeed the smell was stronger here and the cave's position kept it from receiving any wind.

"We must be close to the pit," Zykeiah said.

Ahead of them were five tunnels leading various places, but each had the same uninviting blackness and emptiness. In the distance was the clanking of tools on the almost impenetrable cellac.

"Follow me." Zykeiah picked the center tunnel and Sarah and Kalah followed. Neither of them spoke.

Sarah wondered how Zykeiah knew where to go. Zykeiah had made it no secret that she had escaped from the cages. Indeed, it was the primary reason she had been knighted on Veloris. Sarah had wondered even then, how she had done it alone.

As a soul, Sarah had not smelled the overwhelming stench of the cages. When she had been reincarnated and back in flesh, so urgent was her need to escape that she took no notice of the smell. But now, it threatened to choke the very life from her and reclaim her as its own.

Their shadows followed them, elongated and skinny. They shimmered against the tunnel's surface, dark and empty.

"I know this place like it was the back of my own hand," Zykeiah said softly. "She brought me back and forth through the tunnels with her."

"Who?" Sarah whispered back for she did not want to rouse any suspicion or be overheard.

"Manola. She is Valek's right hand. His sorceress, his confidante and his source for power."

Sarah remembered seeing Manola, but only on a few occasions when she took over for MaxMion in the cages. She seemed to be dead, for her skin was white like the clouds that used to be on Earth. The only color came from her fiery red hair and her painted lips. Even her eyes, an extremely light blue, appeared to be washed out.

Sarah remained quiet, for it appeared that the return to the tunnels and Solis inspired Zykeiah to talk about her past.

"I was her present. A gift from Valek to her for doing whatever evil deed he wanted," Zykeiah went on.

Her voice, although soft and low, was filled with fury and bitterness. "Her 'precious', she called me. She kept me chained to a wall in Valek's bedchamber."

"In his bedchamber!" Kalah shouted out.

"Shhh!" Sarah shouted back equally as loud.

They halted and waited to make sure they were not overheard.

When nothing but the ever-growing sound of hammering and chiseling could be heard, Zykeiah continued her tale.

"Yes. When it did not suit her to leave me, she took me with her. I traveled through the tunnels in little more than a gown."

"But these tunnels are cold, even during the day," Sarah remarked. "Were you still a soul or had you been returned to flesh?"

"Flesh," Zykeiah answered. "A soul could not satisfy her needs."

"Needs? She too is dead." Sarah shook her head in the dimly lit tunnel, causing her shadow to skip across the ceiling.

"She is dead, but undead. Her needs are those of a sexual nature," Zykeiah said flatly.

Single file, they walked through the tunnel and slowed as it came to an end and emptied out into yet another series of tunnels.

"What happened, Zykeiah?" Sarah asked softly.

Zykeiah reviewed the five tunnel openings in front of them. "I stole the key to my chains as she slept and Valek was away. I unlocked my chains and fled to the Allerton Circle. Next thing I knew I was on Veloris."

"That is how Marion found you," Kalah added, "in nothing more than a sheer silk gown and barefoot in the snow. She was close to death from the frost."

"Yes," Zykeiah confirmed.

***

Orono and MaxMion patrolled the cages. Orono grumbled all the more about General Ogroth, Valek, and his missing payment.

"We should visit General Ogroth and demand payment!"

MaxMion said nothing. He thought the General would make a meaty evening meal and more than likely a meaty morning meal.

"How dare he use me for my information but not render payment. He pays Valek without fail and Valek is double-crossing him."

Orono paced and MaxMion sat and counted the souls as they passed on their way back to their cages. Their numbers were low, and he would soon need to compress most of them for another batch of Solance, especially if the deal between Earth 4016 and Valek was confirmed

"You saw Saturn Four. They are loaded with riches. We could live there like kings!" Orono said.

MaxMion nodded eagerly, but deep within he held doubts. Orono had bungled the entire plan with General Ogroth, yet he had gone along with him, feeling that Orono had the superior intelligence. After all, he had only been given the post of patrolling the souls. Orono made the Solance and kept the books for Valek. That took brains.

Or so he originally thought. Now, he had doubts that Orono could pull off their escape and retirement from Valek.

As the last soul returned to his cage, he entered the code and the doors to the block of cages locked. "We are done for tonight."

Orono was supposed to be in the warehouse making Solance. Valek was furious with Earth 4016's king Richard and even angrier at Earth 3012's lack of payment.

His bad mood had paid off in an afternoon treat for MaxMion. The advisor was juicy and fatty. Those were the best. Perhaps staying with Valek wouldn't be so bad. He may even be promoted if he turned Orono in to him

It was something to think about. He removed the torch from the wall, leaving the souls to remain in complete obscurity and followed Orono out of the area containing the cages.

The two left the cages' main entry cave and started towards the castle. The tunnel had been drafty the last few nights, but MaxMion made Orono go first. Tonight, he was eager to be rid of the complaining and whining fool. He should have let General Ogroth kill him.

"…I gave him precious and prized information. I could have easily gone to that other general on Earth 3012," Orono was saying when he heard a shout.

"Quiet!" MaxMion grabbed Orono's wrist and squeezed. "Listen."

He fell quiet for half a second before snatching his arm from MaxMion. "I don't hear any-"

"Shh!" MaxMion hissed. "I heard a shout."

"Manola?"

"No, she is too occupied with her present to be in the tunnels."

"I do not hear anything. Let us go to sleep," Orono said as he continued on through the tunnel ahead of MaxMion toward the castle.

MaxMion stood rooted, listening. He sniffed the air, but smelled nothing different. Yet something was strange and he had heard something. With Orono blabbering on, he could not hear clearly, but it sounded like a shout of a male voice.

"What if one of Richard's advisors is lurking in the tunnels, trying to find the souls?"

"Then it is too bad for Valek that his secret is out," Orono said, making sure to adjust his bulk at the tight corners and narrow spaces.

They reached the tunnel's opening and pulled back the screen to the dungeon. From there, they passed the several empty cells and stopped at the first one closest to the stairs.

Orono yanked the door open and lumbered in. He sat down on the floor and turned to MaxMion. "Are you coming or are you going to chase phantoms tonight?"

MaxMion shrugged and kept his eyes on the two tunnels that emptied out into the dungeon area. The dungeon, albeit dirty and filled with various odors, had a few scents that he had not smelled before. He could smell the slight, almost nonexistent scent of something or someone that was not of Solis.

***

Zykeiah had not spoken in the last few minutes and Sarah's stomach had filled with knots that churned around and against each other. They were getting closer and the hairs on the back of her neck remained standing straight.

Kalah, too, had not spoken as they traveled. They inched ever closer to the scene of their triumph or defeat.

Sarah thought back to Queen Zoë and Octiva's teachings and recitals of the Oracle's predictions. She remembered the vision the Oracle gave her. Then this had to come out for the best.

Right?

***

MaxMion kept his eyes glued to the tunnels' entranceways. The smell grew ever stronger, and he was convinced that there was someone in the tunnels that was neither Valek nor Manola. He would definitely win that promotion if he captured the intruder — or intruders; the scents were combined.

Intruders plus Orono should net him a nice deal or promotion from Valek. He already knew what he wanted, a room in the castle and to be in control of the warehouse, like a normal person.

Plus, all the human bodies he could eat.

***

Zykeiah could see light ahead. It was dim, but the light at the end of the tunnel held more illumination than what they had inside the tunnel. She slowed her pace and gripped her dagger.

If she was correct, this tunnel emptied into the dungeon area, right above the warehouse. If the dungeon was empty, she could go to the warehouse and see if Marion was there. If not Sarah could climb into the other tunnel and head for the cages. Kalah could stand watch while she went up into the castle to search. Valek, Manola and Orono should be asleep by now. In and out within moments and little damage was what she was praying to the heavens for.

Chapter Twenty-Three

The twinkle and flickering dance of the light ahead made Sarah think of Veloris and the hypnotic flames of her fireplace. She was overcome with a feeling of warmth and fluttering deep within her heart.

She saw Zykeiah lift her dagger as their pace slowed to a crawl. They must be approaching the tunnel's end, for Zykeiah had positioned herself flat against the tunnel's wall.

She did the same, as Kalah, too, plastered himself against the wall with his sword drawn. His breathing was ragged and quick. His face was covered in sweat.

Sarah could feel the dampness around the collar of her shirt. The warm feeling still resided inside her heart and for some reason she was not afraid, nervous or scared.

A calm had settled around her.

"Stop!" Sarah heard someone shout as Zykeiah climbed out of the tunnel.

Kalah leapt from the tunnel and she heard more shouts. Running forward behind him, she jumped down from the tunnel's mouth and saw MaxMion racing toward Zykeiah with his mouth opened wide, ready to devour her.

Sarah clapped her hands together and quickly pooled together an orange sphere. MaxMion leapt into the air toward Zykeiah, who had her dagger positioned to strike. Sarah threw the sphere with all her might at the chomping teeth of the sinister little man. Zykeiah raised both her arms to protect herself from the smashing teeth.

The sphere smacked MaxMion directly in the mouth, the force causing him to fly backwards against the wall. The hard impact shattered and cracked various bones and he fell to the floor. Despite the obvious pain, he struggled with both hands to remove the orange gunk of the sphere from his mouth and teeth. The more he pulled, the more the sphere grew and soon his hands were covered in the same material.

Orono, having heard the commotion awakened. He labored to squeeze his frame through the cell's door. "What!"

"Kalah to the castle, up the stairs!" Zykeiah ordered. "Sarah to the warehouse; find him!"

"You won't be going anywhere when I'm done," Orono said as he finally freed himself into the dungeon area. "You!"

His eyes grew wide as they moved from Zykeiah to Sarah and back again. Quickly, he reached into his pocket for his blue spheres.

Zykeiah pounced with her dagger slicing the air until it reached Orono. He tried to turn, but she landed on his back.

As she attacked, Kalah raced past them and up the stairs to the castle.

Sarah, who had seen Zykeiah in action before, turned to the elevator and pressed the button. She only knew the one way to the warehouse and that was from the dungeon.

Orono's growl and screams carved through the quiet night and Sarah knew that before long, the rest of the castle would be awake. She had to hurry and find Marion and Amana, so that they could get out of here before Valek was awakened.

***

Orono grabbed Zykeiah's ears and pulled them hard until he thought they would pop off.

She screamed, but still continued to slice his face with quick, sharp gashes from her dagger.

Soon the pain grew to be too much, and she could feel the skin of her ears pull away from her head. She punched Orono instead and climbed down from his back.

Burning, searing pain filled her head, as she struggled to remain standing. His face was filled with blood and sliced folds of flesh hung down and dripped.

"Is that all you got you silly woman?" Orono spat as he pulled out his blue sphere.

Zykeiah's eyes grew wide for she had seen those blue spheres before, in Amana's hand, in Valek's hand, and in Orono's. She knew what they meant if the light caught her.

"You can do whatever you want. It won't matter; he will be free and you will be skinned alive."

Orono's face turned red as he put the sphere back into his pocket. "You're not worth saving for the cages. A slow painful death is what you're going to get."

He adjusted his bulky frame and started toward her with his two-balled up fists positioned in front of him.

Woozy and in pain, Zykeiah attempted to sidestep the slow-moving, Orono, but he managed to grab her tunic.

He wheeled her around with such speed and strength, that she lost her footing and he slammed her into the hardened dungeon wall.

She collapsed to the floor, unconscious.

***

Orono let go of Zykeiah's tunic as his attention turned toward the dark one who fled up the stairs to the castle. He had to capture him before Valek woke up.

Sweating and bleeding, he hurried past MaxMion, who had become covered in the orange material of the sphere and only his eyes could be seen.

Orono stopped and glanced down at him, but could not help him.

"I will come back for you. I must catch this dark one."

The dark one reminded Orono of the one he had fought at the Circle of Allerton. There was some resemblance between the two men, yet he could not be sure.

It did not matter. He would have his revenge on the intruders for interrupting his sleep and injuring MaxMion. Oh, yes, they would pay dearly — with their lives.

***

Kalah had stayed at the top of the steps for some time trying to decide which room Marion would be in. He had to hurry, yet the decision was overwhelming.

The hallways were poorly lit, and there were doors on the left, but nothing on the right. He had no idea of who was behind each door and he did not want to wake up the entire castle.

He crept down the hallway with one hand stretched out in front of him and the other tightly gripping his sword. He inched along while he wrestled to make a decision.

"I've got you!" Orono's foul breath added its own fragrance to the already horrid odor.

Kalah felt the claw-like hand as it yanked him backward to the floor The force and the sheer strength of the man surprised him. If Orono was here, that meant he must have defeated Zykeiah.

He could not think about that right then, for Orono had pinned him against the hallway wall.

"Who are you?" he demanded as he slammed Kalah's head back against the wall.

He tried to push against Orono. He needed to get his arms free to wield his sword. He struggled but Orono laughed as his cheeks lifted in effort to a smile.

"You're not as strong as the other one," he mocked.

Zykeiah had dealt the monster some serious gashes, Kalah noted as he stared at the flaps of flesh that had been severed from his face.

Orono lifted his huge balled up fist and smashed it into Kalah's face.

Kalah heard a crunch and then the darkness came.

***

Sarah had located the warehouse and managed to blow open the door with the use of her spheres.

The warehouse was not lit and the pitch-blackness made her race back to the narrow hallway and claim a torch. She lit the torch with the flick of her hand and she entered into the warehouse again, this time with light.

The death room was what the souls called it. The storage chamber was what MaxMion called it. The warehouse was what Valek and Orono called it

Sarah wondered if her sister had already been made a part of the latest batch of Solance. The rows were lined with hundreds of bottles. So many souls rested here — their last resting-place was in Valek's warehouse.

She hoped Marion hadn't already been made into Solance.

Sarah crept along, but the need to hurry threatened to overtake her. She had no idea how Kalah or Zykeiah was doing, but she hoped they had found Marion.

***

Zykeiah rubbed the growing bruise on her forehead as she struggled to stand. She investigated and noted that MaxMion had become wrapped in a bright, orange cocoon.

She hurried up the stairs as she heard Orono cackling.

As she took the stairs two at a time, she reached the top step and immediately spotted him with his hand wrapped around Kalah's neck as he shook it violently.

Kalah's skin had a bluish tint. Zykeiah raised her dagger and threw it at Orono with so much force and fury, unlike she had ever managed before. Hate rushed through her body, adrenaline took over her and nothing mattered but winning this fight.

The dagger landed directly into Orono's arm and like a stuck kowlata, he howled in pain. He let go of Kalah and tried to maneuver himself to remove the dagger.

With a running jump, she landed onto his back and began again to beat him on the head with her fists and to pull at the folds of skin, ripping the flesh from his body. She was careful to avoid him getting a grip on her ears.

Coughing and holding his throat, Kalah came to and sat up, gasping to the sounds of Orono howls and screams. He bucked like a raging danker beast as he tried to dislodge Zykeiah from his back. He turned around and ran backwards smashing her against the wall.

Kalah stood up and, with his sword, stabbed Orono in the stomach before collapsing to the floor.

Orono grabbed his stomach and collapsed to the floor not far from Kalah.

He did not move.

"Kalah, are you all right?" Zykeiah kneeled down by Orono and shook him gently.

"Yes," he croaked as he rolled over on top of Orono.

Just then the door closest to the stairs opened. Zykeiah quickly removed her dagger from Orono's arm and held it firmly.

Kalah tossed his sword from one hand to the other and back again as he tried to swallow the searing pain in his throat.

Richard stuck his head outside the door. "Please, keep it quiet We're trying-"

"Who are you?" Zykeiah demanded for she did not recognize the man.

"I am Richard, king of Earth 4016," he snapped. "Who are you-"

He got a glimpse of something down by his feet and noticed a bloody Orono. He stifled a scream and tried to slam his door shut, but Kalah was too quick for him.

He overpowered Richard and the two Minister Knights barged into Valek's guest quarters. Scattered across the two room quarters, were beds and traveling sacks. Several men were sleeping on the floor on makeshift sleeping mats. One bed had the covers turned down and it was empty.

"Richard of Earth 4016, what are you doing here?" Zykeiah asked with her dagger pointed at him.

The advisors bolted upright and some even stood up as they each woke to find two strangers in their room.

"Who are you?" one advisor asked.

"Be quiet!" Kalah barked his voice firm and coarse.

"It is none of your business why we are here," another advisor declared.

Without a second thought, Zykeiah's dagger went singing through the air and directly into the throat of the advisor.

Richard swallowed hard and quickly answered, "We are here to buy Solance. Please do not kill me."

There were no further questions from the remaining advisors. Frozen by fear, they remained in their sleeping mats.

"I am Zykeiah and this is Kalah. We are Minister Knights from Veloris."

"Impossible!" Richard whispered. "No one comes from the ice planet. The Minister Knights died out long ago."

The king was obviously stupid; she ignored his comments about Veloris. "It is true. Valek uses souls to make Solance and he is already selling it to both Saturn Four and Earth 3012."

Richard's mouth fell open and his advisors started to whisper fiercely amongst themselves, but none were brave enough to openly challenge her words.

"We have no issue with you, Richard. But I suggest you leave before this gets worse," Zykeiah announced and gestured for Kalah to follow her. "Leave before the rest of you end up like him."

As she left, she removed another dagger from her sack. Kalah scanned the empty hallway and wondered why no one else had heard Orono's horrifying screams and howls.

"Should we move him?" Kalah asked.

"Where is he?" Zykeiah asked in return.

Kalah turned back to the spot where Orono was and the hallway was empty. A circular pool of blood stained the floor, but Orono was gone.

Chapter Twenty-Four

Orono's screams and howls had not gone unnoticed. Valek had heard them, for he was not asleep. At first, he thought Orono and MaxMion were playing their games and coupling the way they often did...violently and painfully.

Yet, these howls were different and he had sent Manola to investigate. He longed to rest tonight, but the peace of slumber eluded him again.

He felt he had overreacted by killing Richard's advisor; he hated violence. In a moment of clarity, he had offered his castle to Richard for another week. The king had been so shaken he raced past Valek to the corner, where he promptly lost his lunch.

Valek erupted into a fit of laughter, and this only made the king shudder more. So, he tried to smooth

Richard's ruffled feathers with kind words of hospitality and cheer.

Manola had not returned, so she must be having fun with Orono and MaxMion. Either way, she could handle herself amongst those two idiots

He rolled over and tried again to capture sleep.

***

Sarah held the torch high above her head as she turned down yet another row of Solance bottles and inventory. Or was it the same one? There was no way to tell. Each row looked like the last. There was complete silence; the warehouse had been built under the dungeon beneath layers of rock. Nothing could penetrate the warehouse's thick walls. There was no doubt in Sarah's mind that Valek made the warehouse further underground so he could avoid hearing the wrenching souls' screams of agony as they were compressed into his high-priced Solance.

She had completed searching one aisle of bottles. When she turned yet another corner, a flash of bright green light almost blinded her. As she opened her eyes, she bumped into Amana.

"Amana?" Sarah scanned the shadowy gloom behind her for Valek. Her sister had deceived her before; it was a mistake she did not want to make again.

"Yes. Sarah?" Amana responded. "What are you doing here?"

The dullness had faded from her eyes. Sarah wondered if she had escaped Valek's control...and how?

"Amana, what are you doing here?" She lowered the torch for a better look. Amana's honey-colored skin lacked shine, but other than that, it was her.

"I escaped." Amana reached out and hugged her.

She stiffened, and then despite the warning voice that had begun to shout inside her, she gave in to Amana's hug. Her family reunited again.

"I'm glad. Now help me find Marion," Sarah said.

Her grip tightened around Sarah's waist, forcing her to drop the torch. It fell hard to the floor, but retained its flame.

"No, you're not!" Amana growled.

Amana squeezed her; crushing her internal organs together and making her cough and gasp for air as she tried to break free. Her sister was never this strong.

Without warning, her sister released her and with her hands balled into tight fists, punched Sarah in the face with alarming precision.

She reeled back against one of the shelves and it tipped over backward, sending bottles of Solance crashing to the floor.

Amana walked over the broken glass and spilled Solance as if nothing had happened at all. Her eyes remained focused on Sarah and her hands clinched and opened in regular intervals.

Sarah groaned as she felt her cuts and stinging gashes burn as pieces of shard glass lodged further into her back and hands. She struggled to sit up, ripping the palms of her hands on the debris.

Amana gathered a fistful of Sarah's hair and yanked her to a standing position. She pulled back her fist and then punched Sarah hard in the stomach, knocking the breath out of her. She collapsed to the floor again, this time slicing her knees on the glass and sliding on the mixture of blood and slick, wet Solance.

Sarah could feel the blood trickle beneath her shirt and down her legs. Her nose throbbed and her left eye felt puffy. She could still see out of it, but it was closing rapidly.

If she fought back, she might hurt Amana. Amana had no idea what she was doing. Sarah struggled against the blackness that threatened to over take her. She had to stay conscious and aware.

"Fight back! That's right, you don't want to hurt your sister!" Amana laughed hysterically as she reached for a nearly unconscious Sarah

Just then a zinging sound sliced through the air as a dagger slammed into Amana's shoulder where it lodged itself.

"Owww!" Amana cried as she tried to snatch the dagger out of her shoulder.

Before she could free it, Zykeiah had clobbered Amana and the two fell to the floor. They wrestled as Zykeiah proceeded to kick, punch and cut, while receiving blows and bites from Amana.

"No!" Sarah called and began to crawl to the spot where they fought. "Zykeiah-"

A flash of bright, green light shocked Zykeiah and sent her flying across the room as Manola fought to stand where Amana had once been. Her face and shoulders had ripped pieces of flesh and deep cuts, yet no blood trickled or flowed from the open wounds.

Sarah blinked in disbelief as Manola hurried from the warehouse.

Zykeiah landed against one of the shelves and it, too, crashed to the ground from the force of the blast. Moaning, she stood up and said, "She escaped. But I'm not done with her yet."

"Marion," Sarah picked up her torch and limped down the remaining row of shelves. This row was shorter than the others and Zykeiah hurried along beside her. It ended in a little alcove where a small crystal-stained jar rested on a desk.

"Zykeiah!" Sarah called and she quickly approached the desk with her two daggers drawn. "Marion!" She picked up the jar and peered inside. "We've found him!"

"Great! Now let's find Kalah and get out of here," Zykeiah muttered as she took Sarah's torch.

With bloodied hands, Sarah created a sphere and placed the crystal jar inside of it. "This should protect you until we get to Veloris." This last thing they needed was to lose his soul or smash the jar during a battle.

She saw his soul smile, but his eyes were tired and weak. He needed to be reincarnated and fast.

"Let's go!" Zykeiah ordered as they hurried down the aisle toward the warehouse's entrance. She led the way, but slowed to a crawl when they reached the front of the warehouse.

"Manola could be anywhere or anything," Zykeiah said softly as she opened the door to the warehouse and pressed the button to call for the elevator. "We must be extremely careful."

She stepped back from the elevator's doors and crouched down with both daggers drawn. Sarah held Marion in one hand, leaving the other hand free.

The elevator's doors slid open and Zykeiah held her breath, as did Sarah. No one pounced or rushed to attack them, still they entered the elevator cautiously.

"We lost Orono," Zykeiah confided. "That means he still lurks about. He is injured, but he remains a threat. We have him, Manola and quite possibly Valek, to contend with."

Sarah understood and placed Marion in the sack. She tied the sack tightly and slung it onto her back. She needed at least one hand to throw spheres if she needed to. From what Zykeiah had just said she needed to be ready.

"He'll be okay in there?"

"Yes, the sphere will protect him," Sarah said.

"Good."

Zykeiah pushed Sarah to the rear of the elevator as it came to a halt at the dungeon. As the doors opened, she bolted out slicing the air with her daggers.

"Watch it!" Kalah shouted. "I've been waiting for you! What took you so long?" Despite his irritation, he seemed relieved that they were together again.

Zykeiah asked, "Did you not see Manola pass by here?"

"No, I just came from upstairs where I was searching for that Orono creature. No such luck, but I did find your sister, Sarah."

"Are you sure it was her? Manola was disguised as her in the warehouse," Sarah asked.

Kalah shrugged and said, "She was chained to the wall in Valek's bedchamber. I cannot forget her face."

Zykeiah swore beneath her breath, and Sarah gasped. "Did you free her?"

"No, because I heard Valek returning." He turned to look back to the stairs, as the faint sound of footsteps grew louder.

"Someone's coming." Zykeiah stepped in front of Kalah and Sarah "Get ready."

Kalah whispered, "Why wait for them, let's get out of here!"

"What about Amana?" Sarah asked.

Zykeiah shrugged and said, "Give him your sack."

Sarah removed the sack and handed it to him. She looked back to Zykeiah with a look of doubt.

"Go to Veloris, now, Kalah!" Zykeiah ordered.

"I don't know the way to the Circle," he said as he took the sack and contemplated which path to take.

"Stay to the east when you come to the fork in the tunnels. The tunnel that is the furthermost east, take that tunnel and follow it to the Circle of Allerton. It will take you directly to it."

She patted him on the back. He climbed into the middle tunnel and disappeared into the blackness.

"It's just you and me now," Zykeiah said wearily.

Chapter Twenty-Five

Sarah felt her heartbeat increase and her hands were sweaty. Her left eye had completely closed, thus limiting her visibility on that side. She owed Manola. When next they met, she swore to avenge herself without mercy.

"Get ready," Zykeiah said as she kept her eyes focused on the dungeon stairs.

Within moments, Orono's chubby feet were seen as he lumbered down the stairs.

She wasted no time. She threw two daggers, one after the other, towards Orono's feet, striking him in the toes. Each dagger struck their target.

"Oh! Oww!" Orono growled, lost his balance and fell down the remainder of the steps crashing to a stop at the stairs' bottom.

Zykeiah raced over to the twisted Orono and kicked him hard in the face. Next, she lifted her sole remaining dagger and stabbed him several times. Her arm was a blur of slicing jerks and plunges.

Not that Sarah could stand by and watch. She had her hands full with Valek, who had gingerly come down the steps following Orono's landing.

"You!" Valek sneered upon sight of her.

He leapt from the third step, leaving Zykeiah and Orono to settle their own battle. Once he landed, he removed his sword with fluidity and gestured it toward her.

"It seems you've already had your share of a beating today. Allow me to finish by relieving you of your suffering!"

He twirled around, swinging his sword and chopped off the top of Sarah's torch.

She quickly rid herself of the wood and just like the day in the hallway with Queen Zoë's guards, she created a shield made of the same orange substance as her spheres. The battle was on. As they fought, their shadows danced alongside them. Their shouts and grunts could be heard echoing throughout the tunnels. Sweat and fear scented the area.

Sarah's shield protected her from Valek's blows, but she was extremely weak. She had lost more blood than she realized. And he knew it.

"You are weak. I can smell death upon you," Valek spat as he again smashed his sword against her shield.

She cowered beneath her shield, but her mind raced about. She had to do something. Without thinking, she lifted her hand and threw one of her sticky spheres at Valek.

The sphere flew past him as he sidestepped it with the grace of a practiced dancer.

"I see you have powers, albeit an awful aim," he mocked.

Her left eye made it difficult to see him for he kept to her left. She could smell the fresh rosemary in his hair, but if he stayed to her left, he vanished from view.

His shadow revealed his hiding place, but that was not an exact location.

"Who the hell are you?" Valek spat.

Sarah peeked over the edge of her shield to see Kalah emerge from the tunnel's mouth. He had his sword drawn and immediately swung at Valek, the blade ripping through his upper arm.

"I'm Kalah, son of Zoë and brother to Marion whom you kidnapped!" Kalah bellowed as he swung at Valek again.

With Valek and Kalah engaged in a sword battle, she dissolved her shield and turned her attention to Zykeiah and Orono, who were still swapping punches. Zykeiah seemed to be losing strength.

Sarah lifted her palm to the heavens and called, "Zykeiah! Move!"

Zykeiah glanced over her shoulder and saw the pulsating sphere in Sarah's hand. Stepping out of the line of fire, she bowed just as Orono swung a left-handed punch.

He missed, but Sarah did not. She threw the sphere at Orono, who was completely unaware of her. He was so consumed with defeating Zykeiah that he neglected Sarah's presence in the room.

The sphere smashed into his stomach and soon began to spread up his arms and down his lumpy thighs. The more he tried to wipe it away, the faster it spread. Soon, the sphere's material had covered all but Orono's neck and face.

He struggled all the more as panic threatened to overtake him. He fell to the ground, twisting, and fighting. Not too far from the spot where Orono struggled with the sphere's substance, MaxMion, nothing more than a cocoon of tightly coiled material, lay dead; smothered to death by the thick substance of Sarah's sphere.

"Valek, look around you. You are defeated!" Zykeiah called as he took another swing at Kalah.

Kalah's arms had been nicked by Valek's sword more than once. His mouth was drawn into a hard flat line, his face was covered in sweat and his arms decorated in thin streams of blood. He did not stop; he fought on.

Valek quickly scanned the dungeon and found himself surrounded by Kalah, Zykeiah and Sarah.

"Surrender!" Zykeiah ordered as she lifted her two blood-covered daggers and aimed at him.

He lowered his sword and said, "It would seem that would be best."

"Hands up, Valek." Kalah gestured with his sword. "In the air."

"Sure." Valek lifted his hands slowly in to the air, but did not release his sword. His thumb flicked the sword's hidden button. Several small, secret cannons slid out of hidden panels around the dungeon. The tiny cylinders started spraying a mist-like gas into the dungeon area.

"So long, idiots!" Valek called as the dungeon filled with smoke and he disappeared.

"Where did he go?" Sarah coughed as she asked. The room had billows of smoke and she could not see in front of her.

"I don't know!" Kalah called through the dense smoke.

"Upstairs, now!" Zykeiah coughed.

With their hands extended in front of them, they felt and tried to peer through the white, chalky smoke. They stumbled to the staircase.

"Ouch!" Orono moaned as Sarah stepped on him accidentally on her way to the stairs.

She could barely make out Zykeiah's sack in front of her on the stairs as they climbed up.

Coughing and hacking, the three gathered at the stop of the stairs. The hallway led into the main part of the castle. The clearer air allowed them to see each other.

The burning and irritating sting from the smoke in Sarah's throat appeared not to be easily quenched. She swallowed then coughed and neither alleviated the sensation.

"He escaped," she said coarsely.

"Kalah, what are you doing back here? You should be halfway back to the castle by now," Zykeiah said angrily.

"I had to come back to make sure you made it out," Kalah said and shrugged. "It didn't seem right to leave my companions behind."

Sarah was speechless. Kalah had performed a selfless act.

"Fine. Right now I'm not worried about Valek or your return. Let's find Amana and get out of here," Zykeiah said.

Kalah raised his hand and the two followed him down the dimly lit hallway to Valek's bedchamber. As they entered the room, they found it abandoned except for one person.

Chained and naked against the wall, dressed only in goosebumps that blanketed her body, Amana groggily looked up and smiled. "Sarah!"

Kalah quickly searched for the keys to the chains, being sure to avert his eyes from her nakedness.

Sarah hugged her sister, this time for real, and kissed her cheek. As she tickled Amana behind her ear, she erupted into laughter and Sarah knew that this was indeed her sister.

"Here, I found the keys." Kalah came back into Valek's bedchamber and unlocked Amana's shackles.

Zykeiah watched, but remained silent.

He handed Amana a blanket. "I got this from Richard's advisors."

Amana blushed but said nothing as he draped the blanket around her shoulders. She did not look him in the eye, but his eyes never left her face. He smiled softly.

"Come, we must get out of here before Valek or Manola comes back."

The four of them crept out of Valek's bedchamber and into the hallway. Walking quickly, but not running, they reached the stairwell to the dungeon.

Kalah led the way after giving Sarah back her sack, and giving his own personal belongings to Amana. He placed both hands on the handle of his sword, ready to strike.

Zykeiah went next, followed by Amana, and then Sarah who brought up the rear. Somewhere out there, Valek and Manola were waiting to attack.

They had to be ready.

Chapter Twenty-Six

The air had cleared, but smelled strangely of death and burnt wood. Sarah made it to the bottom of the stairs without incident, and the four of them continued on to the tunnel that would guide them to the Allerton Circle and eventually home.

Kalah turned back to look at them as he climbed into the tunnel. Zykeiah followed shortly after him and Sarah helped Amana, who was barefoot and naked beneath the blanket, into the tunnel.

The torches and candelabras lazily lapped as the group made their way through the tunnel. None of them spoke, but Sarah could feel the sense of relief and excitement that coursed from one to the other. They had been reunited. Battered and bruised, they would be home soon.

They reached the end of the tunnel faster than she remembered. As they each hopped down from the tunnel's mouth, they saw General Cullen climb down from the opposite tunnel.

"General Cullen," Zykeiah called to him.

The General's eyes met hers. His eyebrows rose in surprise, but he quickly closed him mouth. For just behind him General Ogroth came through the tunnel followed by several of his soldiers and Valek.

An awkward silence spread and no one spoke as Sarah and the Minister Knights stared back at the two Generals and Valek.

"General Ogroth, we have no issue with you. Allow us to pass on our way home to Veloris," Kalah said.

The hefty General pushed through the soldiers and General Cullen to the front of the group. He walked over to them and inspected each face as he made his way back to his group.

"It would seem there has been a misunderstanding."

"You block our path, General," Kalah repeated, his patience ebbing away.

"We have captured Valek, and we plan to extract the money and lives we have lost due to his selling of Solance to both my kingdom and Earth 3012," General Ogroth said.

General Cullen stepped forward and said, "We owe you a great deal, but allow us to first start with an apology."

"Yes," General Ogroth chimed in. "We owe you an apology and a thank you."

"What do you plan to do with him?" Sarah asked as she watched Valek struggle between the two enormous soldiers from Saturn Four.

"We plan to execute him once we reach Saturn Four." General Ogroth smiled, his pride swollen by his capture of Valek.

"You're going to kill him?" Zykeiah frowned.

"Why, yes." General Cullen smirked. "After I have him for a turn, then we will have an execution during the peace signing."

"You can't kill him," Kalah said. "You're no better than he is if you do that."

General Ogroth blew a stream of smoke from his nostrils and lowly growled. "He double-crossed us and by doing so managed to have thousands of Saturn Four people killed."

"The same is true for Earth 3012," General Cullen added.

Valek smirked and said, "It was fine when you were slaughtering each other's soldiers, citizens, and slaves. Each of you thinking you'd gotten over on the other…"

"Shut up you sniveling maggot!" General Ogroth barked.

Valek, unaccustomed to taking orders, continued to speak. "…Then when you find out you were the butt of the joke, you want to quit. It was only *business*."

General Ogroth wheeled around and without blinking, unsheathed his sword and stabbed Valek in the chest. "I asked you to shut up!"

A flash of green light filled the tunnel briefly blinding everyone. Once it had passed, Valek lay dead between the two soldiers who guarded him.

"You killed him!" Sarah screamed.

"I asked him to stay silent!" General Ogroth explained with a shrug. "I have no tolerance for stupidity."

"You have robbed our planet. Now we cannot extract our penalty for his actions!" General Cullen roared.

"There shall be peace between Earth 3012 and Saturn Four," said General Ogroth, calmly ignoring a furious General Cullen.

"I am glad to hear it. So shall our Queen," Sarah answered as she gazed at Valek's body, collapsed on the ground. She needed to get back to Veloris before it was too late.

"Now that Valek is dead, what's to be done with his castle?" General Ogroth asked.

"There are slaves in the cages below," Zykeiah said. "I shall remain behind to free them."

"You know how to reincarnate them?" Sarah asked.

"Yes. I will also burn the remaining Solance in the warehouse."

General Ogroth and General Cullen turned to look at each other then back at Zykeiah. "There's more Solance in the warehouse?"

"Yes, but it shall not be distributed," she said as she started towards the tunnel that led back to the cages. "Many, many people died to make that stuff."

With that she was gone.

"We will leave, too, and leave the clean up of Valek's castle to you" General Ogroth turned his group around and they crawled back through the tunnel in which they had come. The two soldiers carried Valek's body as one General led the front and the other remained in the rear.

"We must be on our way, Generals," Sarah said calmly and she started towards the east tunnel that would take them out to the Allerton Circle.

***

Zykeiah approached the main gate that led to the cages and sniffed the air, for it smelled strongly of the dead. She picked up the heavy lock and with her dagger started to fiddle with it.

Stabbing and twisting the dagger inside the lock's opening, she was determined to get it opened. She had picked the lock once before, when she had returned on assignment for Queen Zoë. Now, she needed to open it again.

With a click and a hiss, the lock opened. She stifled a cry of joy as she raced into the cages and announced, "You're free! Valek is dead!"

Souls did not sleep, so the remaining souls floated towards the cages' gates to see what the screaming was about.

Zykeiah hurried over to the main controls and with several quick stabs, the cells on the cages slid back setting thousands of souls free. They resembled fog rising in the morning as they spilled out into the cavern

"You will all need to be reincarnated. To the warehouse!"

Solemnly, some were a little hesitant for the warehouse was the place of compression. This could be another of Valek's sick and perverted games.

One of the older souls floated to the front of the pack. Her hair was white and her face wrinkled, for she was a great grandmother when Valek abducted her and took her to the cages so many years prior.

"Zykeiah, is that you?" the older woman asked as she hovered just above the hardened floor.

"Yes, Madam Quivers. I have returned to free you." Zykeiah smiled and as tears gathered in her eyes.

"It is truth that she speaks! To the warehouse for your flesh!" Madam Quivers shouted.

The souls floated past Zykeiah, who held open the main gate to the soul cages and cried.

Chapter Twenty-Seven

The spring had come to Veloris and the ice planet's normally frigid temperatures were kept elevated to a chilly, but amazingly warmer number. Flowers sprouted along the trail that had once brought Zykeiah and later Sarah, to the doorsteps of Queen Zoë's castle.

Queen Zoë sat propped up against fluffy pillows in her bed. Her color had returned soon after Marion's arrival back to Veloris and Octiva had performed the reincarnation of Marion's soul back into flesh.

Sarah remained by the Queen's bedside day and night, leaving for neither food nor water as she waited for the Queen to open her eyes. Octiva started bringing her meals to the room. The Queen had become more of a mother to her than she could remember of her own.

She stayed with the Queen, for Marion's quarters had been closed to visitors. Only Octiva could visit him and he was not to see anyone else. Octiva administered his herbs, food, and water to strengthen him.

Amana had been given a room across from hers and Kalah spent a great deal of his time showing her around Veloris and the castle. They spent much time outside on hikes and danker beast tours. He ate meals with her and took her hunting with him. Sarah was convinced that Kalah had fallen in love with her sister, but she was not exactly sure if Amana knew what love was.

She had not known. She had watched Marion's looks and long glances and thought they were the watchful eyes of an overprotective and dominant personality.

The oracle had peeled the scales back from her eyes and showed her exactly what Marion's true intentions were. The warm fluttering around her heart was love. It was love for him. It was not until his kidnapping that she felt incomplete, empty, and alone, despite Zykeiah and Kalah's companionship.

His presence filled her in ways she had never thought possible for a human to experience. His thoughtfulness, care and love had made her transition to the castle more smooth than it would have been had he not been there. She needed him close to her and she had waited the last few weeks patiently for him to recuperate from his ordeal on Solis.

Queen Zoë chewed on a piece of fig and laughed at Sarah. "You are here again before the day has reached its midway point."

"Yes, but Zykeiah is due back today," Sarah said. "I wanted to see you before she arrives. She sent word that she had finally finished the last reincarnations and that Valek's money has been split between each one of the remaining souls. She burned the warehouse, destroyed the remaining Solance supply, and will be returning shortly."

Queen Zoë nodded. "Octiva has said that Marion should be able to see visitors today as well. It is a good day."

"When will you go down?" Sarah asked.

"After you, of course," Queen Zoë said with a grin.

"Oh, no. You're his mother. He will want to see you." She blushed, unsure of the Queen's intentions for asking her to go first. Surely she could not read thoughts.

"No, he will want to hear what you have to say," she insisted.

Speechless, she did not respond. Her left eye still had some puffiness, but for the most part, her injuries had healed within the past few weeks. She had some scars, but Queen Zoë insisted they would fade with time.

"Where is Kalah?" Queen Zoë asked to change the subject.

"With Amana. They left shortly after morning meals."

Queen Zoë laughed all the more. It was good to hear her laugh and to watch her smile. It was a welcomed sight.

***

After mid-day meals, Queen Zoë took a nap and Sarah returned to her room. In the past weeks, she had made the room all her own. Her clothes were folded neatly in the rocking chair. Her scent was in the room and she had decorated the floor with coverings from the small garden of fresh flowers near the servants' cottages.

On the wall hung a carpet made especially for her by Octiva. It contained a rounded sphere with lights shooting from it, as if it glowed. Beneath the symbol were the words, 'She who saved Solis glows forever in the light of the galaxy'.

Sarah read the inscription and wiped her eyes. Next she sniffed the air, for the smell of rain had seeped into the castle. The day had become cloudy and gloomy. In the distance, she heard the rolling of thunder.

***

"You are feeling okay?" Octiva asked Marion as she watched him eat his evening meal of green poppa soup. It smelled like sweet bread, but tasted sour like the pits of the gradda fruit. He ate heartily, forcing spoonful after spoonful into his mouth. It had been weeks since he had warm foods. Octiva had nursed him back to health on the strength of plants, herbs, and drinks.

"I am fine. Ready to leave this room." Marion shoved in two more spoonfuls of the lumpy, green stuff. "I loved my quarters before, but now it has become like a prison to me."

She raised her eyebrows. "Pardon me."

He snickered. "No offense, Octiva. You have done wonders. I feel reborn." He laughed at his own joke; he *had* been reborn.

Octiva smiled back at him as she started to gather her belongings. The pouches of herbs, the wand of healing and other knickknacks that he had never seen before, threatened to overtake her fragile back from the load. He remembered some of the instruments — the wand was used to measure his temperature, and heal the sores in his mouth when coated with herb and a paste mixture. Even now he could not recall the herbs used to make the paste. Only that it was pink and tasted like peppermint.

"You are healed, great knight. Welcome home." She kissed his cheek; her dried lips rough and chapped against his skin reminded him what a joy it was to feel.

"Thank you, old mother," he grinned.

He watched as she left his quarters and he rose from the bed. Naked, he realized that Octiva had probably seen him in his bare skin. He quickly dismissed the thought as he felt his stomach clutch. She had healed him and for that he was grateful. The rest was immaterial.

He hurriedly grabbed and pulled on his pants and belt from the chair He still felt a little hungry, but he had wiped the bowl clean. The kitchen was still serving. But there was another hunger he wanted to satisfy first.

***

Zykeiah removed her gloves as she made her way up the spiraling staircase She shook her hair to relive it of the raindrops and leaves. The staircase was filled with the subtle scent of death that trailed her. She was glad to be home. She'd feel even better after a bath.

The souls had all been reincarnated back to skin and bones. They celebrated in Valek's office, some even climbing on top of his desk to dance in merriment. Some of the older souls… no, they were people, sat and watched amazed that the day had finally arrived. They could return home to their respective planets, or start a new life on a different one. The choices were endless and their happiness seemed to be as well.

Zykeiah divided Valek's money that had been left in his desk drawer, beneath his bed, and other places throughout the castle, between the people. She hoped the little bit of compensation that she spread amongst them would somehow ease their return to a normal life on other planets She knew no amount would erase the memories or the horror.

After the celebration, each person took up a chisel, hammer or a tool and they all went down to the dungeon. With pent up anger, they destroyed the cages. It had not been an easy task; several had strained muscles, been nicked, and in some situations broken fingers in their haste. When she left, the cages were no more than several ruins and heaps of rocks.

She watched from Valek's office window beneath the moons as they departed with kisses, hugs and many, many tears. As her gaze spread over the office and as she walked into the bedchamber, she rubbed her eyes in disbelief. If she had not been a slave herself, she would not have believed that such horrid things had happened there.

Picking up the torch, she applied the flame to Valek's bed and other furnishings. She walked slowly and decisively as she set various objects aflame. Nothing was to remain, but the castle's shell.

Nothing.

Now, she stood in front of Sarah's door, glad it was over and thrilled to be home once again. Raising her hand to knock, she hesitated as she heard someone coming up the stairs.

"Oh, I didn't know you were back," Marion said as he attempted to mask his surprise.

Zykeiah, too, tried to cover her surprise with a smile. "Good to see you, Marion."

"I can't say how thankful I am that you came for me, friend," he said.

"We all needed you, brother," she said with a smile that reminded him of their former relationship.

"Well, uh-" he shrugged. "Guess I'll be going. I was looking for Kalah."

"What would Kalah be doing up here?" She would not let him off the hook that easily.

"Amana's room is across from-" He stopped, glanced briefly at Sarah's door before going on. "He's usually visiting with her. I think he fancies her."

Zykeiah nodded in agreement, although she was distracted. The air between them felt weighed down as if with boulders. They were like strangers, when at one time they had been very close.

He turned and took the stairs two at a time and headed back down to the main floor.

Zykeiah knocked on the door. She wanted to see both Sarah and Kalah. But first, she needed to see Sarah.

***

"Good day, brother!" Kalah shouted across the hallway to Marion.

He turned and waved at Kalah. He noticed that Kalah escorted the latest castle resident, Amana, on his arm. She had the same beauty that he could not place, just like Sarah, yet the two could not have been more opposite.

From what he had been told by Octiva, Amana lacked Sarah's spirit and overall good nature. She relied solely on whomever could serve her needs best. At the moment, it was Kalah.

They were an ideal couple for Kalah had been known to do the same.

Marion waited while Kalah and Amana caught up to him. He had been told that Amana had been acting on Valek's orders when she came to Veloris and kidnapped his soul. Still, her very presence upset him, causing cold shivers to race down his spine.

Kalah slapped him on the back and said, "Good to see you awake, brother."

"Where are you off to?" Marion noticed that Kalah smiled a lot. Perhaps Amana made him happy. He had

never seen Kalah so taken with just one woman, but many things had changed in the last few weeks.
Including Kalah.
"We are off to the Southern Forest. I am looking for a nice, plumb kowlata to make Amana a cloak. And you?"
Marion remembered he still had his satchel in his hand. "To Stocklah. You should be very careful, Kalah. Remember what happened the last time you went there."
"Of course," he laughed, "have fun at Stocklah."
Marion stepped back as the two made their way down the hallway, past the central baths and down the stairs to the stables.
He went into the Great Hall and up the stairs to his mother's room. The royal guards had been dismissed and the gloom of the afternoon had settled in the hallway, making it bleak and gray.
Without knocking, he strolled into his mother's quarters then back to her bedchamber. He came to a halt at the doorway as he watched her sleep. Her breath, slow but consistent, went in and out, making her chest rise and fall in a rhythm all its own.
Quietness settled upon the land with the approach of the oncoming storm and the birds waited in the trees for the downpour. He could hear the voices and shouts of the servants in the kitchen far away and he felt homesick already.
Sighing, he left. He would have to see her after his ride to Stocklah. Thoughts and ideas swirled around in his head. His mother had understood when he had ideas and talking them out with her always cleared his head.
Zykeiah had been going to see Sarah. From the smell of her she had just returned from Solis. If that had been the

case, the first person she would want to see would be the person she missed the most.

Sarah.

He had been a fool to think that she could love him. Sarah and Zykeiah had fought side by side, spent numerous nights together while he remained an encased slave. There had been plenty of time for a bond to be established between them.

He had to get out of the castle.

As he jogged down the stairs to the stables, he found it empty except for the danker beasts. Without waiting for the servant to return, Marion picked his favorite one and left for Stocklah.

Chapter Twenty-Eight

"Zykeiah, what are you doing here?" Sarah asked, shocked. Reaching out, she grabbed a fistful of Zykeiah's shirt and pulled her into the room. "I'm so glad to see you!"

Zykeiah smiled wearily at her and said, "Me, too."

They moved to the bed and Sarah sat while Zykeiah paced in front of the fireplace.

"I have something I need to say to you now that we're back on Veloris."

Sarah didn't like the way that sounded. Zykeiah's eyes would not meet hers and for the first time, that troubled her.

"I wanted to say thank you for saving me back on Solis," Zykeiah began.

She waved her off. "We are a team."

"There's more. I wanted to say that I understand and support your decision to be with Marion."

Sarah waited for her to go on as she tried to figure out what Zykeiah was talking about. Finally, she decided to ask her.

"What are you talking about?"

"I know that he's in love with you. I also know that you are in love with him. I respect that." Zykeiah stepped back, close to the fireplace with an expression of amusement at Sarah's confusion.

Sarah stood up slowly and held Zykeiah by the shoulders. "Did you just say that Marion was in love with me?"

"Yes, didn't you know?"

"Are you sure?" Sarah's heart started to pound and she could hear the *thump-thump-thump* speed up the more she thought about Zykeiah's words. "How do you know?"

"I know him. I have known it since you first arrived. Plus, I could read it in his eyes. Even just a few moments before in the hallway, his eyes still held love for you."

Sarah shook Zykeiah lightly before letting her go. "He was in the hallway?"

"Yes," she replied, surprised.

Sarah stepped back from Zykeiah and opened the door. "Where is he?"

"He left," she said calmly.

Sarah didn't bother to ask where as she raced into the hallway, down the stairs and down the main hallway to Marion's quarters. She had no idea that he would be up and about today. Not only that, but if what Zykeiah said was true, he was still in love with her. The urge to talk to him, to sort out his feelings and hers was too great to delay.

She ran down the hallway, too eager to walk politely. His door had been closed and she knocked hard and waited for him to beckon her in.

No answer.

Again and again she pounded on his quarters' door without success.

She checked the Great Hall.

He was not there.

She checked the queen's quarters. Octiva told her that Marion had not been to the Queen's room that day.

"Are you well, child?" Octiva asked.

"Yes. I need to find him." Sarah panted for she had been running around searching for him.

"Is he in danger? You are out of breath."

"No." Sarah smiled. "He is not in any danger."

She left the queen's quarters disheartened. As she emerged from the Great Hall, Zykeiah came out from her quarters.

"No luck?"

"No," Sarah said sadly.

Just as the two were talking, Kalah and Amana were coming up the stairs from the stables. Amana trailed behind Kalah and they soon joined them.

"Zykeiah, good to have you back on Veloris." Kalah playfully punched her in the arm.

"Have either of you seen Marion?" Sarah asked heatedly.

Kalah raised his eyebrows in surprise. He had never heard her tone become so irritated and forceful. "Yes. He said he was going to Stocklah."

Stocklah.

Sarah pushed past them and fled down the stairs to the stables. She picked Majaga, climbed on and hurried out

into the residing afternoon day. He could not have gotten far. Zykeiah had only been in her room for a few moments.
She encouraged her Majaga with hard, stinging shots of the whip. She howled in protest and pain, but sped up.
Sarah could see him as she approached. His broad back, dark shiny skin and black pants made a stark contrast to the blankets of white, puffy snow. She called out to him.
"Marion!"
He turned around. She saw he had on his tinted glasses. She remembered how he looked the first time she saw him with those glasses and her heart pounded hard and fast against her chest.
She finally reached him at the base of the trail to Stocklah. The wind had picked up and it blew with force and strength, scattering her hair and giving her chills.
"Kalah said you were headed to Stocklah?" She smiled, as her stomach grew nervous. What would he say to her now?
"Yes, I need to clear my head. How is Zykeiah?"
She thought it odd that he would ask about Zykeiah. "She's fine."
He nodded gravely. He had not smiled since seeing her and Sarah began to wonder if Zykeiah had lied to her.
"I'm glad to see you're out and about," she said lightly.
Marion merely nodded and gave a half-hearted shrug.
"What's the matter? Do you need me to go get Octiva?" she asked as she placed her hand on his arm.
"I am fine," he replied, as he felt her hand on his arm; it was soft and warm. He was not fine. He fought back the urge to kiss her.

Sarah gazed up at the heavy cloud coverage and their darkened state. "It looks like a big storm is approaching. Perhaps you should not go to Stocklah alone."

"I plan to move to the Southern Forest…alone. I might as well get used to it," he sighed. "Besides, Stocklah clears my head."

"What?" She felt as if the air had been knocked out of her. Fear took its icy fingers and squeezed her heart. "Why? Aren't you happy here?"

"I - I," he faltered and turned away from her. "It is what I want."

"Is it?" Sarah muttered. "I love you. Don't do this."

He turned back to her. "What did you say?"

"I said don't do this," Sarah said slowly.

"No, before that," he pleaded.

Sarah tried to remember for it seemed extremely important to him. He had shoved his tinted glasses to the top of his head and his eyes burrowed into hers intently.

"I think I said, 'I love you. Don't do this'."

Marion's face seemed to crack into a smile as he reached for her, bringing her into his embrace and covering her with kisses. "Oh, Sarah. I love you, too!"

He picked her up and swung her about as if she was a three-year-old child.

"Did you mean it Sarah?" Marion asked as he let go of her.

"Yes," she said with a laugh.

He joined her and was soon laughing, too. If felt good to laugh, to *feel*, again. He took her hand and helped her onto her danker beast, making sure to allow his hands to linger about her waist. "I love you, Sarah."

He appeared to walk on clouds as he made his way back to his danker beast and climbed on. Joy seeped from him as he smiled and kept his eyes on Sarah.

They rode back to the castle and arrived just in time for evening meals.

Queen Zoë sat at her familiar spot at the front of the Great Hall and Octiva stood behind her. The Minister Knights, Sarah and Amana took their customary seats at the table closest to the queen.

Queen Zoë raised her glass. The Minister Knights did the same. "Dear loyal servants, knights and guests. Valek has been defeated, the enslaved souls set free and the war between Earth 3012 and Saturn Four a thing of history. Raise your glasses, cheers and voices in celebration of the Minister Knights and Sarah."

Cheers erupted and the celebration was underway. Sarah danced with Marion throughout many songs. Kalah and Amana drank ale and danced some as well.

Zykeiah found herself cornered by both Mary and Tate, who wanted to hear the stories of the rescue mission.

Queen Zoë watched all carefully, but with an expression of joy.

Epilogue

On the moon of Chaka, Manola covered her body with another blanket. The sun never reached the western side of Chaka, so the air was cold and all other life had been cut short or failed to exist at all.

She cursed the darkened night sky. It could be morning for all she knew; it was always dark on Chaka.

The abandoned wooden shack had been ideal. There were blankets and several stoves to cook food and warm the room. She didn't need that, nor was she in danger of starving to death. She had died many centuries ago, but her powers kept her spirit alive.

Her wounds had closed up shortly after Zykeiah had made them. She could not be killed. She smiled as she thought of how vigorously her precious had fought.

She got up from the floor and reached into the empty cabinet. She removed the orange-colored box that once belonged to Valek. She placed it on the makeshift table constructed of various discarded parts and garbage.

She peered inside and winked.

Valek's soul spun around to face her and floated closer to the glass

"Get me out of here!" he roared.

Manola licked her painted lips and said, "Soon, my precious."

crystaldreamspub.com
P.O. Box 698 Dover, TN 37058

Crystal Dreams Publishing
Order Form

Quantity	Title/Author	Price

Subtotal $

Shipping and Handling
$2.50 US, $3.50 International 1ˢᵗ book. Add $1.00 for each additional book.

Total

☐ Enclosed check)
☐ Please bill my Credit Card
　☐ Master Card
　☐ Visa
　☐ American Express
　☐ Discovery
☐ Money Order

Note:
A physical street address MUST be provided. All books are shipped via United Parcel Service (UPS). UPS will not deliver to PO Boxes

Merchandise will not be shipped when paying by personal check, until the check clears. Returned checks will be subject to a $25.00 returned check fee.

Mail to:
Crystal Dreams Publishing
PO Box 698
Dover, TN 37058

Printed in the United States
52914LVS00004B/93